Kpegnan: Twilight of Destiny

Jules Sehi

This book is based on the author's personal experiences. Some details may have been changed to protect privacy.

ISBN:

Ebook: 979-8-9935513-5-7

Paperback: 979-8-9935513-6-4

Published by **American Publishers, LLC**: 2026

www.americanpublishersllc.com

Dedication

To my grandmother **Nanhan Matoma**, and to all those who loved me and who, unfortunately, left us too soon for the hereafter, and whom I have always held in high esteem.

For Tianna Sehi, my princess, love beyond the moon.

For Maman Goulia, rest in eternal peace.

For my mentors Ethleen, Chris, and Ablasse, your support meant a lot to me.

Acknowledgements

This book was born of perseverance, faith, and brotherhood.

My deepest gratitude goes to God, who gave me the strength not to give up.

To my brother and friend, Engineer Kadet, companion of my sleepless nights, who stayed with me until the very last pages, your commitment and your rigor were decisive in bringing this work to completion.

To my pastor and friend Lehi, whose prayers, words, and constant support kept the flame alive whenever discouragement tried to take over.

To my sister Fatima, for her love, her quiet yet essential presence, and her unwavering trust.

To my friends Konneh, Cashauna, Mama, Maguy, Tete, Yvette, Delago, Edem, Azeh, Rachou, Rania and Harold. I am forever grateful. Stay blessed.

To all my female and male friends whom I cannot name one by one, thank you for your affection, your encouragement, and your belief in this dream.

To my family and to my future readers: this book is also yours.

Jules Sehi Nickin

Table of Contents

Part 1

In the peaceful little village of Tenably, tucked away in the western part of the land of lagoons, life flowed to the rhythm of age-old traditions. Every morning, the piercing cry of the rooster shattered the silence of dawn. The children, barefoot and carefree, dashed through the dusty, reddish alleyways, while the young and the grown prepared their machetes, ready to head to the fields.

The clay houses, topped with thatched roofs and palm leaves, seemed to rise naturally from the earth itself, wrapped in the morning mist and bordered by lush fields of coffee, cocoa, rice, and corn. From sunrise onward, the small market square in the heart of the village was already bustling. The beignet sellers set up their stands, while the schoolchildren, a few coins clutched in their hands, looked for something to buy for breakfast.

All this gave the early morning a unique kind of buzz. It was a place where flavors, sounds, and smiles blended together a true mirror of Tenably's soul. At sunset, as the village slowly prepared to welcome the night, the conversations grew softer and more intimate. In the darkening sky, the stars began to appear one by one, forming a constellation of thousands of glittering points. The animals, tired from wandering all day, returned to their shelters, and the village found its calm once again.

Hurricane lamps, torches, and candles glowed inside the huts, casting a warm, dim light through the windows. As the night deepened, the children after being lulled by the evening stories were urged to join their beds, while the couples retreated into the intimacy of their homes. The village then sank into a deep peace, disturbed only by the whispers of the night and the soft rustling of nocturnal creatures.

It was in this authentic world that Kpegnan and Djekobou grew up, two inseparable souls since their early childhood. Kpegnan, lively and curious, was a fearless dreamer, always on the lookout for new adventures. Djekobou, for her part, matched him in boldness, but her wisdom often kept his impulses in check. Together they formed an unbreakable duo, united through every burst of laughter and every challenge they tackled. When they weren't at school, they spent their days climbing trees, playing near the marigot or along the little river winding around the village, and helping their parents with the fieldwork.

Their school, a modest structure made of clay bricks, was the place where their minds woke up day after day. At the back of the windowless classroom stood a large blackboard, often covered with the fine white dust of the teacher's chalk.

Kpegnan discovered a true passion for numbers there, solving arithmetic problems with surprising ease, while Djekobou found herself captivated by words and reading. But it was in the courtyard, during recess, that their bond truly came alive. Kpegnan, barefoot and kicking around a makeshift ball made of rags and string, led the other children in lively, chaotic football matches.

Djekobou, meanwhile, traced wide squares on the clay ground with charcoal and guided her friends in endless rounds of hopscotch. Their crystalline laughter rang through the air light, joyful, almost dancing.

Every evening, after a long day, Kpegnan would join Baha, his grandfather, around a crackling wood fire. There, under the moonlight, Baha would launch into his stories tales of ancestors, full of wisdom and enchanting mysteries that captivated the children gathered around him. This was how Kpegnan and Djekobou grew up: cradled by their village's traditions and carried forward by their dreams of the future.

With his raspy voice and theatrical gestures, Baha brought the old stories back to life. Among them, the adventures of Sanwan the spider held a special place, for they fascinated the young ones and sparked their imagination.

One of old Baha's favorite tales was this one:

A long time ago, in a remote village, lived a merchant named Sanwan, the spider. Big and prosperous, he was known for his greed and his talent for twisting others around his finger. But one day, misfortune befell him.

A terrible famine struck the village, destroying the crops. Sanwan's business collapsed, and he no longer had enough to feed his large family. Worse still, he was drowning in debt, having borrowed from every villager… except four:

The termite, the hen, the hyena, and the hunter.

That's when Sanwan, sly as ever, cooked up a plan.

Early one morning, Sanwan went to see the termite and, with his sweetest, most charming smile, exclaimed, *"My dear termite! All through the forest, they praise your generosity. I don't doubt it, but I'd like to verify it myself. Would you be so kind as to lend me a few cassava tubers? I'll repay you without fail on the first day of next month. Be at my house at 6:00 sharp, not a minute longer, otherwise the debt will be canceled!"*

Flattered by such honeyed words, the termite agreed at once and handed Sanwan ten sacks of cassava. His starving family devoured them within a few hours. But soon, they wanted more.

Without wasting a second, Sanwan went to see then:

"O, you, tireless worker, whose little ones are never hungry! If only everyone were like you. They say your granary always overflows with rice and corn. Help me, I beg you! Give me a few sacks, and I'll repay you on the first day of next month. Come by my house at exactly 6:05. Not a second more, or the debt will be cancelled."

Caught off guard, the hen immediately gave him a few sacks of rice and corn. Within fifteen minutes, everything had been devoured at Sanwan's home.

Sanwan couldn't let his family starve.

So he went to the hyena and pleaded:

"Ô big hyena, with a generous heart, I know how sensitive you are to the suffering of others. Help me feed my family. I will repay you on the first day of next month, at 6:10 sharp. Be right on time; otherwise, the debt will be canceled."

Moved by such apparent sincerity, the hyena gave him large chunks of meat. In barely five minutes, everything disappeared into the ravenous bellies of Sanwan's children.

There remained only one last option: the hunter.

Sanwan searched for him in the forest and, when he found him, delivered a grandiose speech:

"Ô Gladignon, the great hunter, the man with the immense heart! My family is on the brink of death. I wandered the forest for days to find you. Help me, and I swear I'll repay you on the first day of next month, at 6:20 sharp, not a second longer or the debt will be cancelled."

The hunter, impressed by Sanwan's strict sense of punctuality, gave him a fine gazelle.

Days passed. The month came to an end. The dawn of the first day arrived. Sanwan was ready.

At exactly 6:00, the termite showed up, right on time.

"Good morning, my brother Sanwan! I've come to collect what you owe me."

Sanwan smiled slyly.

"Ah, my dear termite! My wife has the money; she went to the marigot but will be back any moment. In the meantime, sit down and relax!"

But Sanwan knew one crucial thing: The hen despised the termite.

And at 6:05 sharp, as expected… the hen came running. The moment she spotted the termite; she lunged at him and swallowed him in one swift peck!

Sanwan nodded with a satisfied grin.

"My dear hen, as a token of gratitude for your punctuality, I saved this little feast just for you. Now wait a bit my wife will return with the money."

At 6:10, the hyena appeared. Immediately, she pounced on the hen and devoured her.

Sanwan, unbothered, said:

"That hen was merely an appetizer. Just wait a little; my wife will be back soon. But in the meantime, hide behind that bush one never knows, a hunter might be lurking."

At exactly 6:20, the hunter arrived.

Sanwan started chatting casually, then asked:

"Tell me, do you know the technique called Fire on the bush?"

"Of course!" replied the hunter proudly.

"You should try it on that bush over there. I saw a hyena prowling around..."

The hunter didn't hesitate. With one blast of his rifle, he killed the hyena on the spot.

Sanwan rejoiced inwardly.

"Ah! My dear friend, thanks to me, you've just caught a hyena! We're even now no need for repayment!"

The hunter, furious, realized too late that he had been tricked. He carried off the hyena's carcass, swearing to never help Sanwan again.

Sanwan, having fooled everyone, thought he was safe. But news travels fast in the forest. No one ever wanted to lend him anything again.

Little by little, he fell into famine. Deprived of food, he weakened, shriveled, grew skinny as a twig... Until he became nothing but that tiny creature with long legs...

And since then, he spends his days and nights weaving his web, desperately trying to trap his prey... Because no one trusts him anymore.

In the village, during their childhood, Kpegnan and Djekobou took great delight in accompanying the women and youth on nighttime termite hunts. As soon as night fell, an air of adventure settled over the place. Armed with lamps, torches, and baskets, they dashed along the misty paths in search of termite mounds.

Once a mound was spotted, the ritual began. A bright fire was lit nearby. Using twigs and dry grass, they created a thick smoke that they directed into the entrance of the mound with handmade bellows.

Suddenly, swarms of winged termites burst out, panicked, whirling around the light like a living tornado. A frenzy seized everyone. Baskets, gourds, bowls anything that could hold them was used to scoop up the insects. Kpegnan, for his part, didn't bother waiting; he grabbed them with his bare hands and crunched them alive, to the amused or disgusted reactions of the others.

Rich in protein, termites were a delicacy in Tenably. They were dried or roasted, and their smoky taste was truly delicious.

Harvest season had come to an end in Tenably. The time of hard work gave way to a period of rest, when nature itself seemed to catch its breath after months of effort. That morning, before dawn had even touched the horizon, thirteen-year-old Kpegnan slept deeply, wrapped in the quiet of the still-slumbering village.

A whisper suddenly pulled him from sleep.

"Get up, we must go." It was his uncle Téhé.

Still half-asleep, Kpegnan rubbed his eyes, splashed some water on his face, cleaned his teeth with an old toothpick, then stepped into the cool morning air. He asked no questions. He knew he simply had to obey, without trying to understand just as custom dictated between children and elders in his village.

Téhé took the lead, and the two of them followed the winding path through the bush. The thick, heavy silence was broken only by the chirping of nocturnal insects and the rustling of leaves beneath their feet.

Kpegnan did not know where he was being taken, nor for what purpose, but a growing premonition tightened inside him. As they walked, shapes began to emerge in the dimness: other boys his age were already gathered there. Their presence, far from soothing him, made his heart thump even harder. He met their eyes some were frozen with fear, others kept their heads lowered, unwilling to face what awaited them.

The group was led to a clearing, not far from a small stream. The place had been carefully cleared and cleaned. Everything had been prepared with meticulous attention, the unmistakable sign that a solemn ceremony was about to take place.

It was then that Kpegnan noticed a frail-looking man, bare-chested, his muscles sharply defined. He stood at the center of the clearing, motionless. In his hands, a sharp blade glimmered faintly under the first light of dawn. A cold shiver ran down Kpegnan's spine. He understood then, without anyone needing to tell him. Today, he would undergo a trial even though he had no idea what form it would take.

The boys stepped forward one by one, advancing with contained fear. When Kpegnan's turn came, he approached on hesitant feet, almost stepping backward, breathing rapidly, his heart pounding like a war drum. In a split second, the blade came down cleanly, doing its work with imparable precision. A searing pain tore through his body. A strangled cry escaped him before he collapsed into sobs, shaking with uncontrollable shivers.

But he was not alone. Around him, the other boys marked by the same ordeal stood wavering between pain and a budding sense of pride. Their eyes trembled, unsettled, yet in this shared suffering, an invisible bond now united them.

Suddenly, a cry split the air, making the leaves of the bush tremble. The Zoho, master of the initiation, had just announced the end of the ordeal. Almost instantly, the news spread throughout Tenably. Shouts of joy erupted from all sides. A wave of elation swept through the village.

The families of the new initiates, relieved and swelling with pride, rushed to the gathering place, ready to celebrate this major milestone in their sons' lives. Drums came alive, beaten by skilled hands, and songs resounded in unison. The elders congratulated the parents, reminding them that their children were no longer little boys, but men now.

The pain gradually faded, replaced by something greater, a new sense of belonging. Still trembling, Kpegnan lifted his eyes toward the sunlit sky. He knew he had just crossed an invisible threshold, the one separating childhood from adulthood.

While the festivities were in full swing, the young initiates prepared to return to the village. Two Klinbos young men who had already undergone initiation and were appointed to supervise and guide their juniors led the procession. The initiates' respect for the Klinbo was absolute. These guardians, often unmarried, bore the heavy responsibility of assisting their young brothers in the days to come.

On the path back, Kpegnan and his companions held a wooden stick firmly in their hands. At regular intervals, they swung it downward, slicing the air in front of their genitals.

"This prevents the sorcerers' spiderwebs from reaching the wound and poisoning it," they had been told.

Superstition or not, none of them dared to ignore the instruction.

Once back in the village, Kpegnan and the other boys were taken to a communal hut called Klingbou. It was a sacred space where they had to remain until their wounds healed completely. Their arrival was announced by the Toué Gnangboho, the guardian of the circumcised, who blew a ritual melody through his flute:

"Toué dé, toué dé, toué dé, toué dji wai oh"

"Toué ai pon Kpélé ko"

The Toué was a mysterious figure surrounded by legends. It was said he had no legs, that he moved by crawling, dressed in a raffia skirt, and that he suffered from leprosy. His role was sacred. He ensured that the rights of the initiates were respected, and no one dared to defy him.

The initiates ate from the same dish, and their meals were brought to them. The Klinbos, responsible for watching over them, had to observe strict sexual abstinence and avoid any contact with the outside world.

Their days were filled with songs, discussions, and games. Once a day, they were taken into the bush to receive treatment and wash. Then finally, after several weeks of seclusion, the healing was deemed complete. The raffia they had worn as clothing was removed and replaced with a strip of cloth. The old raffia was burned in a symbolic ceremony, marking the end of their transformation. On the eve of their return to their families, one last event had to take place.

During the night, a feared force appeared: the Founglo. People said this powerful entity, like a furious storm, destroyed everything in its path. Its arrival marked the end of the initiation cycle. Women and non-initiates were forbidden to see it. Even speaking its name was taboo, and only the initiates could face it silently.

At dawn, the faces of the young men were coated with kaolin clay, the sign of their passage into adulthood. Their homecoming was a grand celebration: their families welcomed them with songs, dances, and abundant meals.

For several days, festivities continued, celebrating their courage and transformation. From now on, Kpegnan and his companions were free to have sexual relations if they wished.

But more than a mere passage into adulthood, circumcision was a test of courage. To accept suffering without complaint, to endure the Zoho's blade without flinching, was proof of bravery. To refuse this trial was to be condemned to contempt and shame. Worse still, the women of the village often refused to sleep with an uncircumcised man.

This ritual was not only about physical maturity it was a mark of honor and social belonging.

A month later, it was the turn of the young girls who had reached puberty to face their own initiation rite. The rite was approaching, and for days, a cloak of tension suffocated the village.

Gaston, a Jehovah's Witness and father of Djekobou, had become a feared man. Ever since he had sworn that his daughter would never undergo excision, he was carrying alone the weight of an entire village's anger.

When Sohou, his wife, admitted she still wanted their daughter to undergo the ritual, he exploded.

His voice tore through the silence:

"Never! My daughter will not endure that suffering!"

The elders whispered, women murmured, men frowned. But he stood tall and walked straight to the chief's hut. His steps echoed on the packed earth.

"My daughter will not be excised," he declared, his eyes locked with Guehi's.

The old man, expressionless, replied:

"In two days, she will undergo the rite. The women are ready. To refuse is to spit in the faces of our ancestors."

Gaston clasped his hands behind his back.

"My ancestors were men. My Creator is Jehovah." "So *you call us impious? You think you know better*

than those who have preserved our customs since the dawn of time?"

"I know what the Bible says: everything God made is perfect. To mutilate my daughter is to profane Jehovah's work."

Guehi stepped forward, raising his staff toward him.

"And when your daughter is rejected? Mocked?

When no man will want her?"

"I would rather she remain whole and approved by God than married at the price of her blood."

The staff struck the ground dry, sharp.

"Here, tradition rules. Not your God from elsewhere."

Téhé intervened:

"Even Oulai, with his church here, does not behave like you. Be careful."

Unshaken, Gaston replied:

"It is not the honor of men that will save me, but Jehovah's approval."

A heavy silence fell. Looks grew even darker. He walked out, alone, as murmurs trailed behind him.

Old women shook their heads. An elder spat on the ground.

"Keep going like this, Gaston," a young man called out. *"A lone man does not stand long against a village."*

"The night is long, and doors are not always solid," added another.

He did not slow down. At the entrance to his courtyard, an old neighbor stopped him:

"*The village knows how to bring a misguided son back to reason.*"

The door slammed behind him. He bolted it firmly, then in the dim light, took his daughter's hand and whispered:

"Jehovah, protect us tonight."

Outside, voices still prowled like hyenas.

His refusal had shaken the village. Some admired him in secret; others called him a traitor to his culture.

Then one morning, while he was far from home on a mission distributing his brochures, the worst betrayal occurred.

Taking advantage of his absence, Sohou handed Djekobou over to the women of the clan.

When Djekobou realized that, despite her father's promises and loud refusals, tradition would prevail, her heart began to race. Her legs trembled beneath her, unable to support her, and she clung desperately to her mother's cloth wrap.

"No, Mama, it hurts, I don't want to do it. I'm sorry." Her voice was only a broken breath, the cry of a child searching for tenderness protection she did not find. Her tear-filled eyes searched her mother's face for a spark of pity, a doubt, a final remorse, a moment of humanity, a change of heart.

But her mother's face remained stone. A stone worn down by the weight of custom, a stone shaped by fear of judgment, a stone deaf to the tears of her own daughter.

Djekobou collapsed to her knees, her sobs tearing through the silence of the hut.

"Papa said no. Papa promised!"

But her frail, fading voice drowned beneath the dull pounding of the mortar outside, and the whispers of the women already gathered for the ritual.

Fear curled inside her belly. A brutal betrayal thundered in her heart. And in her hands, clenched against the packed earth, there remained only the raw helplessness of a little girl being robbed of her right to choose.

Her mother crouched beside her, her voice soft but unyielding:

"Do not fear, my daughter. We all went through this me, your grandmother, your aunts. Today we are happy, and our husbands do not complain. Your father thinks he knows everything with his Cepe, but he knows nothing. This is our tradition; others have theirs. If God wanted us all to be the same, He would have made us identical. But since He chose to make us as we are, it is because He wanted us to have our own destiny."

Dawn slowly rose over the village. That morning, a strange silence floated in the air. The men carried on with their activities, indifferent or pretending to be, while in the dim shadows of the huts, the women moved in secret, preparing the rites of an ancient tradition.

The day before the ritual, the young girls were gathered in a communal hut.

They were not alone. Older women, called Sahédés, guardians of the tradition, watched over them.

The night stretched endlessly, filled with songs and stories under the flicker of oil lamps. The future initiates sat awake, their eyes wide, captive to a heavy anticipation.

Their gazes met uneasy, torn between excitement for the unknown and fear of what awaited them. Some huddled together, whispering barely audible prayers. Others forced themselves to smile, trying to imitate the courage of their elders.

The Sahédés, guardians of the rite, asserted their authority with a commanding presence. They repeated tirelessly:

"Tomorrow, you will become women."

There was no room for doubt in their tone.

At dawn, the door opened onto a village already awake. The elderly excisers were there, draped in worn cloths, waiting as they sat on woven mats. In their hands were the ritual tools, worn by time and history.

The girls were called one by one. Their steps were hesitant; their hearts pounded in their chests. Djekobou felt the invisible weight of destiny press upon her shoulders. When she was finally led before the excisers, her whole body tensed.

Exhausted from crying, Djekobou felt their hands grip her without a word. The hands of women she knew. Neighbors, aunts, women who had smiled at her just the day before. But on this morning, they seemed reduced to mere instruments of tradition. Their fingers were hard as iron, their movements deliberate.

Djekobou struggled, screamed, begged again. Her voice, hoarse and broken, rose into the air but no face flinched, no eyes sought hers.

They laid her down on a mat, her knees pinned, her wrists held firmly. The sky above her was a brilliant blue cynical in its indifference.

The blade appeared thin, cold, glinting in the morning light. Djekobou screamed one last time a scream that seemed to travel through time, carrying within it the pain of all those who came before her.

Then came the burning, a searing bite that tore through flesh and shattered her spirit. Her breath caught; her mind staggered between fear, pain, and bottomless darkness.

She closed her eyes so she would see nothing so she could flee to a world where her father would save her, where his voice would rise stronger than all the voices that betrayed her.

But silence returned. The ordeal was done.

And Djekobou, lying on the soiled mat, was no longer a child nor quite herself. Something had been stolen from her.

According to custom, Djekobou like all the other girls who had undergone the ordeal was taken to an isolated hut on the edge of the village. A dark shelter where light barely entered, where wounded bodies healed in silence among whispers and the scent of medicinal plants. There, they would remain hidden from the eyes of men until their wounds closed.

But Gaston was not a man to accept a forbidden boundary without a fight. As soon as he learned where his daughter was, he ran to the hut, breathless, his eyes wild with fear and fury. He wanted to see her, hold her in his arms, tell her she had nothing to blame herself for, nothing to fear, that he was there, that he loved her. He wanted to take her away, bring her home, far from this imposed suffering.

But as soon as he reached the door, several men from the village rushed at him. They seized him, trying to reason with him, to push him away:

"It's tradition, Gaston! You have no right to enter!" He fought like a lion, shouting his daughter's name. *"Djekobou! Djekobou! I'm here!"*

Inside, Djekobou heard her father's voice. A soft warmth spread through her chest. But she did not dare answer. The women watching over them gave her a hard look the look that reminds girls they must be strong and obedient.

Outside, Gaston fell to his knees under the weight of the men, exhausted from struggling, his heart shattered. He struck the earth with his fist, letting out a cry, a cry of love and despair.

"Forgive me, my daughter. Forgive me."

Then, in the silence that followed, he swore before God, before the ancestors, before everything sacred in heaven and earth that he would devote the rest of his life to breaking this chain, uprooting this tradition, so that no other girl would ever have to endure what Djekobou had suffered.

He even planned to take the matter to the authorities.

In the hut where they stayed, the newly excised girls were under the protection of the Sahédés, who watched, enforced silence, and demanded obedience.

Their food was specific: rice drizzled with palm oil, dishes rich in spices, all meant to speed healing.

Time stretched on, punctuated by songs and stories about the importance of the passage they had just completed. After several weeks, when the day of their reintegration arrived, the Sahédés prepared the girls carefully.

Their faces were painted with white kaolin, traditional patterns drawn on them. Their bare chests were covered in white clay; their skin, coated with scented oils, gleamed in the sun. They were no longer the children they once were. They were women.

The whole village gathered, eager to see the new initiates.

They sang, danced, and performed complex movements with stools in hand. The pain seemed to no longer exist. Their bodies moved gracefully. But one final test remained.

In front of them, a blazing fire crackled. They had to leap over it running, without hesitation.

It was the final test:

If they succeeded, it proved their wounds had healed. If they failed, they would be taken back to the hut until fully recovered.

Djekobou inhaled deeply. She watched the others go before her. Some hesitated, but they had no choice. Then her turn came.

Without thinking, she ran. The fire flashed beneath her feet.

She did not stumble. She was free.

Everyone cheered for the survivors. The onlookers didn't hide their delight. They commented, laughed, whispered. A little farther away, an old woman shrieked like someone possessed, running in every direction and demanding a few coins from the spectators. She was a spectacle all on her own. The young girls could now be reintegrated into the community.

At the end of the ceremony, Gaston was there. Standing in the middle of the crowd, his eyes filled with tears. Suddenly, he pushed his way through with determined steps and opened his arms wide.

"Come, my daughter, come." His voice trembled, caught somewhere between the joy of seeing her again and the pain of knowing what she had endured.

Djekobou ran toward him, forgetting the pain in her feet. She threw herself into his arms, burying her head against his chest. There, against that heart beating so hard, she felt safe at last. Gaston's arms closed around her like a soft wall, a fortress of love where no one could hurt her anymore.

Around them, the murmurs faded. No one dared to comment. For within that embrace was something stronger than tradition itself: a father's unconditional love for his child.

"Forgive me..." he whispered into her hair. *"I should have protected you better, never left you alone with your mother… But the harm is done. From now on, I'll be here for you."*

Djekobou didn't answer. Her tears fell, but this time, they were not tears of pain. They were tears of love rediscovered.

And in that suspended moment, under the watchful eyes of the entire village, Gaston and Djekobou were no longer just a father and his daughter. They were the embodiment of hope for a new future.

That September morning, Tenably awoke under a soft, calming coolness. The previous day's torrential rain had left behind a heavy humidity, filling the air with the scent of wet earth. Slowly, the village emerged from its quiet slumber.

The women, straw brooms in hand, swept the yards of their homes, restoring a fresh cleanliness to their spaces. The men sharpened their tools, preparing to return to the fields where the work of the land awaited. Animals joined the morning commotion: sheep and goats wandered in search of leaves and stems to nibble, while pigs rummaged noisily through piles of refuse. Freshly released from their enclosures, roosters, hens, ducks, and guinea fowl scattered about, chirping with their feathers still damp with dew.

A morning like so many others in Tenably.

And yet, for Kpegnan, nothing felt the same anymore.

The holidays were drawing inevitably to an end. Soon, he would again leave the village, leaving behind the family cocoon to return to the big city where Modern High School and the discipline of studies awaited him. But this time, the transition felt different. He was no longer a child. He was now sixteen, preparing to enter his final year of school.

Nostalgia already tugged at him as he thought of the last days spent here, in the village that had watched him grow. He thought of his grandparents, the anchors of his childhood, who had lovingly raised him after his parents passed away. He thought of his childhood friends, with whom he had laughed, run, and played under the big tree in the village square. But more than anyone else, he thought of Djekobou.

Djekobou his unwavering friend, his lifelong ally. They had shared everything, from hesitant first steps to long wanderings through the surrounding nature. Their friendship had grown as they grew, strengthening with every challenge, every secret whispered under the moonlight.

How could he leave without her? How could he face the chaos of the city without that familiar look and voice that had always accompanied him?

The morning wind swept softly through the village, clearing the last traces of the night's rain. Kpegnan knew he had little time left. Before leaving, he had to see Djekobou one last time, before distance came between them.

Djekobou was a bright, quick-witted girl with a promising academic future. But like many girls in the village, she had been forced to quit school to help her mother in the fields. Around her, many of her friends had seen their futures decided without their consent: some married off by force, others resigned to domestic and agricultural chores. Only her friendship with Kpegnan had survived the wear of time and sacrifice.

Around them revolved a carefree group of friends: Kemessié, Bayala, and Kouia.

Kouia nicknamed Kouiyou, *"little white boy,"* by the village kids, was the oldest of the group, already in his twenties. His light skin and mixed features bore the mark of a father from elsewhere: a European timber operator who had built his fortune buying land cheaply from destitute villagers too desperate to realize what they were giving up.

That father, as wealthy as he was arrogant, had met a brutal end crushed under a log he thought he controlled, like everything else. Kouia never spoke of him. He preferred to laugh loudly and ride around rather than dwell on memories heavy with forgotten lessons.

Books and notebooks had never meant much to him. Every new school year, he promised to try, only to flee the classroom for open air and friends. After several failures, he quit school entirely, trading blackboards and roofless, oven-hot classrooms for his Vespa a rare marvel in the village or the wheel of the old tarp-covered Peugeot left by his father.

The wooden house perched on the hill, with its huge fruit trees and massive fence, was all that remained of that ambiguous inheritance. But Kouia wasn't made for fences or boundaries. His true kingdom was the village paths, the empty lots where time was killed, and the evenings where he reigned like a prince, with his booming laugh and fearless swagger.

Among the inseparables was Bayala, tall and wiry, always in motion as though afraid that a moment of stillness would pin him down forever. Son of a man from the far north and a mother from Tenably, he carried two heritages, but his heart beat to the rhythm of the village where he was born.

From childhood, he embraced the local culture, mastering the dialect with ease and sharing the same dreams as his friends. He had even refused to follow his father back to his homeland when the man was summoned to serve as village chief there. They called him *"Petit Mossi*," a nickname honoring his father's origins, which he wore proudly a sign of his complete integration and strong bonds with those who had watched him grow.

But it was above all on the football field that Bayala truly shined. Agile as a panther, he slipped past opponents with feline grace, dodging defenders with a simple step- over or a twist of the hips, to the cheers of children and young girls perched on tree stumps or leaning against the straw belt that circled the field like a fence.

His tandem with Kpegnan was formidable, making village boys self-appointed match commentators lose their voices: *"Bayala Garrincha! Garrincha Bayala! Garrincha... goooal!"*

Together, they were inseparable, capable of turning a match around or alongside Kouia creating unforgettable chaos in the village. Bound by a silent brotherhood, one that needed no words, they shared everything: victories and defeats, laughter and teenage secrets, long nights spent dreaming of a future bigger than their native hills.

And then there was Kemessié a true whirlwind of energy, a barefoot tornado who burst into the group without warning, shaking them up with crude jokes and explosive laughter. A self-proclaimed tomboy with a Pelé-style haircut, she played football with a ferocity that demanded respect. They called her Pelé, and she was a starter on the village's main team.

But behind that warrior's fire, Kemessié hid a magnetic grace. As soon as the rhythms of Têmatê or Aloukou pulsed through the air, her body *became* music. She danced with the fluidity and suppleness of a reed. During village festivals, she captivated the entire crowd, turning dust into a stage and the moment into a performance.

Her reputation as a dancer spread far beyond Tenably. In neighboring villages, her name was whispered with admiration, and the organizers of *Booms* those improvised youth parties never hesitated to invite her to *"set the place on fire,"* because a Boom with Kemessié was an event you didn't want to hear secondhand.

Her story was as rebellious and untamed as she was. After a tumultuous stay with a strict aunt in the city, she was sent back to Tenably due to her nocturnal escapades that raised eyebrows and stirred gossip.

Today, she raised her twins on her own. Two bundles of energy she proudly carried around the village never revealing the name of their father. Gossip? She brushed it aside with loud laughter or a sharp comeback. Kemessié never justified herself. She kept moving, free and upright, in a world that had tried to break her.

In the group of five, she was the flame, wild, burning, and above all, impossible to extinguish.

Kpegnan was an intelligent young man with unmatched speaking talent. Tall and slightly bow-legged, his skin was bronzed and luminous. He had a beautiful smile and never hesitated to show it.

An only child and an orphan, he had never known his father, who died young from tuberculosis. His mother died after being bitten by a venomous snake when he was just five.

A brilliant footballer, he was nicknamed Garrincha for his mesmerizing dribbles. He was the least turbulent of the group and above all, the peacemaker.

If Kpegnan found it so difficult to leave the village, it was mostly because of Djekobou.

She was beautiful and graceful, with a deep, polished dark complexion, big bright eyes filled with intelligence, and a dazzling smile. But beyond her beauty, it was her strength of character, her respect for elders, and her discipline that made her unique. Despite the limitations imposed on the village girls, she carried herself with unshakable dignity.

Her future, however, seemed already mapped out. Like all girls her age, she had undergone the rites of passage, and her father planned to marry her off to one of his loyal friends much older than her. But what about *her* dreams?

Kpegnan and Djekobou's friendship had been sealed one adolescent night in a rush of euphoria and recklessness. That evening, intoxicated by a hard-fought victory on the worn-out field of Bably stadium, they made a decision they would soon regret. Instead of taking the long, monotonous main road home, they chose a shortcut through the forest, a path only the daring used after nightfall.

But nature, fickle and unpredictable, had other plans. As soon as they ventured deeper into the woods, a strong, cold wind rose, howling through the branches like a warning. The sky, streaked with blue lightning, rumbled with contained fury. In an instant, the darkness thickened. Rain poured down mercilessly, torrential and stinging, whipping the leaves and soaking their clothes.

Around them, the trees seemed to twist under the storm's violence, branches cracking in the wind. Each lightning flash revealed an unreal landscape bare trunk, bristling bushes, unsettling shapes. Kpegnan, jaw clenched, held tightly to Djekobou's hand. She, despite her trembling steps, refused to give in to panic.

They were no longer alone. They were at the mercy of the elements and especially of the forest and its mysteries. The most feared danger might have been lurking close by: the terrible boa-serpent.

That long creature the villagers believed immortal. Silent, lurking in the shadows, it would strike, coil around its prey, and swallow it whole. Even the fiercest hunters dared not confront it.

Every rustle in the underbrush made Kpegnan jump.

Djekobou could barely breathe.

The village was only a few steps away, but one final obstacle stood before them: a swollen stream, raging with rainwater. There was only one way across, a slippery tree trunk laid over it like a makeshift bridge. Without a torch, they could barely see. The deafening thunder drowned out their voices. One wrong step and they would plunge into the black water, full of reptiles, stirred by treacherous currents and tangled roots. So they said their last prayers, called upon the ancestors, and, resigned, clung to each other, shivering, in silence.

Then, in the distance, a light. Voices. Silhouettes moving through the night. Their friends, seeing they had not returned, had gone looking for them. Armed with flashlights, machetes, and a shared courage, they crossed the stream and pulled them out from the cold embrace of the forest.

It was a moment of indescribable relief. Soaked to the bone, trembling but alive, they finally reached the village, their hearts still pounding from fear. Upon their arrival, they faced the anger of Kemessié and Kouia, exasperated by their stubbornness. That night, the forest had tried to test them. It failed. Instead, it only strengthened the bonds of their friendship.

That morning, Nan, Kpegnan's grandmother, had risen before dawn. As always, she swept the courtyard with slow, steady steps, tracing little circles in the clay soil with the serene calm of age. Then she placed her large pot on a fire made of three bricks of baked clay. She filled it with water to heat it for Baha, her husband, who never began his day without a scorching hot bath, a habit he had kept since he married her.

Inside the house, all was still quiet. But Kpegnan knew these peaceful, stress-free moments were coming to an end.

Soon, he would have to leave this simple life where time seemed to stretch without constraints, and go to the town of Daloda its crowded hallways, its classrooms, its demanding teachers. A totally different world where Djekobou would no longer be by his side.

Days passed quickly in Tenably, and every moment spent with his family was a treasure he wanted to hold onto. In a few days, he would board a filthy old Badjan to travel to Daloda. But before that, he wanted to savor every second.

He wanted to hear the rooster's morning song one more time, feel the damp earth beneath his feet, and most of all, and see Djekobou one last time.

Despite their deep friendship, Kpegnan secretly harbored feelings for Djekobou. He had never dared tell her, afraid it would break the unique bond they had always shared. But now, with his departure approaching, he felt unable to leave without telling her the truth. Two days before leaving, he asked her to meet him, fully aware of the turmoil this might cause. Anxiety gnawed at him as he pictured her reaction, but he no longer wanted to hide. Better to face reality, no matter how painful, than continue carrying this burden in silence. He hoped without deluding himself that even if she didn't share his feelings, their friendship would survive.

That evening, after a football match and a last- second defeat against Touzon, a game where he had played poorly, distracted and unfocused Kpegnan finally confessed his plan to his friends Bayala and Kouia, still groggy from disappointment.

He hinted that he wanted to talk to Djekobou, to finally tell her how he felt.

At first furious, Bayala shook his head, then sighed, gradually calming down.

"Listen, my guy, my heart is boiling bad, what is it even? That's why you missed all those goals, eh? Honestly, tell her you're tired of going in circles and that you want more than friendship. Me-self, if it wasn't because of you, since long time..." Bayala grumbled.

"*Stop. Since long time what?"* asked Kpegnan, slightly irritated.

Sensing tension, Kouia jumped in and shouted:

"Oh guys! What kind of madness is this? All this because of one defeat? You disappoint me seriously!" Then he turned to Kpegnan, calmer: *"Brother, be honest with Djekobou, but go gently like joking, you see? Test the ground. Use Kissinger's small-steps method."*

Kpegnan, unable to stay angry for long, burst into laughter and teased:

"*You talk like you're flirting experts! Thanks for your advice anyway, but I'll do it my way. And if it all goes bad, I'll say you two pushed me!*"

The trio exploded in laughter, falling back into the carefree, joyful harmony that made their friendship so strong.

Back home, he swallowed the foutou balls his grandmother had prepared without tasting them, his stomach tight with worry. Then, gathering his courage, he headed to the meeting place near Boukary's shop. Djekobou was already there, her eyes filled with curiosity. Without a word, he gently took her hand and led her to their usual hiding spot the quiet corner where the whole group used to meet to invent worlds away from prying eyes.

This time, they were alone. The moment hung heavy with unspoken words.

The time had come. He wanted to tell her everything. But now that she was there, beside him, he froze. Eyes lowered, searching for words, he murmured in a trembling voice:

"*Djekobou, I need to tell you something.*"

"*What again? What's your problem?*" she replied.

"I hope you won't be upset by what I'm about to say," he warned.

"*Talk then! You're making my heart go gboom gboom like that,*" she said.

"*That's exactly why I'm scared to tell you,*" he added.

"*You're there turning, turning only... Speak now!*

Are you not a man or what?" she teased, giving him a little nudge to reassure him.

"Well, it's that..." he began.

"Ah that one! I remember, my teacher told us that in English you no start sentence with 'well, it's that...'' she interrupted, laughing.

"*Look, stop your nonsense, I'm serious. Last night, I had a dream. I dreamed of a girl with dark skin, so pleasant and so beautiful. Her skin was soft like silk. We made love all night and it felt so good. That girl was you,"* he said with a long sigh.

"Ei Jihiii! What kind of dream again is that one? Since it's only dream, it's not bad. I hope you didn't come inside, eh!" she laughed.

"*You're crazy. Be serious just once! Yes, I know... but I want my dream to become real,"* he insisted, emotion burning in his eyes.

Djekobou sighed, half-serious, half-amused:

"*My Kpeg, the thing you no can finish, don't start it. This friend-friend matter sweet oh. No jealousy inside. And you know my papa! He say I must not do anytin' before marriage. That one why he hot-hot to marry me by force to Uncle Prosper."*

But Kpegnan didn't give up. He looked at her intensely and whispered:

"*Djeko, since our paths crossed, I've felt something strong for you. It's not just friendship... it's more. I always wanted to tell you, but I never had the courage. Now, I want us to be more than just friends."*

Djekobou stared at him, surprised.

"What do you have? You talk like person who is crying?" she asked, touched against her will.

She bit her lip, then added with a nervous laugh, eyes on the ground:

"Me-self, truly, since we always play together, I also want... but you are like my brother now. Look for a girl who knows book. I will teach her how to cook Kpélé and okra sauce. Me, I'm a village girl oh!"

A sting of pain hit Kpegnan's heart, but he didn't give up.

"I understand. But let's do it just once and then stop. If you like it, we continue. Forget this village-girl matter. I love you and that's all that counts," he murmured, almost begging.

Djekobou's eyes widened.

"What? You want taste and see? You think I be Banji?" she exclaimed.

"*Me, if you taste, you keep,*"

Kpegnan added.

"*Djekobou, I really love you. Your eyes move me, your softness captivates me. You are everything I desire. At school, plenty of big girls like me, but you're the one I prefer. I want you to be the queen* of *my heart. Just imagine, you and me, together for life.*"

Djekobou looked at him silently, unsure. He continued, wanting to touch her heart:

"*You know, as a Jewish proverb says: giving friendship to someone who wants love is like giving bread to someone who is thirsty.*"

A spark of delight lit Djekobou's eyes, thrown off- balance by his eloquence.

"Hein! All that big english for me alone? Boy can sweet-talk, deh! After that it's to knock-and-leave!"

But her tone softened. She lowered her eyes and added, more seriously:

"Kpeg, what you're saying is a bit hard for me, but I won't lie you please me too. I don't want to spoil a friendship that is so good. What is sure, I go think first and then I go tell you. Eh! Kpegnan, wetin you put me inside like this? Will I even sleep today? You don scatter my head!

A silence settled between them. Then, in a spontaneous impulse, Kpegnan leaned forward and placed a quick kiss on her lips.

Djekobou froze, stunned. Her heart pounded wildly. Without another word, Kpegnan turned and ran, his heart light, a smile lingering on his face. He had just done what he had always dreamed of doing.

And above all, Djekobou had not rejected him. To him, that was a good sign. Maybe, after all, his dream wasn't impossible.

That night, sleep eluded Kpegnan. Lying on his mat, he replayed the events over and over. Every glance, every word exchanged with Djekobou was etched into his memory, imprinted on his soul like a sweet yet painful burn.

In the courtyard, Nanhan, his grandmother, was already awake. True to her habits, she swept the earth floor before preparing breakfast with the previous day's leftovers, a hearty leftovers rice served with okra sauce and palm-seed oil. Later, she would return to the camp, where she spent most of her days.

As for Baha, his grandfather, he had become a shadow of his former self. Once strong and vigorous, he now spent his days lying in his hammock, a fly-swatter in hand, weakly fending off the insects that disturbed his rest. Illness was eating away at his body, and Kpegnan knew his time was running out.

The next morning, as usual, Kpegnan accompanied his uncle Téhé before heading to the fields. Together, they went to extract Banji (a sweet white palm wine) and check the traps they had set the day before.

Téhé was a giant of a man, with muscles like steel and a stare that could make even the bravest men look away. People said he had once subdued an enraged bull with his bare hands. Others swore he possessed mystical powers inherited from his ancestors.

His teeth, once white as ivory, were now stained by kola nuts and eroded by the tobacco he chewed tirelessly every day. He never smiled. To him, smiling was a weakness, a luxury real man didn't have the right to afford. He spoke very little, and his silence was louder than a thousand shouts. When he did speak, faces turned away, not out of disgust, but out of respect, almost fear. Yet beneath that stone armor beat a heart that even hardship had not managed to harden. He didn't speak of love; he proved it.

One day, when Kpegnan was barely ten, curious and stubborn, he dared to challenge the village river with his friends. The current amused him. He wanted to prove he was the bravest. So, when no one was watching, he ventured too far, barefoot on slippery stones.

Suddenly, he slipped. The scream was brief, carried away by the wind. And the child disappeared beneath the waves.

But Téhé, fishing not far away, lifted his head. He did not hear the scream he felt the fear. He rushed toward the rocks where the raging water crashed.

A few meters away, he saw a small arm struggling against the current. And then he saw a shape. Long. Terrifying. Swaying.

A gigantic crocodile.

Téhé did not hesitate. He leapt into the water without a weapon, without fear. He swam against the current, his muscles shaped by a thousand battles fighting the fury of the river. He grabbed Kpegnan with one arm, lifting him out of the water.

But behind him, the monster's jaws opened.

A flash a roar and Téhé turned. With a single strike, he hit the beast on the snout. A violent blow filled with the rage of an uncle ready to die to save one life. The crocodile recoiled, growled, and sank into the dark waters.

Panting, Téhé emerged from the river, the child tightly against him. He fell to his knees, Kpegnan alive, trembling but safe. Water streamed down his body, but his eyes were dry, burning. He stared at the river for a long time and murmured:

"Not today. Not while I live."

The day before his departure, after a hearty breakfast, Kpegnan went to the fields with his uncle as usual. The morning air was still fresh, and the smell of damp earth floated around them. In front of them, Pohe, their loyal hunting dog, trotted with its nose alert, ready to signal any prey.

The first trap had caught a partridge. Farther on, spotting another, Téhé an expert hunter needed no rifle. He loaded his slingshot, aimed, and with precise skill brought down the bird perched on a branch. The partridge collapsed, its feathers still trembling from the impact.

"The day is off to a good start!" Téhé exclaimed, picking up his prize.

They continued their route, checking each trap one by one. The second had captured a rat, the third a well-fed agouti.

"The day is very fruitful, my boy!" Téhé said with satisfaction.

"Yes, uncle," Kpegnan answered timidly, his body present but his mind elsewhere. His heart was clinging to the hope of a reply from Djekobou.

As they approached the last trap, a rustling sound drew their attention. Pohe rushed toward them, foam at its mouth, a sign that something was wrong. Téhé froze, scanning the surroundings. He cut a sturdy branch and handed it to Kpegnan.

"Be ready."

He then armed his bow, fitted an arrow, and in an instant, a pangolin hiding in a thicket fell under a precise shot. Kpegnan's eyes widened. His uncle was a formidable hunter, but he had never seen such a swift and efficient shot.

"A pangolin is a good omen. The ancestors are blessing us today," Téhé said as he retrieved the animal.

Yet the dog remained nervous, refusing to approach the last trap. It paced back and forth, licking its master's feet before retreating cautiously. Téhé knew this was a bad sign.

As they approached, he saw the rope pulled to its limit. Then, movement in the bushes. Téhé advanced carefully and discovered a huge cobra caught in the trap. Its body twisted, its scales shining in the morning light, and its fangs dripping venom. The snake fought fiercely, trying to escape the steel wire that tightened around it.

Téhé glanced at his nephew. It was time to test his courage.

"Finish it. Show me you are a worthy son, a true Tchiglo."

Kpegnan did not back down. He tightened his grip on the branch, and with a powerful first strike, he smashed it onto the serpent's head. The animal thrashed violently. Without hesitation, he struck a second time, then a third. Finally, the cobra fell still.

Téhé nodded, satisfied.

"I recognize a worthy son. You are a true boy. From now on, when they see you, they will flee."

Kpegnan looked at the lifeless snake, his jaw clenched.

"I hate these animals. If I could, I would wipe them all out. One of them took my mother's life."

Téhé drew him close.

"You are right, my boy. The snake is a cowardly and dangerous creature."

Without delay, he cut off the snake's head to be sure it was dead, dug a hole, and buried it. In their tribe, they did not eat snake meat.

With the bag full of game, they headed back, the silence between them broken only by birdsong and the whisper of the wind in the leaves. This hunting day would remain engraved in Kpegnan's memory not only for the abundance of the catch, but for the trial he had just overcome.

Back in the village, they took their game to Nan, who would prepare the next day's meal. Téhé went off to sell the Banji, and Kpegnan, lost in thought, returned home.

As soon as he stepped inside, Baha called him loudly:

"Come here, my boy, I have something to tell you."

Kpegnan nodded.

"I'll wash quickly and come, Grandpa."

Baha dreamed for him a future as a sub-prefect or a great politician. But Téhé had other ambitions. He wanted him to join the Blahons, the secret brotherhood of panther- men, surrounded by myths and legends. They were said to be invincible, able to bewitch anyone who crossed their gaze.

But Kpegnan did not dream of invincibility. His dreams were turned toward the sky. He dreamed of airplanes, of becoming a pilot, of flying far away, of challenging the heavens.

That day, he rushed to shower, dried himself, then grabbed a stool and sat beside his grandfather, ready to listen to his wise words.

"My boy," Baha murmured, coughing, *"my life is coming to an end, while yours is just beginning. I don't know if I will still be here when you return to the village."*

When he spoke of their lineage, his voice grew deeper. He looked the boy straight in the eyes, as if trying to carve his words into him forever.

Kpegnan felt his heart tighten. Tears welled up. "*Why do you say that, Grandpa*?" he asked, voice

trembling.

Old Baha placed a hand on his grandson's and

sighed.

"I can feel it, my child. My time is short. Only God

knows why He delays the inevitable."

Kpegnan shook his head vigorously.

"*No, Grandpa! Nothing will happen to you. This illness is defeated in God's name.*"

The grandfather paused, caught his breath, then continued:

"*I have a few pieces of advice to give you, my boy. Life is full of obstacles, but with wisdom, you can go through it more peacefully. Listen carefully and write them down if you want to keep them."*

Kpegnan took a notebook and pen, ready to record every word.

"*Know that life is much simpler than we think,"* the old man began, his voice calm but full of wisdom. *"We are the ones who complicate it unnecessarily."*

Kpegnan listened thoughtfully. Baha paused again, letting the weight of his words fill the air. Then he continued with a serene smile:

"*Do not seek for things to happen as you want them to. Accept them as they come, and you will find peace."*

Kpegnan frowned slightly, puzzled.

"*Grandpa, are you telling me to be fatalistic?"* he asked with sincere curiosity.

The old man smiled knowingly, as if he had been expecting the question. He shook his head, his eyes filled with the clarity of someone who had lived long and seen much.

"*Not at all, my child."*

He took a deep breath, his piercing look drifting toward the horizon, drawing from the vastness of his experience before replying:

"*It is not about fatalism, but inner balance.*"

He turned back to Kpegnan and continued:

"*Always do your best without expecting anything in return. Win each day. Do what you can with what you have, and let God handle the rest.*"

Though skeptical, Kpegnan felt warmth spread through him at his grandfather's words. Baha continued:

"*Look at the course of a river. It does not stop flowing when faced with obstacles. It does not stop to fear them it goes around or through them, but it stays true to its nature. It does not force its path; it accepts what comes, and that is how it reaches the ocean.*"

He paused again before adding:

"*Life is like a river. Constant effort, but without forcing, without wanting to control everything. Accepting what comes, even if it is not what you imagined, is the key to inner peace.*"

Kpegnan reflected in silence. He had a tendency to force things, to impose his will on events, but something in the way Baha spoke touched him deeply.

"*Should I always wait and not take initiative?*" he asked.

"*No, my child,*" Baha replied gently. "*I am not*

speaking of passivity, but of wisdom. Do everything you can, with honesty and integrity, and let the rest unfold. Life, my child, is as unpredictable as the wind. What you can control is your own conduct. Do not lose sight of that."

Kpegnan felt calmer. He took a moment, then nodded slowly.

"I understand, Grandpa. It's not about giving up my dreams, but accepting that some things are beyond my control."

Baha smiled, his voice soft but firm:

"That's right, my child. In that acceptance lies true freedom a freedom that allows you to live fully, without fear, without regret. Accept life as it is, and you will see it become much simpler.

My son, listen carefully to this: instead of assuming, learn to seek reassurance. Ask questions, try to understand. Never remain a prisoner of your own interpretations. When I was across the ocean during the war, an old sage used to tell me: 'Wisdom begins with the admission of ignorance.' I never forgot that sentence.

Choosing to seek reassurance instead of assuming means preferring rigor over ease, truth over illusion. It is a demanding path, my son, but it avoids many conflicts born of misunderstandings. And above all, it will lighten your heart and free your mind from worries you would have created yourself." With a grave tone, Baha added:

"I should have started with this, for it is very important. My child, never be afraid to ask or to say clearly what you want. A refusal should never frighten you. Everyone has the right to say yes or no. And you have that right too."

Kpegnan lowered his eyes, slightly embarrassed. *"That is my biggest flaw. I never manage to say no, and it exhausts me."*

Old Baha nodded kindly.

"I understand, my son. But mark my words: knowing how to say no is an act of self-love. Saying no means preserving what truly

matters to you. It's about setting healthy boundaries and looking out for your heart, your time, and your energy."

Kpegnan felt a weight lift off his shoulders: *"I was afraid people would paint me as the villain."*

Baha smiled: "*Ah, kiddo, you've still got a long road to travel before you reach wisdom! I understand,*" said Baha. *"But when you say yes to everything, simply out of fear of letting people down, you end up losing yourself. And that breeds fatigue, anxiety, and sometimes even a quiet rage that you bottle up inside. So keep this in mind, my son: a 'no,' delivered with gentleness and respect, can work wonders. It clears the air, nips misunderstandings in the bud, and allows you to stay true to who you are."*

"So a clear 'no,' said calmly and respectfully, is better than a forced 'yes'?"

"Precisely."

He continued: *"Be humble and kind, but don't grovel like an earthworm. If you make yourself into a doormat, people will eventually wipe their feet on you. And remember this: don't blow your own trumpet. Let others sing your praises for you.*"

Kpegnan cracked a smile. *"That works out perfectly, since I'm very modest myself,"* he threw back with a hint of amusement.

The grandfather grinned, lightly tapping his fist on his thigh. *"Always look before you leap. Every decision you make will always have consequences. You can't control everything, but your reaction? That belongs to you. If you let anger, pride, or fear take the wheel, you're done for. But if you practice patience, calm, and discernment, you can always choose how you face adversity."*

Kpegnan replied: *"Is that the best way to not fall victim to circumstance, Grandfather?*"

"Exactly, and above all, respect your neighbor and your word. It makes the man."

He stood up slowly and paced a little, as if chewing over the very words he had just spoken.

"When you give your word, it must be sacred. A man without his word is like a broken branch. Useless. Trust is fragile and, once shattered, it's a hard thing to fix. Words are what bind men together. If you want to be a man of honor, don't make promises you can't keep. Because a broken promise cuts deeper than silence."

Kpegnan remained mute, thinking about the commitment he was preparing to make with Djekobou. Then he looked up at him: *"Grandfather, do you mean we must always stick to our commitments, even if the temptation to break them is strong?"*

"Yes, my child," Baha nodded. *"Temptation will always be there. But he who gives in to empty promises will never find peace of mind. True dignity lies in honesty and loyalty."*

"Grandfather, some temptations are irresistible, especially women. But I will try to put your advice into practice."

Kpegnan, now more mature in his thinking, felt stronger. These words, though simple, carried great depth, and he swore to put them to good use for the rest of his life.

"Thank you, Grandfather, I will try to follow your advice to the letter."

"That is all I ask of you, my son. Don't forget that wisdom doesn't lie in what we do, but in how we do it. And the way we choose to live."

He wanted to get up, but Baha held him back by the hand. *"Wait, my son, that's not all. You are the only member of the family going to school. Make sure to bring honor to the family and hold the lineage's name high. Take good care of your grandmother."*

Baha rummaged through his old leather satchel, worn by time, and pulled out a small pendant: a panther's tooth suspended from a hand-braided cord. He handed the object to Kpegnan.

"I have one last secret to entrust to you. This belonged to your great-grandfather. He wore it through the great crossings, the famines, the epidemics, through the war. He gave it to me when I was recognized as a man. Today, it is your turn."

Kpegnan held out his hands, almost trembling. He felt the weight of the object, modest, yet heavy with meaning. Baha gently tied the pendant around his neck, then placed his hand over his heart.

"This isn't just a piece of jewelry. It's a reminder. Whenever you are tempted to forget where you come from, or who you are, touch it. It will bring you back here, under this tree, to those who love you and came before you."

A silence wrapped around the two silhouettes. Kpegnan lowered his head and whispered: *"I will do you proud, Grandfather. I promise you. But promise me you'll be here for Christmas break. Hang in there, you still have time left to live."*

After listening religiously to his grandfather and taking plenty of mental notes, Kpegnan hugged old Baha.

Then he ran toward his grandmother, who was busy finishing the evening meal. Nanhan, who knew her little one's tastes, had cooked his favorite meal: a rich *Palm nut soup* tinted with black mushroom juice, with agouti meat, accompanied by a good *foutou* of unripe plantain.

Kpegnan was hungry, but every bite seemed tasteless. His mind was elsewhere, haunted by Djekobou's words and her gaze. He knew he couldn't leave the village without hearing her answer.

Night was softly blanketing Tenably. The air was thick with the familiar smell of wood fires and damp trees. Kpegnan still had a few loose ends to tie up before his imminent departure, but his heart beat for only one thing: Djekobou's answer. He hurried to finish his meal, his eyes fixed on the horizon.

For her part, Djekobou had spent the night thinking. Her mind was torn between the fear of the unknown and the intensity of the feelings binding her to Kpegnan. Finally, she made her decision and sent her little brother Tahi to warn Kpegnan that she would wait for him at eight o'clock in the school courtyard.

When the time for the meeting arrived, Kpegnan was already there. Alone at the rendezvous spot, he kept a lookout for her arrival, his heart pounding out of his chest.

The minutes ticked by slowly. Thirty minutes passed, and ants were in his pants. Yet, he remained calm, convinced she would eventually show up.

And then, finally, she appeared.

Djekobou approached, her demeanor fleeting but determined. A sweet perfume floated around her, a subtle scent that awakened a thousand memories in Kpegnan.

She was dressed in a see-through mini-skirt, with nothing underneath, and a small white sleeveless top that struggled to contain her firm, round chest.

When she spotted Kpegnan, a wide smile stretched across her face. A smile that spoke volumes about her intentions.

Kpegnan, for his part, felt a sudden heat invade his body. Earlier in the day, he had drunk *Banji*, a fermented drink mixed with a green, slimy, and terribly spicy concoction. The effect was immediate: he was having a hard time controlling his desire, his Adidas shorts struggling to hide his excitement.

The two young people sat side by side, hand in hand, on the donut seller's table.

Without waiting for Djekobou to express her decision, Kpegnan leaned in gently and began to lick her neck, while slipping a chicken feather into her ear. She shivered at the touch but stayed calm.

Kpegnan, feverish, felt his palms sweating. He wanted to speak, but his words seemed to vanish into the night air. Djekobou lowered her eyes before raising her head with visible hesitation.

Then, in a soft voice, she whispered: *"My brother, my friend, my everything, are you really sure this is what you want? Love, It's not joking matter oh!"*

While Djekobou tried to explain that she was afraid of being let down and that she cared deeply for their friendship, Kpegnan, carried away by emotion, moved closer, his gestures becoming tenderer. He whispered in her ear, in a soft and reassuring voice:

"I've been waiting for this moment for a dog's age. If you feel the same way too, then don't fight your feelings. There is no harm in loving, in letting yourself be carried by what you feel. We are made to feel, darling... so trust me."

With a delicate motion, he pulled Djekobou to him and kissed her. She closed her eyes, swept away by a wave of new and troubling sensations. Their hearts beat in unison, and without really understanding how, she let herself be carried away by the moment. It was a unique moment, a discovery both sweet and intense.

When their breathing calmed, they remained embraced for a moment before heading back, walking arm in arm through the gentleness of the night.

«What a thrill*!* » Kpegnan exclaimed, wiping the sweat beading on his forehead.

Djekobou frowned, perplexed. *"What?"*

Kpegnan burst out laughing, shaking his head. *"No, no, I wasn't talking about that! I just meant that I loved this moment with you.*

Djekobou sighed, relieved, before smiling shyly. "*Ah… I thought you were pulling my leg.*"

They exchanged a look of conspiratorial understanding before continuing on their way, savoring the silence charged with meaning, now bound by a memory they would never forget.

"*No, darling, I could never do that. I love you sincerely and I don't want to lose you. Just imagining my life without you scares me to death. I don't know what would become of me if you were to disappear."*

Kpegnan spoke with visible sincerity, his eyes locked into Djekobou's. She bent over with laughter, amused by his seriousness.

"Oh, really? You mean I'm the one who's going to kick the bucket before you?"

"*No, no, that's not what I meant!* » he corrected himself immediately. « *I just mean that if one of us had to check out first, I dare not even imagine…"*

He paused, searching for the right words, before adding:

"*I just pray that God keeps us together for as long*

as possible. You are my wife from this day forward, and nothing can tear us apart. I was born to love you, and since I know you adore me, we will cherish each other for eternity."

Djekobou raised an eyebrow, a mischievous smile playing on her lips.

"Hmm... I sure hope you aren't just saying all that to sweet-talk me! We know you boys. Sweet mouth like honey. Don't come chop me for free then throw me away, eh!"

Kpegnan shook his head, annoyed. "*We say 'make love,' not what you just said. You love profanity too much; it dirties the mouth and stains the soul."*

Djekobou giggled, provocatively. "*Oh really? 'It's English, no? Or what?' Even the white people created their word, and then you guys are ashamed to say it.* 'Sorry, oh my dear.'"

"You understood exactly what I said, 'Don't do plan, don't pretend, eh!'"

"Yes, but you need a little modesty all the same. Your vulgarity bothers me sometimes. Do you even know the etymology of the word you just used?"

She rolled her eyes, exasperated. "*Ah, please, l*eave me small here with your big-big English."

"What I mean is that I am not a woman you take and toss aside like a rag. I have always said: the one who is first with me, we will die together. You know me well! So from today on, you and me, c'est collé-serré, until the bitter end."

She spoke with disconcerting assurance, and Kpegnan couldn't help but smile.

"Alright, don't worry. If it were up to me, not even death would part us. I'd like to have four children with you: two girls and two boys. I've even already picked out their names: Potey, Gnahe, Dehi, Gnansou."

Djekobou roared with laughter and teased him: "*You, you're really jumping the gun! But if it's a boy, I want us to call him Gaspard!"*

Their laughter rose into the night, carrying promises and hope.

"Stop cracking me up, I'm dead serious."

Kpegnan's tone was grave, sincere. He looked Djekobou in the eyes, trying to anchor the truth of his words there. Then he burst out laughing again. When he regained his composure, he said:

"Djekobou, I have never been so sure of anything. I want you to know that you matter more than anything to me. I adore you, you can't understand. And if I ever do anything that hurts you, may the full rigor of divine law fall upon me."

Djekobou raised an eyebrow, a mocking smile on her lip. *"There is a law matter inside this thing again?"*

"You, starting today, you and me, it's for life. If I die, you die with me, okay! "Don't come later and say I no know paper, eh!"

She laughed heartily, and so did he. But behind the laughter, they knew. It wasn't just a game, not just empty words. It was a promise. They gazed at the bright moon, letting the silence speak for them. Then, gently, they parted ways.

Djekobou returned home, her heart fluttering, a smile on the edge of her lips. Kpegnan went back whistling, drunk on a happiness he had desired for far too long.

Since that day, Kpegnan had never stopped thinking about Djekobou.

When Kpegnan got home, the household was asleep. Only Nanhan, his grandmother, faithful in her love and her worry, was still waiting for him.

"Where were you, my son? I was worried sick."

Kpegnan smiled. "*Nan, there's nothing to fear. I'm a big boy now. I was just at Mister Amani's watching 'Télé pour* nous'."

Nan nodded, not entirely convinced. "*You leave tomorrow. Is your luggage ready?"*

Then, like a mother who thinks of everything, she added: *"Your nephew wanted to steal your pair of crepe- soled shoes and your silk shirt. I hid them behind the mattress, don't forget them. Also, old Gbéhé entrusted a package to you for his daughter in the city. Put it safely with your things, you're too absent-minded."*

Kpegnan smiled. "*Thank you, Nan. I'm going to rinse off and hit the hay."*

The next morning, at the first crow of the rooster, Nanhan was already up. She prepared *''riz couché''*, a leftover rice dish much appreciated by Kpegnan before a long journey.

Tenably was located five kilometers from the main road, and the only truck serving the village stopped there once a day around noon. Those who missed it had to either hoof it the whole way or wait until the next day.

Noon was creeping up. In front of Bakary's shop, which served as the bus station, the whole family had gathered. A heavy wait hung in the air, palpable in the shifting glances. Everyone was scanning the horizon. Only Djekobou was missing. Since dawn, she had locked herself in her hut, overwhelmed by confusion and shame. The night before, she had abandoned herself to Kpegnan, her childhood friend, the one with whom she had laughed so much, shared so much. in an instant, innocence had tipped over. She had broken the promise made to her father, the one to keep her virginity until marriage. Since then, a deep embarrassment gnawed at her, mixed with painful confusion. A thousand questions spun relentlessly in her mind. Would their friendship survive this shift? Would Kpegnan still love her? Would he marry her one day? Or would there remain only silence, and the weight of a memory too heavy to carry?

Kpegnan stood a little apart from the group. He scrutinized the road without really seeing it, arms crossed over his chest. He could easily guess why Djekobou wasn't there. He wasn't caught off guard, but he was deeply troubled by it.

He replayed their gestures, their mingled breath, the clumsy tenderness of the night before. Nothing had been premeditated; everything had imposed itself with a gentle and irresistible force. But the weight of that moment weighed heavily on his shoulders.

He blamed himself, without really knowing why. He had always respected Djekobou. Their friendship was a rare thing. Had he ruined everything? Was it too soon? he asked himself.

His eyes turned toward the hut from which she did not emerge. He would have liked to talk to her, to tell her that he regretted nothing, that she had no reason to be ashamed, that he loved her perhaps more than he had ever admitted to himself. But he was afraid too. Afraid of what she really felt, afraid that the silence had already begun to drive a wedge between them.

Then, the roar of an engine split the silence.

Moussa, alias Café Noir, had just arrived.

His apprentice, Ladji, adjusted the wheel chock while Moussa, a Gitane cigarette in the corner of his mouth and a glass of black coffee in hand, shouted: *"Ladji, you must put the wedge good there! Hey you people, do fast fast or I go leave!"*

Kpegnan climbed into the back of the vehicle, his step heavy. Around him, faces were frozen in mute sadness. His friends tried to mask their pain, but their eyes spoke for them.

When the engine grumbled, breaking the silence of departure, a cry rang out behind him. It was Nan, his grandmother. She broke down in tears, arms outstretched toward him, trying to hold him back one last time.

Kpegnan looked away, a lump in his throat. He wanted to maintain his dignity, to hide the tears welling up. He knew people were watching him. Everything about him screamed attachment. He had never known how to love halfway. His natural tenderness, his frank smile, his spontaneous generosity. All of this made him a deeply loved being. And that is why he was leaving a void.

As he started up, Moussa spewed a cloud of dust and smoke over the people present at the station. He knew this road like the back of his hand and knew how to dodge every pothole that littered it. Moussa loved the adrenaline rush that speed gave him. He couldn't care less about the screams of the passengers, who tried to convince him to slow down and drive carefully.

Sitting by the window, Kpegnan let his thoughts wander.

Nanhan, the children's laughter, the paths between the huts, the nights studded with stars, the whispered promises. Everything danced in his mind. A long, deep sigh escaped his lips. He was only leaving for three months, and yet, deep down, it felt as if he were leaving a whole world behind for an eternity.

Crossing through the village, his gaze rested in turn on the church, the school, then on the sandy field that served as a football stadium, with its wooden goalposts of uneven sizes, witnesses to the fierce matches played during the holidays.

Moussa's rickety bus lurched forward in a cloud of dust, bumping along the potholed track. Despite the jolts and the deplorable state of the road, he floored it, swallowing the five kilometers separating the village from the crossroads in no time flat.

At the crossroads, a few travelers were waiting in the shade of a tree. They hopped on in a rapid ballet of greetings and bags thrown onto the roof. Then, without dilly-dallying, the bus started up again, coughing out a plume of smoke, heading for the city.

Kpegnan, glued to the window, tried to breathe the outside air, but every bump of the vehicle kicked up a wave of stifling smells inside: stale sweat, damp fabrics, and whiffs of poorly digested food.

The bus had been rolling under a blazing sun for a few hours. The passengers were packed like sardines, some dozing off, others sitting on stools in the aisle, griping about the lack of space.

Arriving at a makeshift rest stop, the *Badjan* came to a halt with a dull rumble, kicking up a cloud of reddish dust that clung to clothes and stung the nostrils. As soon as the wheels stopped turning, Moussa shouted in a loud voice:

"Fifteen minutes rest! If somebody wanna eat, pee or shit, he must do it now, quick quick!"

Immediately, passengers leaped out of the vehicle. Others made a break for it toward the sparse bushes, eager to release the tension built up by hours of bumps and stifling heat.

Some vanished into the tall grass, diving into the wild vegetation, while others, less concerned with modesty, simply turned their backs to the minibus to relieve themselves against the first tree they saw. A little further away, a woman, her loincloth tied tightly around her hips, crouched behind a pile of garbage, casting nervous glances to each side, haunted by the fear that prying eyes might violate her fragile privacy.

A young man, clearly in distress, caught attention against his will. Seized by a sudden and violent attack of the runs, his features tense, he tried to sprint toward a nook, hand pressed to his stomach. Alas, he didn't even have time to drop his trousers. A split-second hesitation, a grimace, and the drama unfolded, discreet but fragrant. Ashamed, he stood rooted to the spot for a few seconds, legs trembling, before limping away, eyes on the ground, in an awkward silence that no one dared to break.

Fortunately, in this rather ghastly theater, a kind- hearted passenger approached without saying a word, opened a plastic bag, pulled out an old pair of sweatpants, and handed them to him. The garment, too big for the young man, billowed around his hips, but no matter: it covered the essentials, and at that moment, that was all that mattered.

This stop was truly a sticky situation for some travelers. Not far away, another passenger, down on his luck, stepped with all the clumsiness of fate onto a pile of excrement hidden under a banana leaf. A squishy sound, then a cry of disgust made those around him jump. He lifted his sandal, looking horrified, searching in vain for something, anything to wipe off this foul gift. Around him, some burst out laughing, others turned their heads with a grimace.

The air, already thick with dust, sweat, and smoke from the surrounding fields, thickened with another smell, more brutal, more sickening: that of excrement left there by entire generations of travelers. A treacherous breeze picked up, carrying the acrid bitterness of fresh urine baking in the scorching sun. Kpegnan looked away, a grimace distorting his usually serene face. This degrading ritual of long hauls to the big city had always repulsed him, but it was part and parcel of the journey.

Near the vehicle, a few women were hustling, their shrill voices calling passengers to come buy something to curb their hunger. Hot bread smeared with pâté, pieces of grilled meat still smoking over a flickering fire, braised plantains, roasted peanuts. But even the mouth-watering aromas couldn't mask the foul stench of the makeshift latrines. Despite everything, a few travelers rushed over, their stomachs stronger than their sense of smell, shamelessly trading their dignity for a bite of survival.

Kpegnan leaned against the minibus door, arms crossed, eyes lost on the horizon shimmering in the heat. It was just one pit stop among many. But each stop carried within it a raw slice of this unvarnished life, that of the roads, empty stomachs, and stubborn smells that whisper the tales of those forgotten as soon as they move on.

When the horn tore through the air to call the straggling passengers, Kpegnan hopped back into the minibus, eager to flee this suffocating halt. He pulled his handkerchief over his face, a gesture that had become second nature to filter the air saturated with smoke, sweat, and lingering odors. When the engine roared, the wheels spat out a shower of dry earth, and the vehicle lurched forward again, swallowing the bumpy track with jolts that made the passengers shudder.

The journey was still long, and this stop surely wouldn't be the last. But as the landscapes rolled by before his eyes, Kpegnan felt both wonder and melancholy. Every nook and cranny of this land, which he had traversed on foot to participate in football tournaments, reminded him of a memory, a story, an unbreakable bond with his village that he was leaving behind, at least for a while.

Kpegnan let his eyes float along with the passing landscape, trying to capture every fragment of this land whose faces, sufferings, and secrets he knew.

Crossing through a village, he noticed the cemetery appearing on the left, calm, and almost ghostly. The graves, devoured by time, seemed to be fading little by little under the bite of the wind and the assault of wild weeds. Leaning wooden crosses still fought against oblivion. Here, the dead slept without witness, rocked only by the breath of the wind slipping through the dry grass. Kpegnan shivered. This cemetery was the mute memory of the village, a memory crumbling gently under the weight of indifference.

Further on, life reclaimed its rights. He spotted a procession of women, marching with a steady step on the path, some barefoot or wearing sandals full of holes. They carried heavy buckets of water on their heads, balanced with disarming elegance. On their backs, babies slept, rocked by the natural sway of their hips, in perfect harmony with the majestic rhythm of their walk.

Others carried immense baskets overflowing with provisions or massive bunches of bananas. Their loincloths, worn and blackened by sweat and dirt, danced in the burning light; every step drew ripples of bright fabric, merging with the dust rising under their feet.

They spoke little, but when a sentence burst forth or a laugh escaped, it was like a discreet song, a fleeting melody flying toward the sky. Kpegnan watched them, fascinated. He saw in this rhythmic march a lesson in courage, poetry without words, and the very soul of the village beating its rhythm, unyielding and beautiful.

As the bus moved on, the landscape changed again. As far as the eye could see, dense forest bordered the road, its great trees casting their majestic silhouettes against the sky. In places, cornfields stretched to the horizon, rippling in the breeze.

A little further, rice paddies glistened under the sun, their shimmering waters reflecting the blinding daylight. Bent figures, equipped with sickles and baskets, worked the earth with the quiet endurance of those who follow the immutable rhythm of the seasons, pulling up weeds or transplanting young seedlings.

But another battle was playing out within these fields: the one against pilfering birds. Boys perched on wooden platforms waved pieces of cloth attached to long poles to scare away flocks of sparrows and starlings eager for ripe grain. At times, a piercing cry split the air, followed by the sharp crack of stones launched by homemade slingshots.

These ceaseless struggles were part of the daily grind for the peasants, a stubborn fight between man and nature, where cunning and perseverance were the only weapons against the voracity of hungry birds.

Arriving at the bridge over the Sandra River, Kpegnan shuddered. He had a visceral fear of water ever since, as a child, he had nearly drowned while swimming with Djekobou and the others. Every crossing of the old suspension bridge over the Sandra River reawakened this buried anxiety.

As soon as the vehicle drove onto it, he closed his eyes, tense in his seat, holding on for dear life to whatever he could. Every jolt, every creak of concrete under the wheels gave him the impression that the whole thing was going to collapse. The heavy silence of the other passengers, their faces taut with palpable fear, only heightened his unease. When the bus finally cleared the bridge, Kpegnan heaved a heavy sigh. Those five minutes of crossing felt like an eternity to him.

Part 2

After hours on the road that seemed to drag on forever, he finally arrived in Daloda. The Daloda bus station was a world unto itself, a bubbling theater where a thousand scenes played out at once. The moment Kpegnan set foot on the ground, he was struck by the hustle and bustle that reigned there. The laterite soil, kicked up into dust by the ceaseless coming and going of vehicles and passersby, was alive with a constant hubbub.

Green taxis, the color of the city of gazelles, honked incessantly to elbow their way through the packed crowd. Their worn-out bodywork bore witness to years of loyal service on the city's chaotic roads. Drivers haggled loudly with passengers, with their arms resting nonchalantly on open windows.

Nearby, sweating porters struggled to push their push-carts loaded with heavy goods: sacks of rice, crates of yams, bunches of bananas, jugs of red oil. They shouted at the drop of a hat to alert pedestrians:

"*Wotro, Wotro, get off the road, let us pass!*"

Some, shirtless and muscled from the exertion, sporting *gris-gris* on their forearms, wiped their brows with scraps of cloth, while others negotiated with female customers who had voices like foghorns.

Under a corrugated iron shed, the transport company's counters were under siege. Endless lines of travelers stretched out before small wooden openings, where employees wrote out tickets by hand.

A crier, perched on a stool, chanted the next destinations:

"Bamakro, Bamakro! Departure imminent! Only three seats left!" "Bobokry direct, with a layover in Conagnoa! Hop on, make it snappy!" "Nabidjan, direct!"

The *Badjans* buses, heavy and rickety, awaited their passengers, their roofs groaning under luggage piled slapdash and held together by ropes tied in a hurry. Their bodies, painted blue and white, sported evocative names like "*God Only Knows*" or "*The Hand of the Eternal,*" a reflection of the drivers' faith, given the sometimes-dodgy state of their vehicles.

Near the entrances, food vendors were making money hand over fist, drawing in a famished crowd. The mouth-watering aroma of sheep skewers, braised bananas, and yellow bread stuffed with vermicelli wafted through the air, mingling with the fumes of gasoline and exhaust.

Agile and crafty street hawkers weaved through the passersby, shouting:

"*Hot cakes, sweet breads!" "Caramel candies, cigarettes, matches, popito*!"

Off to the side, mechanics, looking like grease monkeys in dirty outfits with hands blackened by oil, were busy around a broken-down bus. One of them, a wrench clenched between his teeth, cursed as he tried to tighten a stubborn bolt.

At a busy intersection, while some stood lookout, young opportunists were busy selling party cards for the single party, often expired to illiterate passersby, mostly unsuspecting folks from neighboring countries. Exploiting their ignorance, they presented these documents as golden tickets, playing on fear and the necessity of political belonging to offload their merchandise.

A police officer in a khaki uniform and black kepi prowled the station, keeping a suspicious eye on the gatherings. He occasionally exchanged a few words with the drivers, tossing out warnings or demanding a few crumpled bills to turn a blind eye to an overloaded vehicle.

In this organized chaos, every element had its place, every actor played their role in this ceaseless ballet. For Kpegnan, the scene was both fascinating and tedious. This place, teeming with life, where everything seemed to unfold in a noisy but perfectly masterminded disorder, marked the beginning of his stay in Daloda every single time.

Waiting for him at the station was Kamone, one of his late mother's nieces.

Kamone was a woman of elegance and refinement. A German teacher at the middle school, she enjoyed the finer things in life, living in a plush villa located in an upscale neighborhood near the *"40 Logements."* She drove a Citroën, a symbol of her independence and success.

Fair-skinned, with a slender silhouette and average height, she radiated a natural beauty enhanced by a warm smile she wore come rain or shine. Yet, behind this confidence, she kept mum about her private life.

Rumor had it, however, that she was engaged to a businessman living in the United States, twenty-five years her senior, whom she had met on a flight to Hamburg, Germany. Their relationship, though kept under wraps, was sincere. She loved him deeply, and he, despite the distance, regularly shuttled between the USA and Daloda to be by her side.

Despite the excitement of the reunion, Kpegnan knew that Daloda would be a far cry from his village. Here, everything moved at a breakneck pace; the urban effervescence contrasted with the tranquility of his village. This year, he was determined to make the grade, to honor his mother's memory, and to show himself worthy of the trust his family placed in him.

After retrieving his khaki canvas suitcase and a precious old briefcase, a gift from his grandfather, Kpegnan scanned the crowd until he finally spotted Kamone.

There she was, leaning with a casual air against her freshly washed white Citroën, dressed in a fitted denim suit that highlighted her natural elegance. She exuded a quiet confidence with her sunglasses carefully perched on her nose.

When she spotted Kpegnan, with a fluid gesture, she raised her hand to wave, before walking toward him with a warm smile, radiating her signature kindness.

"*Kpegnan, my boy! Welcome to Daloda*!" she said, ruffling his hair.

"Thank you, Tantie Kamone."

"Did you have a good trip? Not too worn out?"

"A little, but I'm okay. The road was long and the station... it was a total circus!" he replied, laughing.

Kamone shrugged with amusement. *"Ah, yes, with the bad roads, it's no walk in the park. You, who go to the village all the time, should be used to it by now."*

She popped the trunk of her car, and Kpegnan stowed his things.

"*Well, my dear nephew, in three days, you start your final year. It's the home stretch, you need to buckle down.*"

"*I know, Tantie. I'm going to do everything to pass my baccalaureate. Grandfather is counting on me."*

She nodded with satisfaction before continuing: *"In a few weeks, you'll join the boarding school. But in the meantime, you'll stay at the house. Use this time to recharge your batteries. I want to see a student in top form, studious and diligent again this year."*

Kpegnan smiled shyly. *"Yes, Tantie. I'll give it my best shot."*

Kamone shot him a knowing look as she started the car. *"Don't worry, I'm sure you'll succeed. But avoid getting a swelled head, because the bac exam is nerve- wracking. With a little discipline and a lot of hard work, nothing can stop you, my son."*

The Citroën slowly pulled away from the station, leaving the bubbling hubbub of the city behind them. Sitting in the front, Kpegnan watched in silence as the carefully aligned trees along the road and the well- maintained grass bordering Daloda's paved streets rolled by the window.

In a contemplative mood, he said to himself: *"This city truly earns its nickname, the Green City."*

On the first day of school, the high school was abuzz. Students were returning from the four corners of the country. Tales of the holidays were flying around: romantic conquests, football tournaments, wild parties. Some proudly sported their brand-new khaki outfits. Others, more low-key, hid their worn and wrinkled uniforms. And then there was the fresh meat, the new students, lost and intimidated by the high school racket.

At the start of every school year, the new sixth- grade students were subjected to a humiliating shakedown session.

Even prodigy students didn't escape the high school rituals. Kpegnan had known this ritual a few years earlier. They had forced him to improvise a love speech to the rusty statue that sat enthroned in front of the teachers' lounge, in front of a hilarious crowd. He had come out of it with flying colors, turning the prank into a performance. Kpegnan's poem, which had won over the entire assembly and commanded immediate respect from the seniors, went like this:

To love... a tender word, a vast word, that we think we know, but which always slips through our fingers. It is not merely a simple affection, It is a flame, a source, a mystery.

The sages of old, the lexicographers of martial times, have scrutinized its roots, plumbed its etymology, To decipher the enigma of the human heart.

In the school of grammar, to love is conjugated thus: I love, you love, he or she loves, We love, you love, they love.

But in the secret language of souls, Love invents other conjugations: I love you, you adore me, we cherish each other, and every heartbeat becomes a living verb.

Yet, to love is not reduced to words declaimed on bended knee: "Oh my angel, queen of my heart, Your regard bewitches me, your eyes burn me! I would die for you!"

Often, the heart is far from these monuments of swollen words. To love is less about speaking than living, Less about promising than giving, Less about dazzle than building.

Today, it was his turn to watch the newbies go through the wringer. He had neither pity nor cruelty for them; he simply knew it was the rule of the game. Here, no one grew up without learning to laugh at themselves.

Amidst this tumult, Kpegnan seemed strangely absent. The noise of the first day reached him like a distant hum, drowned out by the inner voice of his memories. He was thinking of Djekobou, of Nanhan, of Baha, of the winding paths of Tenably, and of that promise buried in the dust of his native village.

He knew that this year would not be like the others.

Kpegnan was no ordinary student. His sparkling intelligence had carried him through the grades like a leaf pushed by the wind. In primary school, he had skipped 2nd grade, and later 5th grade. At only 17, he was already in his final year, ready to snag his baccalaureate.

But what was most striking about him was this two- sided nature: on one hand, a brilliant student capable of solving complex equations without breaking a sweat; on the other, a carefree teenager, always dressed to the nines, passionate about fashion and football. Where some hid behind poverty or lack of time to explain their sloppiness, Kpegnan took care of his appearance, refusing to let his modest origins define his look.

Kpegnan had a gift that fascinated as much as it unnerved: he learned without effort. His classmates whispered that he hid a talisman, a bewitched pen that wrote the answers for him. His math teacher, amused by this reputation, had made a habit of slipping a *"Special Kpegnan"* question into every exam. A personal challenge that the student rose to every time, adding more fuel to his legend.

He had a circle of loyal friends, and especially Aimso, his inseparable sidekick, the son of a high-ranking official and self-proclaimed prince of fashion. He showered Kpegnan with gifts in gratitude for his help with studying. Thanks to him, Kpegnan sometimes wore designer shirts, tailored trousers, and even flashy watches that set tongues wagging among the girls.

On the first day of class, when the bell rang, drowning out the shouts and laughter for a moment, Kpegnan looked up at the sky. Behind the heat, behind the dust, somewhere between Tenably and this high school, he was looking for a sign. Perhaps the promise that one day, this life of a small schoolboy would become the first chapter of a great story.

While Kpegnan was lost in his thoughts, two familiar silhouettes emerged from the crowd: Aimso and Léopold, his eternal partners in crime.

Knowing that for this first day, the khaki uniform wasn't mandatory, Aimso, true to form, wore a checkered shirt in bright colors, a flashy watch, and shoes polished so bright they could blind the sun. Kpegnan, more discreet but just as sharp, wore sky-blue Wranglers, a bottle-green Lacoste shirt, and a pair of two-tone Ferradinis, dark brown mixed with black. By his side, Léopold, always the picture of sobriety, sported an immaculate Coq Sportif tracksuit, blindingly white.

"*Heeey, the genius of Tenably, look what the cat dragged in!*" shouted Aimso, opening his arms wide; a theatrical exaggeration that only he knew how to pull off.

Kpegnan cracked a smile. Aimso hadn't changed a bit. Always loud, always extravagant, always ready to make a scene out of every moment.

Behind him was Léopold with his short hair, still glistening with sweat, and his frank smile lighting up his face.

"*Kpeg, my brother, you're still alive*!" he exclaimed, giving him a friendly slap on the back.

The three friends met under the great acacia tree that reigned over the courtyard. This acacia was more than a tree: it was their headquarters, their sanctuary, their improvised conference table where they set the world to rights at every recess.

"So, spill the beans! Did the big city make you important or are you still that villager in love with Djekobou?" asked Aimso, a mocking glint in his eyes.

Kpegnan laughed softly, but his smile froze for a split second at the mention of Djekobou. *"Nothing has changed. Except maybe my nights... they're longer without Nanhan's foutou and without your nonsense."*

Laughter erupted, breaking the tension, at least for a moment. As was their habit, they started walking toward the small stands of the school vendors, where oil sizzled joyfully and the smell of golden fried plantains and fried fish enveloped the courtyard.

Léopold grabbed an abandoned ball and, with a precise kick, sent it to Kpegnan, who intercepted it with the agility of a player used to improvising. The trio crossed the courtyard, between clumsy juggling and bursts of laughter, carefree on the surface, but each internally dragging a skeleton in the closet that the first day of school couldn't quite erase.

After receiving their schedules, it was time to hit the books.

The first class was history with Monsieur Zokou. Zokou was a small man with a dark complexion, long hair, and a thick beard. Always with a cigarette dangling from the corner of his lips, he sweated profusely and displayed an open contempt for the current government, which he never missed an opportunity to criticize. As a leader of the teachers' union, he used his classes to grind his axe and share his frustrations with his young students, who were hungry for knowledge. He spent his time telling stories and, in their naivety, these teenagers took his words as the gospel truth.

Zokou was a pseudo-pan-Africanist, systematically blaming all of Africa's woes on the "damned white colonists." Yet, irony of ironies, he had married the high school gardener, a woman of French origin, thanks to whom he had obtained French citizenship.

Through a twist of fate, she had even become a French teacher at the high school due to a shortage of staff. Despite his declared hatred of Westerners, he never missed an opportunity to jet off to France for the holidays.

"This year, our curriculum includes: the Israeli- Palestinian conflict, the United Nations and their role, and so on. But with me, my children, we are going to talk about real history. Not the one they feed you in textbooks written by foreign hands! No! We are going to speak of the memory of the vanquished! Of those who were silenced while others wrote history in their place."

At that moment, Kpegnan worshipped the ground he walked on. That fire in Zokou's eyes, that sacred anger, that burning passion turned every class into a political soapbox where past and present blended without borders.

But Aimso, for his part, let it all go in one ear and out the other. He was too busy straightening his collar and casting charming glances at the girls in the front row. Léopold, meanwhile, was discreetly fiddling with a pen cap, rolling it between his fingers.

Zokou continued: *"And you, my dear future leaders, what will you do with this history? Watch it pass by like you're watching a funeral procession, or dare to rewrite it with your own hands?"*

He slammed his hand onto the desk out of the blue, making half the class jump out of their skins.

"Kpegnan! Tell me, young man, what is the difference between a historian and a parrot?"

Kpegnan stood up calmly, not batting an eyelid. He knew the answer by heart. It wasn't the first time Zokou had thrown out this question, always intended to wake up sleeping minds.

"The historian analyzes. The parrot repeats." he replied.

"Exactly! So be historians, not parrots!" thundered Zokou, before scribbling a few words on the blackboard.

Zokou continued his fiery speech on decolonization and betrayed struggles, but for Kpegnan, the words were becoming a distant hum. That day, his mind was miles away.

Aimso, sitting next to him, gave him a nudge. "*Stay with us, brother! It's the first class, are you already lost in the clouds?"* he whispered with a smirk.

Kpegnan replied with an absent smile, and Zokou, who had eyes in the back of his head, pointed a finger in their direction. *"The fashion lovers over there! If you think history is changed with well-ironed trousers, you're in the wrong century!"*

The whole class burst into laughter. Aimso raised his hands in a sign of innocence, and Kpegnan shook his head, taking their teacher's dig with a grain of salt. He knew the drill: in Zokou's class, you had to learn to take a punch as well as you could think.

Kpegnan harbored a genuine fascination for Monsieur Zokou, his history and geography teacher. A passionate orator and fervent defender of revolutionary ideals, he claimed to be an anti-colonialist, never hesitating to pass on a politically engaged and critical view of the world to his students. His charisma and fiery speeches commanded as much respect as they did reflection.

Kpegnan admired Mr. Zokou and knew his impassioned speeches by heart, even going so far as to adopt some of his favorite expressions, particularly when he described ministers as "undertakers," getting rich on the backs of the population. This fascination for his teacher fed a contempt for politics within him, to the point where he flatly refused to join the student movement aligned with the state party.

When the bell rang to end the class, Kpegnan let out a slight sigh. He was back in high school, yes… But this year would not be just another year.

After the bell, the class returned to its usual hubbub, with chatter flying in all directions. However, Kpegnan remained low-key. He slowly packed his things, trying to delay the moment when he would leave the room and dive back into the hustle and bustle of the high school.

It was at that precise moment that Mademoiselle Saplet made her entrance.

She made no noise, yet the whole room seemed to come to a standstill. She walked down the hallway with a light step, almost on tiptoe, and when she crossed the threshold of the room, her perfume announced her arrival. A soft and enveloping scent, a subtle blend of white flowers and spicy notes, both delicate and unsettling. Kpegnan didn't need to turn around to know; that scent was familiar to him. It still lingered in the room after every English class.

Mademoiselle Saplet was the picture of grace. Always dressed with simplicity, she exuded a natural elegance that stood in stark contrast to the austerity of the student uniforms and the sloppiness of some teachers. Her scarf was always tied with care, her smile discreet, and above all, her voice. A soft, lilting voice that made irregular verbs sound as seductive as love poems.

Kpegnan tried his hardest to stay focused, but he knew it was a lost cause. He felt as though every word she spoke was addressed to him alone, and her perfume wrapped around him completely.

"*Good morning, class!*" she said, her usual smile lighting up her face without being flashy, carried by her American accent.

"Good morning, Miss Saplet!" the class replied in chorus, some more enthusiastic than others.

But that day, Miss Saplet, in her tight black leather pants and white shirt, seemed even more beautiful to him, softer, and paradoxically less accessible.

While she explained the differences between the present perfect and the past simple, Kpegnan couldn't help but watch her gestures and her allure. Deep down, a thought crossed his mind: "*If only I were a little older... I would have poured my heart out to her.*"

She liked to circulate between the rows, questioning students to keep them on their toes. When she stopped near Kpegnan, her perfume hit him full force, a sweet dizziness that made him lower his eyes. He didn't dare look her directly in the face, for fear she would read in his eyes everything he could no longer hide.

At the end of the class, when the door closed behind Miss Saplet, Aimso leaned toward Kpegnan, a mischievous smile on his lips: *"My brother, if perfume alone could kill, you'd be six feet under by now!*

"Perfumes, my mother has a collection she brings back from Paris every time she goes. I'll send you a good one, which you can give to your sweetheart when you go to the village, so you can leave other people's wives alone."

And Leo added, laughing: "*Tell her: Miss you perf... how do you say perfume in English? Good. I love you.*"

Kpegnan burst out laughing, a laugh a little too loud to be sincere. "*You really are an idiot.*"

During recess, Kpegnan and his gang of friends had a very particular tradition called *"no pay, no eat.*" Everyone contributed, and with the money collected, they bought a plate of *alloco* which they took turns sharing. Only those who had chipped in had the right to the feast, an unchangeable rule they respected religiously.

A few weeks later, it was time to move into the boarding school.

The high school boarding house, where Kpegnan would now spend the lion's share of his time, was a true microcosm where strict discipline, complicity between students, and daily struggles to stand out all mingled together. It was a mixed boarding school, a rarity in those days, which added to the complexity of interactions between boys and girls.

The dormitories were long rooms with faded walls, where metal beds were lined up like rows of soldiers. The mattresses, thinned by the years, often revealed twisted springs beneath their tired foam. Each student had a rickety locker where clothes, notebooks, and books were piled up.

In the dormitory, lack of privacy was the name of the game. They lived packed like sardines, sharing the air, the secrets, the dreams, and the nightmares.

At the far end, near the window, Kpegnan's bed and Aimso's were pushed right up against each other. A large mosquito net, fixed by bits of string and a few rusty safety pins, covered them together, forming a sort of refuge of friendship, their little kingdom in the heart of the night.

Nights at the boarding school were rarely peaceful. Between loud snoring, late-night whispering, and the clandestine comings and goings of the most daring students, sleep was a luxury. There was always some strange noise in the night: a bed squeaking, a student mumbling in their sleep, or a supervisor making rounds with a flashlight, on the hunt for *"nocturnal runaways"* trying to sneak over to the girls' dorm.

Meals were served in a crowded refectory, where the smell of morning coffee and spices at noon mingled with the stench of the gutters and trash cans not far away. The line for food was a battlefield: the biggest and strongest pushed the younger ones around to get served first.

Portions were meager, and the craftiest students had developed all sorts of schemes to get seconds.

The menu changed every day. But the most dreaded remained the day of yam porridge accompanied by a clear fish sauce. Prepared in a rush, often undercooked, the sauce lacked flavor and the yam, if not eaten immediately, turned as hard as a rock, transforming the meal into a real ordeal.

The boarding school was a place of severe discipline, where studies were at the heart of daily life. Every morning, before the crack of dawn, the thunderous bell resonated throughout the establishment, announcing wake-up time.

Mandatory study hours were dreaded: under the uncompromising supervision of the educators, everyone had to keep their nose to the grindstone. But some disruptive students amused themselves by distracting others. The fact that the boarding school was mixed added a special tension to daily life. Encounters between boys and girls were strictly monitored, but that didn't stop the boldest from attempting escapades and hitting on the girls during study hours.

In the evening, after the mandatory study session, a curfew was in place. Students had to head back to the dorms on the double.

At ten o'clock sharp, like an unchangeable ritual, the boarding school plunged into an imposed silence. The supervisors did their final rounds, their heavy steps echoing in the dark corridors, hunting down the slightest whisper, forbidden lights, or rebellious souls refusing to give in to the curfew. Every light had to be out, every student had to feign sleep, even if, behind these appearances of docility, the night belonged to the boldest. Aimso and other reckless students dared to defy the rules.

Rather than returning to their dorm after evening study, some students preferred to venture along the walls of the girls' dormitory.

Their goal? To catch a glimpse, through the darkness, of those feminine silhouettes fresh out of the shower, drying themselves in the corridors, unaware of the eager eyes watching them.

Aimso pushed the envelope even further. Crouched in the tall grass, he stoically endured mosquito bites, his stare fixed on the dimly lit openings. He would later brag in the dorm about having seen the nakedness of almost every girl in the high school.

But woe betide the one who got caught: the sanction was immediate, often humiliating, and the shame remained etched in minds for a long time.

In the dormitories, no sooner had the last supervisor walked away than the room woke up in a different way. Furtive whispers were exchanged under the sheets, by the flickering light of a candle stolen from the refectory, carefully hidden behind a notebook. Secrets were born, jokes flew around, dreams were murmured. Sometimes, an insomniac or tormented student stared at the shifting shapes on the walls, hoping that one day, life would offer him something other than this straitjacket of rules and punishments.

But among all the troublemakers, none surpassed Aimso, the undisputed master of nocturnal chaos. His favorite pastime? Letting rip thunderous farts in the middle of the night and pinning it on an innocent bystander.

"Hey! Who was that?! Who ate a rotten egg?" he would cry out, snickering under his blanket. *"It's you, we know you! Every day, it's the same old song!"* a classmate would protest, trying not to burst out laughing.

But Aimso always had an excuse ready. *"No, it's not me! It's Alain over there! Look at him, he's playing possum."*

The dormitory was a sanctuary where indestructible friendships were forged, where every student found a way to survive. Solidarity was an unspoken rule, sometimes forced, but always precious. Between bullying and punishments, you had to know how to roll with the punches, but it was the stolen moments, the fits of laughter, and the small clandestine victories that made boarding school bearable.

On weekends, Kpegnan and his buddies met under the "sacred" tree, the theater of their favorite rituals. There, verbal jousting took on the appearance of duels, or the game of "*gâte-gâte*", that battle of friendly insults triggered roars of laughter.

Nearby, others got fired up in passionate debates about Asec and Africa, the two rival clubs whose clashes unleashed passions. And then there was the grapevine: those savory stories, those juicy pieces of gossip circulating about a goofy-looking teacher whose enigmatic behavior fascinated and amused them in equal measure. Made-up love stories between teachers.

But nothing equaled Aimso's art of storytelling. His favorite anecdote? The day he had been caught in a trap in the middle of an essay by his French teacher. The man was slightly cross-eyed, and Aimso, thinking he was looking elsewhere, had taken the opportunity to discreetly pull out a cheat sheet hidden in his pants.

Bad calculation. The eye that seemed to be wandering in the void was actually fixed right on him. Caught red-handed, Aimso still hadn't been able to stop himself from laughing. And every time he told the story with the gestures that only he could pull off, his friends laughed until their sides hurt.

The true Holy Grail, the object of all desire, was the Walkman. To possess this technological jewel was to enter another dimension, to access absolute privilege.

At the boarding school, in addition to the supervisors, there were also the live-in supervisors (*maîtres au pair)*.

The *maîtres au pair* occupied an ambiguous position in the boarding school: simultaneously feared very little and respected, they were often students at the end of their cycle and a bit older who had become monitors, with limited authority that sometimes made them more understanding than the supervisors. But among them, some took their role very seriously.

This was the case with Bouazo, a karate master, a rigid and uncompromising young man who followed discipline to the letter. Every morning, he walked the corridors, transistor radio in hand, religiously listening to the news broadcast on *"The Voice of America,"* which gave him the air of a high official surveying his territory.

His severity was legendary, and Kpegnan paid the price for it one day, after a grueling PE session. Under a blazing sun, he had just spent an hour running on the field where dying grass gave way to a sea of gravel. His body sweating buckets, his skin irritated by the heat, the discomfort had become unbearable: he needed to take a shower immediately.

So, he sneaked toward the showers and, without thinking, turned on the tap to rinse off under the cool water. Instant relief.

But his peace was short-lived. Just as he was enjoying this moment of freshness, a scathing voice rang out behind him: *"You there! Who gave you the green light to take a shower outside of hours?"*

Kpegnan flinched and turned slowly. Bouazo was staring at him, arms crossed, one eyebrow raised. *"Sir... I was in PE... I was soaked in sweat, and I was itching..."* he tried to explain.

But Bouazo was not a man to be sweet-talked. *"Rules are rules! And to teach you to respect them, on Sunday morning, you will clean the courtyard before sunrise!"*

And without waiting, he turned off the tap, leaving Kpegnan covered in suds, soap sticking to his skin and hair. And that is how Kpegnan spent two hours sweeping the boarding school on Sunday while his classmates were still sleeping, bitterly regretting his premature shower.

While Aimso loved to joke, he wasn't always discreet about his flings. One evening, when everyone was supposed to be in the dorm, the supervisor stumbled upon him and Blandine, a junior student, in a very compromising position behind the refectory.

"*But... but it's not what you think!*" stammered Aimso, trying to get dressed in a flash. *"I don't want to hear it! Tomorrow morning, you will face the principal.*"

The next day, the news had already spread like wildfire through the boarding school. *"Hey, Aimso, you too, behind the refectory! Couldn't you find a better spot?"* joked a classmate. *"Ahh, I'm dead meat... my mother is going to kill me if she hears about this!"* groaned Aimso, in despair.

In the end, they were punished with a month of chores but avoided expulsion from the boarding school and the high school.

In this harsh universe, there was Yvette, Kpegnan's "boarding school mother." She was a true guardian angel for him. At 25 years old, a final year student like him, she had taken the young boy under her wing and looked after him like a protective big sister.

She made sure he ate well, that he didn't let people walk all over him, and above all, she knew his biggest problem: Kpegnan hated the fish served at the boarding school.

Every time the menu featured boiled fish with a questionable smell, Kpegnan made a face. *"Oh no, Yvette, I can't eat that, I'd rather starve."*

"My son, I'll handle it."

Yvette, who knew a vendor at the high school, often went to buy him good fried fish, nice and crispy, accompanied by a well-garnished *attiéké*. "Here, eat this and stop moping," she would say, slipping him his plate in secret.

"Yvette, you're the best! If I pass the bac, it's thanks to you!"

And Yvette would burst out laughing. *"It's not free, you know! You have to help me pass the bac this year."* But for Kpegnan, these small kindnesses made all the difference.

In Daloda, as soon as they got a pass to leave the boarding school, Kpegnan and his buddies headed for the airfield, nestled on the outskirts of the city. This modest place held a fascination for them. It was nothing like the grand airports they saw in magazines: here, everything was simple and rudimentary.

The arrivals hall was just a simple concrete block building whitewashed with lime, topped with a corrugated iron roof that groaned at the slightest gust of wind. Inside, a few wobbly wooden benches, a counter worn by time, and a lazy fan turning nonchalantly were enough to set the scene.

As for the runway, it looked like a long dusty ribbon of reddish gravel, bordered here and there by tufts of rebellious grass that seemed to resist abandonment.

When a plane was expected, a battered old Land Rover would appear out of nowhere, kicking up a cloud of dust as it sped down the runway to ensure no man or beast would hinder the landing. The rumble of its tires on the stones was the alert signal.

The boys, hiding in the grass, held their breath. The machine descended slowly, propellers roaring, wheels ready to bite the earth.

It touched the runway in a cloud of gravel and smoke, in a racket as brutal as it was fascinating.

It was a suspended moment, raw, a bit surreal, and Kpegnan loved it. For him, this little airfield felt like a door left ajar to the unknown, a window open to an *elsewhere* he dreamed of joining. A vaster world, bigger, which he hoped to conquer one day as a pilot.

Meanwhile, back in the village, it had been two months since Kpegnan had left for the city. Two months that Djekobou hadn't seen her period.

The anguish was rising within her, excruciating. Not knowing who to confide in, she went to see Kemessié, her best friend, the only one who could understand her torment.

"Kemessié, my menses don't come for two months. I dey fear."

Kemessié shrugged, looking relaxed. *"Just wait small, e dey happen like that. Anyway, why you dey worry? You be virgin oh, you never know man."*

Djekobou looked away." *"But if I want it to just come, what do I go do?"* she asked, desperately looking for a solution.

"Nothing. Just wait. Even me sef, it does me like that sometimes."

"Okay... but no tell anybody, you hear?" she whispered, a lump in her throat.

Kemessié nodded, but she sensed a strange tension in her friend's voice.

Despite her love for Kpegnan, she had succumbed. Amani. The school director. She didn't love him. She had always despised him. But how do you refuse his advances when you have so little, when he offers gifts and promises the moon? She had let herself get swept away. And now…

Her breasts were swelling. Her belly was hardening. The smell of okra sauce, which she used to love, made her stomach turn.

It didn't take long for her mother to notice the signs. One evening, she called her out, straight to the point.

"My daughter, you are pregnant. Who did this to you?"

Djekobou froze. Her breath caught in her throat.

"You heard me! I want a name. Who got you pregnant?"

Silence. Then… *"Mama, I... I don't know,"* she breathed in a trembling voice.

The slap came out of nowhere.

"You don't know? So, you're sleeping around with every Lehi, Tiehi, oula, and Guehi, is that it?! Talk, you little toutou. Talk, or I'm going to put pepper down there!"

Djekobou closed her eyes. Her back was against the wall. She murmured, ashamed, broken: *"Mama, sorry- sorry, na the director Amani."*

Her mother's eyes went wide, then, against all odds, she smiled. "*Amani?! That's a good thing then. Tomorrow, you pack your bags and go move in with him. He's going to step up to the plate."*

Djekobou felt her world crumble. Her heart sank.

She wanted to scream.

"Amani... you no even know him yet oh! That man bad-bad, deh!"

The next evening, she went to Amani's house. He received her distractedly, barely concerned. Then she dropped the bombshell: *"Sir... I get belle."*

Amani went pale as a sheet. *"Pregnant?! Since when?!"* he growled. *"I don't know. It's now Mama says I get belle."*

"And I'm the one you come to accuse just like that?!"

"Yes what?! When you were doing it there, you no forget?"

A flash of rage crossed his eyes. "*You little slut! Is it my home you came to ruin?!"*

The blow came out of nowhere. A brutal slap. Djekobou fell backward, shocked. *"Tomorrow, you're going to get an abortion. I have a nurse friend at the sub- prefecture. This problem will be taken care of!"*

Djekobou felt a shiver of horror run through her. She whispered, her eyes dark with determination: *"What's sure, just keep shouting. When I talk everything finish, we go see if you be man."*

She ran to Kemessié's place, in tears, and spilled the beans. When Kemessié learned of Amani's intention to force her to abort, she hit the roof. *"You will NOT abort!"*

Her voice trembled with anger. *"If Amani doesn't want it, me, I will take this child as a gift! My aunt in the city is looking for a child with a torch in broad daylight and she can't find one!"*

Djekobou, despite her distress, smiled weakly.

"This pregnancy, you will keep it Tchoco-Tchoco!"

Then, with tears in her eyes, Kemessié continued: *"Child like that, it is God given. He has the right to live! Do you think about the number of women who would give their right arm for a child but can't make one?!"*

She made Djekobou sit down. *"And you, you want to kill this little being?"*

Djekobou shook her head, on the fence. *"But I be afraid..."*

"Scared of what? Scared of who?! Me, I am here. I will help you."

Then, after a silence, she added with a mischievous smile: *"But between us, since when are you going out with Amani, little bandit?!"*

Djekobou laughed in spite of herself. **"***E almost one month now. We do am only one time...***"** she murmured, ashamed.

Kemessié shook her head, half-amused and half- exasperated. *"One month only? But you said it's been two months since you've seen your period. Are you sure it's one time only you did? You there, when they say still waters run deep, it's true hein!*

Djekobou, annoyed, shot back: "*Eh hé, Kemessié, you dey ask plenty question. So you wan say na another person then?"*

She paused for a moment and thought, then added: *"Wait, Kemessié, make we count well small. Na last month Amani force me. If today I get belle, e no fit be him? Explain me well."*

Kemessié smiled before teasing: *"When it rots, it will smell oh! Me, I am here, I am just watching!"*

"Wetin go spoil? That day we do it clean-clean, I fall for belle straight, so na him sure-sure!"

The two young girls burst out laughing and went their separate ways.

A few days later, a letter arrived from the high school. It was Kpegnan. Djekobou tore the envelope open feverishly and scanned the lines with hungry eyes.

My dearest Djekobou,

It has been more than two moons that your silence has embraced me, and every day without you drags on forever. I miss you, Djekobou, with a longing that eats away at me, that burns, that steals my sleep. I long to see you again, to find that smile that lights up my nights, to hear your voice slide softly into my ear. I think of you with every beat of my heart. I think of us. Of that night suspended between heaven and earth, where the stars seemed to watch over our secrets. I see the glow of the kerosene lamps again, the dust dancing under our steps, the warm breeze grazing our faces while we set the world to rights under the old tree. I miss all of that. You, me, this village that sheltered our dreams.

Here, the city swallows me up, noisy, blind, indifferent to my memories. Crowds brush past me, but no presence touches me. This void, Djekobou, this void has taken on your face.

School keeps me standing, even if every class feels like another step away from you. In Terminale C, the rigor is relentless. Monsieur Coudet, with his piercing eyes and marble expression, teaches mathematics without mercy. I hang on, even if sometimes, my thoughts flee toward you, toward Tenably, toward that simpler life I left behind, in the village.

The days fly by, hard and austere, and the nights fall, cold. Without you to warm me with your laughter and your little teasing, there remains only a burning absence, an absence that gnaws at everything.

And you, over there, how are you? How are Nan and Baha? And Kemessié, still as mischievous, always ready to make the elders burst with laughter under the palaver tree? Tell me about all of that,

Djekobou. Tell me about the life that goes on, the wind running over the cornfields, the shadows stretching at sunset. Tell me that the earth of Tenably still bears our footprints, even erased by the rain.

I would give anything to see that dust redden my feet again, to run by your side on paths wet with dew, to breathe that air that smells of dawn and childhood.

May time pass quickly, may the season bring me back to you. In the meantime, be gentle with yourself, keep your smile intact, and if the wind carries my thoughts to you, welcome them like a caress, or a prayer whispered in your ear.

I love you, Djekobou, with a love that defies roads, days, and silences.

Your Kpegnan, the one who loves you beyond every instant.

Djekobou placed the letter against her heart. Her tears welled up, unstoppable, beading at the corner of her eyes before rolling down her cheeks. She wanted to answer him right away, to tell him that she loved him, that she was counting every day that separated them. But the truth, the naked truth, weighed heavy between them.

That unforgettable night Kpegnan spoke of. She remembered it and it shook her to her core. So, a thousand questions spun in her head: Should she keep this secret under her hat until it was too late? Or should she, on the contrary, tell him everything, right now, straight from the shoulder?

Lost, she had turned to Mathieu and Bayala, seeking a wisdom she lacked. *Kpegnan will understand. It's not your fault*, they consoled her.

They saluted her courage. The courage to keep this child despite the storm it announced. Where others, out of fear or despair, would have put an end to it in the secret of a night, resorting to risky methods that break bodies as much as souls, she had chosen to face the unknown, head held high.

But a question remained hanging, as fragile as a spider's thread in the dawn: how would Kpegnan react to this dizzying truth?

She decided to inform him all the same.

Kpegnan,

It's me, Djekobou. How you dey there? I know you dey learn-hard. God give you strength. Here for village, we dey manage small-small. But Sokpai e sickness don catch am strong.

Kpeg, I wan tell you something. Abeg, no vex for me. Two moon now, my menses no come. I tell Kemessié, she say make I wait small. But Mama say na get belle, she beat me sef for that matter. Me, my head don twist finish. I no even sure who be the papa.

My hand dey shake as I dey write you, because I sabi you. I fear say this news fit spoil your school. Kemessié say make I keep am, she say na God wey give pikin.

Abeg Kpeg, no be my fault. When you go come back village, we go sit talk well. This belle matter, I believe say na your own, but... I no talk am to anybody. When belle go finish and pikin come out, we go see who e resemble.

Abeg, forgive me for God sake. Learn well there. Me, I go manage pregnancy like that. If this thing make you no want me again, e go pain me deep, but I go understand.

Since that day, I just dey cry. I no even sabi wetin I go do again. I stop here for today.

Your own woman, Djekobou

Night had fallen over the high school, blanketing the boarding house in its vibrant silence, made of sighs, stifled laughter, and conspiratorial whispers. The windows with broken louvers let in a warm wind, heavy with the smell of wet earth and smoldering charcoal.

Léopold had set himself up just opposite, sitting in a sleeveless undershirt on his mattress, his flashlight between his legs, tinkering with an old deflated ball.

Kpegnan seemed miles away; he wasn't jovial and teasing like usual. The weight of the letter still hung over him, invisible to his classmates' eyes, but tormenting his brain.

"So, genius of Tenably, do you plan to tell us what's eating you or are you going to keep playing the brooding philosopher?" Aimso threw out, his voice a bit muffled by the pillow he had buried under his head.

Kpegnan hesitated. But the darkness made confessions easier. He took the letter out of his shorts pocket, unfolded it gently. The paper, already crumpled, rustled like a dead leaf being crushed underfoot.

"Djekobou wrote to me…" he murmured.

Léopold looked up, suddenly attentive. Aimso sat up, leaning on one elbow. *"So what? It's not the first time..."*

"No. This time, it's different."

He paused, staring into the void. *"I'm confused. She says she is pregnant. But she says she's not certain of the identity of the pregnancy's author. She doubts, and me, I'm blindsided."*

A heavy silence settled in. Kpegnan continued, short of breath: *"Yet I am her only boyfriend. I'm the one who took her virginity,*

I know it, I feel it. We promised each other fidelity. And now, she's planting seeds of doubt. It hit me like a ton of bricks. Is it my child or not? I would like to know, right away. I don't sleep anymore, I think only of that. I love her more than anything, but why this doubt?"

His voice broke and he burst into sobs, his head in his hands. The silence, thick as a blanket, was only disturbed by the stubborn song of crickets outside. Léopold let go of his ball, eyes fixed.

"Hey, what kind of story is this, my brother?" he finally managed to whisper.

Aimso, usually always ready with a joke, sat with his mouth hanging open, flabbergasted. *"Hey! But this is serious! Women, really, you can't trust them. You'll see, she's going to take a villager's pregnancy and pin it on you."*

Kpegnan raised his head, eyes red, but determined. *"No. I know her, she's not like that. But I feel it. I feel she's hiding something from me. And it's not April Fool's Day."*

Kpegnan, sitting on the bed, held the letter in his clammy hands. Aimso, lying nonchalantly, chewed on a twig. Kpegnan, whispering, just to himself: *"She is pregnant and I am sure it is mine."*

Aimso sat up abruptly, a sneer on his lips: *"Ah! That's what all the girls say. But open your eyes, genius of Tenably. You think because you are her first, she can't go look elsewhere? Women, we can never trust them, I tell you."*

And he added: Kpegnan, frowning, offended: *"No, not her. I tell you I know her, Aimso. She's not like the others. She looks at me as if I were her whole world."*

Aimso snickered. *"Her whole world, really? Me, I say she's going to take the pregnancy of a passing villager, a guy with a few bills, and you, you're going to carry the cross like a saint because you have a bright future."*

Léopold, shaking his head, a bit embarrassed by Aimso's words: *"Stop with your stories! She would never do that. Not all girls are the same."*

Aimso insisted: *"But brother, in this play-play thing, if the pregnancy is for you, you've become a papa just like that before even getting the baccalaureat. That's heavy, hein! You'll have to enter directly into the CAFOP to take care of the child. All X, Y, it won't matter. You're going to drop equations to solve real problems."*

He chuckled and tried to tickle Kpegnan, but the latter didn't share his mood. His face, closed off, betrayed a weight much heavier than Aimso's joke could lighten.

Léopold, more pragmatic, cut him off dryly*: "Aimso, knock it off. This is serious."*

Then, after a short silence, he asked the burning question on everyone's lips: *"What do you plan to do now, Kpeg?"*

Kpegnan stared at the ceiling, where a few cobwebs danced in the wind. *"I don't know yet. But I'm going to talk to her when I go back to the village. I can't leave her high and dry like this. I'd like to know more before making a decision."*

Kpegnan had a thousand-yard stare. He didn't dare look his buddies in the eye.

Aimso, seizing the opportunity, mocking: *"However, what? You feel well that she is hiding something from you. Otherwise, why would she doubt you? A child doesn't lie. But if she herself isn't sure..."*

Kpegnan, with mixed anger and sadness: *"Enough, Aimso! Do you want to drive me crazy? I love Djekobou more than anything. I am sure of her, well... I think."*

A heavy silence settled in. Kpegnan crumpled the letter and stuffed it into his pocket. Aimso, satisfied with his little provocation, lay back down, snickering in the shadows.

Then, with a serious air: *"You know, sometimes, I envy you. You have this simple life, this love that has followed you since childhood. Me, I have all the clothes I want, all the girls I desire... but deep down, no one who really waits for me. As soon as a girl gets pregnant, she rushes to abort without my consent."*

He paused, then, in a voice more bitter, and dejected, he added: *"Sometimes, I question myself if they really love me or if they are using me?"*

He let out a sigh and looked away, before dropping in a bitter tone: *"Plus, Papa never lets me go to the village, to discover this simple life, even though he himself was born there."*

Léopold shook his head, a disillusioned smile on his lips. *"Love, it's sweet when it starts, but it becomes bitter when doubt settles in or when responsibilities arrive. Take heart, bro."*

They remained there, in the twilight, three boys suspended between childhood fading away and adulthood knocking too early at the door.

Kpegnan folded the letter with care and slid it under his pillow. *"Thanks for listening. I just wanted you guys to know."*

Aimso reached out across the blanket and briefly squeezed Kpegnan's hand. *"We're with you, my brother Come hell or high water. Above all, don't force her to abort."*

And then, slowly, fatigue took over. Breaths became slower, deeper. Sleep carried them away one by one, but Kpegnan stayed awake for a long time, his eyes lost in the darkness, listening to the breathing of his friends, that fragile shield against the fear of tomorrow.

The next morning, the sun barely up, the boarding school woke to the brutal sound of the General Supervisor's whistle, Monsieur Tra Bi, a dry and nervous man whose voice carried further than the high school siren. That whistle, you heard it even in your dreams. A merciless ringing that separated the boys' and girls' night from the discipline of the day.

Kpegnan, still groggy from his short night, folded his mosquito net while Aimso, as was his habit, took his sweet time. He watched himself in the small cracked mirror they had hung on the wall, meticulously adjusting his shirt a shiny silk piece, khaki color, but a khaki far too elegant, far too *"city,"* far too Aimso.

"Are you sure about that?" murmured Kpegnan, keeping his voice down. *"You know how Tra Bi goes crazy over a uniform story."*

"Let him go crazy!" replied Aimso with that insolent smile that was his legend. *"Khaki is khaki, isn't it? It was never said it had to be poor quality cotton."*

Léopold, already ready, let out a fit of laughter.

"You, you're going to get us into trouble again."

They left the dormitory together, the morning sun gilding the boarding school courtyard. Everywhere, clusters of students were busy fixing their hair in a rush, shining their shoes, or ironing their trousers on an improvised board.

They hadn't gone ten steps when the stiff silhouette of Monsieur Tra Bi popped up in front of them. Hands crossed behind his back, stare sharp behind his round glasses, he looked like a gendarme tired of permanent disorder.

His fixed look swept over the trio, but it stopped dead on Aimso. His right eye twitched. He approached slowly, like a big cat stalking its prey.

"You!" he said in a low voice.

"Yes, Sir." replied Aimso with a perfectly polite smile, that smile that made Tra Bi boil all the more. *"What is this... this masquerade?"* He pulled slightly on the sleeve of the shirt. *"Since when do we wear silk to go to class? Where do you think you are?"*

Aimso shrugged. *"But sir, it is a khaki shirt. The rules say 'khaki shirt.' You can see well that it is khaki, right?"*

Kpegnan felt his stomach tie in knots. Léopold turned his head to stifle a laugh. Around them, students had stopped, smelling the imminent confrontation. Monsieur Tra Bi's expression changed, stuttering his words.

"You little brat", Who do you think you are? Here, it is not your father who commands! Go change immediately or you will be confined all week!"

But Aimso didn't budge an inch.

"Sir, with all due respect, this is the only khaki shirt I brought this week. You wouldn't want to force me to break the rules by wearing another color, would you?"

A murmur of admiration rippled through the crowd. Tra Bi took a step forward, short of breath, but Kpegnan stepped in smoothly to diffuse the situation.

"Sir, it's true he's pushing the envelope a bit... but it is khaki. If you punish him for that, the other students will say you're being unfair."

Tra Bi narrowed his eyes, torn between anger and weariness. He knew Kpegnan's reputation, the brilliant student who, despite his quiet demeanor, always knew how to pour oil on troubled waters. He grunted:

"Very well! But I never want to see that again. Let me make myself clear!"

He did an about-face and walked away, while a sigh of relief swept through the trio. *"You're playing with fire, my brother!"* whispered Léopold, bumping Aimso with his shoulder.

During the Christmas break, without wasting a single day, Kpegnan set off for Tenably. The journey to the village was long, but fatigue didn't even make a dent. Every mile swallowed brought him closer to Djekobou, to his childhood, to this little world he had left behind. The air became hotter, denser, saturated with that familiar smell of sun-baked earth, flowering trees, and wood smoke. As the bus bumped along the dirt track, impatience burned in his chest.

When he finally caught sight of Tenably, a wave of nostalgia washed over him completely. Almost nothing had changed. The thatched-roof huts still formed a crown around the village. The trees spread their generous shade over the beaten paths, and the comforting smell of simmering *sauce Kpélé*, scented with spices and dried meat, wafted through the air.

No sooner had he set foot in the family courtyard than Nanhan, his grandmother, burst out like a tornado of tenderness. She hugged him with all her might. *"My son has returned! May God protect you and help you grow even more!"*

Under the large acacia tree where the weaver birds were knitting their nests in an indescribable racket, Baha, his grandfather, welcomed him with a nod, dignified and reserved. But in the crinkles of his smile, Kpegnan read a silent pride.

"And school, is it going well?" he asked, his deep voice rolling like a bush drum. "Yes, Grandfather. I am learning, I am keeping my nose to the grindstone."

He barely had time to put down his bag before the rumor of his return had already spread like wildfire. Téhé's wives flocked in, their loud voices mingling with warm greetings. The village children, fascinated by this big brother who had returned from the big city, ran around him, laughing and eyeing him with envy.

And as the day waned, Kpegnan understood that the village was waiting for him, whole, with its noises, its smells, its heat, and perhaps too, its truths that he would have to face.

The first few days were marked by festivities. A goat was killed in his honor, and a grand feast was prepared. Kpegnan reunited with his childhood friends: Bayala, Kouia, and of course, Kemessié, who didn't miss a beat in teasing him the moment she saw him.

"*Eh, the big city student, you're forgetting us already, hein?"* she joked, nudging him lightly. *"Never! Tenably runs in my veins,"* he replied, laughing.

But behind this newfound warmth, he sensed a lingering tension. Heavy glances, conversations cut short as soon as he approached. It took him a while to realize that his return was not awaited by everyone with the same lightness.

The rumor about Djekobou and Amani was spreading like a contagion. At every corner of the village, he caught whispers as he passed. Then came the moment when he could no longer bury his head in the sand. Djekobou. He had to see her, hear her, understand.

In the schoolyard where they shared so many memories, he waited for her.

The Christmas festivities seemed far away, drowned in the tumult of his thoughts. His heart beat heavily in his chest. This long-awaited return no longer had the sweet taste of reunion, but the bitterness of painful truths to be faced.

That evening, he could wait no longer. His eyes scrutinized her intensely. *"Djekobou. You wrote me things that are tearing me apart. How can you doubt me? You know very well that I am the only one,"* said Kpegnan, his voice trembling.

Djekobou bit her lip, her eyes filling with tears. She wanted to speak, but the cat got her tongue. Kpegnan knelt before her, grabbing her by the knees. *"Look at me! If it's not me, then who? Tell me! Because the whole village is talking. They say Amani is the author of your pregnancy. Tell me the truth."*

She shot back: "*They dey gossip. "But apart from that, nothing dey."*

A long silence. Only the birds fluttered in the branches above. Then, in an inaudible breath, she confessed, her voice cracking: *"Na Amani. The school director."*

Kpegnan froze, his fingers loosening their grip. *"Amani?! But how?"*

Sobs were already shaking Djekobou. She buried her face in her hands. *"He call me to his house, he say he want make I cook for him. I couldn't say no, he be the director oh. And when I reach there..."* She collapsed, unable to continue.

Kpegnan, pale as a ghost, whispered in a strangled voice: *"Did he force you?"*

Djekobou swearing between her sobs: *"Yes, I swear, Kpegnan. It was just one time. I no want, never! Na you alone I love."*

Kpegnan put his hands to his head, short of breath, his mind adrift. The world around him seemed to wobble. *"Why... Why didn't you tell me anything? Why let me believe..."*

Djekobou, throwing herself against him, desperate: *"I shame! I fear you go leave me. You be everything for me, Kpegnan. Please, do am because of God."*

Their sobs mingled. But in Kpegnan's heart, an immense doubt, a dull pain, and a feeling of helplessness were already digging an abyss.

Kpegnan remained silent for a long time, his head in his hands. Djekobou's words were playing on a loop in his head. Amani, one time only, shame. But suddenly, a detail came back to him like a light in the darkness.

He abruptly raised his head and, with sudden assurance, asked: *"Wait. You say it was one month ago only?"*

Djekobou nodded timidly, tears still streaming down her cheeks. Kpegnan, pressing, almost calculating, added: *"And it has already been two months that your period hasn't come."*

Djekobou, eyes wide, understood immediately. The penny dropped.

Kpegnan, with a breath of relief mixed with contained anger: *"Then it's not his. This pregnancy is mine, Djekobou! It's me, not Amani. Do you understand?"*

Djekobou burst into sobs again, but this time from relief. She threw herself into his arms. *"Yes yes, Kpegnan, I know oh, but I no sure."*

He held her tight, but his eyes remained dark, inhabited by another idea. And, in a deep voice, thinking out loud: *"Listen to me carefully. That bastard Amani took advantage of you. He deserves to pay. And he is going to pay. You are going to let him believe the child is his."*

Djekobou pulled back, surprised. *"But why?"*

"Because he has money, power. You are going to push him to help you, to support you. Let him think he is fixing his mistake. And everything he gives you... that will be for us," he said, fixing her with a cold, determined stare. *"Do you understand? We are going to turn the tables on him."*

Djekobou hesitated, shaken by this plan, but finally nodded. *"For you, Kpegnan, anything I go do."*

He caressed her cheek, mixing tenderness with calculation, then whispered: *"Then this secret stays between us. To the world, Amani will be the father who pays. But you and I, we will know the truth. This child is ours."*

The breeze made the branches of the kapok tree tremble. In secret, a pact had just been sealed: a mixture of sincere love, pain, and vengeance. *"Remember what I told you,"* he murmured. *"Don't accuse him. Make him believe that he is the one who wants to make amends. Receive, but never give in to his advances."*

Djekobou nodded. Fear trembled in her fingers, but also the resolve of one protecting an unborn child.

A few days later, as night was falling and a bright moon illuminated the village, Kpegnan and his friends were preparing to organize a big *Aloukou* night. The atmosphere promised to be festive, laughter was flying around, and everyone was busy with the final preparations.

Not far away, Youl Bloffeur, the famous local singer, was rehearsing with his musicians. The drums resonated in the air, strings vibrated under expert fingers, and voices were warming up in anticipation of a memorable night.

Then suddenly, everything went south.

A scream tore through the silence. A scream of pain, followed by resounding weeping. The excitement came to a screeching halt. The drums fell silent, discussions ceased, worried glances were exchanged. A leaden silence fell over the village; only the weeping was audible.

Troubled, Kpegnan rushed toward the source of the commotion, his heart pounding like a hammer. And there, the unthinkable was revealed to him: Marvin, a promising young executive of the village, had collapsed in the middle of the party. Moments later, he had breathed his last.

The announcement hit like a bolt from the blue. The festive atmosphere transformed into a pall of sadness and disbelief. No one wanted to believe it. Marvin, so young, so full of life, had just disappeared brutally, shattering the joy of a night that had promised to be radiant.

The village, under the pale light of the moon, had just plunged into mourning.

Marvin was the pride of Tenably. The whole village saw him as a beacon of success and dignity. A generous and humble man, he was the patron of the local football team, organized inter-village tournaments, and never hesitated to support those in need. His meteoric rise to the position of director of a public company inspired an entire generation.

His sudden death left the village in shock. No one wanted to believe it. In less than thirty minutes, an immense crowd pressed in front of his villa, the largest building in Tenably.

When Madeleine, affectionately called Mado, his young wife in tears, took the floor to recount the circumstances of the tragedy, emotion gripped every heart present.

"He was talking with his parents..." she sobbed, her voice broken by pain. *"He complained of the heat, of a pain in his chest... We laid him down on a mat... We fanned him with a van... But a few minutes later, his eyes rolled back... He blinked one last time... and then nothing."*

She burst into sobs, and the crowd, helpless, let their grief explode. Wailing rose up, lamentations saturated the air. An abyss of sorrow opened in the hearts of those who had loved him.

Marvin, cut down in his prime, could not have left like this without reason. According to local beliefs, such a sudden death could not be natural. "It is the work of sorcerers!" people shouted in the crowd.

The next day, as tradition required, a four-day mourning period began. His widow, Mado, had to submit to the imposed rites. Her hair was undone, surrendered to the wind as a sign of renunciation. Her body was smeared with mud. Dressed in rags, she was forced into seclusion, isolated from everyone. For four days, under the uncompromising eye of old Mawa, she ate only cassava and boiled banana, every bite steeped in bitterness, for her grief was infinite...

The whole village fell into a respectful silence, but if calm dominated, the pain continued to grow.

On the day of the funeral, Tenably was unrecognizable. An impressive flood of humanity poured in from all the surrounding regions. No one wanted to miss this farewell.

Traditional masks performed sacred dances, a final tribute to the deceased. Dance troupes vied in skill, transforming pain into mesmerizing rhythms. As a sign of the deceased's importance, the sub-prefect and an official delegation marked their presence. His colleagues and friends from the capital mingled with the mourning crowd. And among the assembly, his numerous female conquests, draped in tears and regrets, wept for the one who had made their hearts beat so fast.

Despite the immense sadness, the night was punctuated by singing and dancing, for tradition dictated honoring the memory of the deceased by celebrating life.

At dawn, the maternal nephews, tasked with digging the grave, came to announce that preparations were complete. A final meeting took place between the maternal and paternal families. After long discussions, the burial was approved.

Marvin's body was washed with hot water and wrapped in a traditional loincloth. The two families chose the deceased's final loincloth together. A few gifts were offered to old Zou, guardian of the body, in exchange for his "release" for his journey to the great beyond.

In Tenably, they never forgot those who had left their mark. And Marvin would remain, forever, a legend.

Before the burial, a final tribute was paid. His body was displayed one last time, allowing every villager to say goodbye. Some placed silver coins, a final gift for his spiritual journey. Others placed a piece of loincloth on him, so that he would be well-dressed on the other side. Gifts in kind and in cash were given to his family to ease their pain.

The women of the village prepared a symbolic meal and placed raw rice in a basin near the body. Each woman then took a handful of this rice to put back in her own plate, a ritual meant to guarantee abundant harvests. A goat, destined for sacrifice on the grave, was given to the maternal nephews. Everything was ready for his passage into the afterlife.

As the rites were coming to an end, a final question floated in the air: was Marvin's death really natural? Some still whispered about occult forces. Others spoke of a curse. But beyond the speculation, one thing was certain: the void left by Marvin would be hard to fill. And in Tenably, his name would resonate for a long time, carried by those he had inspired.

Just as they were preparing to close the coffin, Derou, one of the deceased's brothers, wanted to place his fine suits inside, a final gesture to honor Marvin. But the family firmly opposed it. *"According to tradition, only the chosen loincloth must cover the deceased. No material wealth can be taken into the afterlife."*

As the procession prepared to leave the compound for the cemetery, a rebellion broke out. Kpegnan and the village youth, angry, blocked the body's departure. They demanded that Marvin *"reveal"* the identity of the sorcerers responsible for his death before undertaking his final journey. *"He did not die naturally! He must show us the guilty ones!"* they chanted.

They wanted to parade the coffin from hut to hut, convinced that in the presence of the culprit, the coffin would refuse to move forward. Heated arguments broke out. The atmosphere was electric, voices rising from all sides. Finally, the tension simmered down after the intervention of the sub-prefect, who threatened to call in the gendarmes to disperse the crowd.

The dreaded moment arrived. Marvin was going to join the ancestors. Absolute silence settled in. Then, heart- wrenching weeping rose up as his coffin disappeared underground.

While Marvin was joining his final resting place, his wife, Mado, having remained locked in the house throughout the mourning period, was led to the edge of the riverside marsh (*marigot*) to undergo the purification ritual. An old woman, guardian of traditions, poured several cups of water over her head while reciting: *"May misfortune never returns upon you."*

Then, her head was shaved, and she was washed entirely. Once back in the village, to symbolize her return to normal life, she was served a bowl of rice. She was now free. But she had the choice to marry one of Marvin's brothers if she wished.

The days passed and the frenzy of the funeral gave way to a calmer atmosphere, tinged with melancholy. The village gradually found its usual rhythm, but a shadow still weighed on hearts. The end of the holidays was approaching, and with it, the inevitable separation.

Kpegnan spent his last days between moments of bonding with his family and moments of farewell with his friends. Every corner of the village seemed more precious to him now that he knew he would have to leave it again.

On the eve of his departure, he sat under the great tree, where he had shared so many memories with Djekobou. He knew he had to speak to her one last time before leaving, but words failed him. The weight of recent events, the still-fresh pain of Marvin's loss, all of this made the moment even harder.

"I'm going to miss you, Djekobou," he murmured. She lowered her eyes, playing with a pebble under her fingers. *"You too. But you, you dey go to the city over there. Me, I am not moving with belle matter that is tiring me."*

A heavy silence settled in. He wanted to promise her that he would return soon, but he knew that nothing was certain.

The next day, at the crack of dawn, his grandmother prepared a final meal for him. His grandfather, true to himself, slipped him a few words full of wisdom before handing him a small sum of money, the fruit of their savings. *"Study well, my son. Knowledge is your only true wealth."*

On the way to the bus station, his friends accompanied him, joking to lighten the mood. But when the bus arrived, a blanket of silence fell over the group. Kpegnan shook Bayala's hand, patted Kouia on the shoulder, and hugged Kemessié, who was struggling to hold back her tears.

"You there, don't forget to send us letters from time to time from the city, hein?" Kemessie threw out, laughing nervously.

"Promised."

Then, he boarded the bus and, as the engine roared, he cast a final glance at the village. Tenably was fading away little by little, but his heart remained attached to this land, to these familiar faces, to these memories engraved forever.

Back from the Christmas holidays, at high school, Kpegnan distinguished himself in the eyes of the teachers by his seriousness and analytical mind. Whether in mathematics, English, philosophy, or natural sciences, he excelled with an ease that commanded respect. Yet, instead of being content to shine alone, he dedicated a large part of his time to helping his classmates, especially those who were having a hard time keeping up with the pace set by the teachers.

Among those who depended on him the most were Aimso, a full 21 years old, and Yvette, both in their final year but having great difficulty absorbing the lessons. Aimso, despite his eternal carefree attitude and taste for jokes, struggled mightily in mathematics and physics. His patience wore thin quickly when faced with the most elementary demonstrations.

"My brother, this story of X, Y, and vector là, it is for the Whites! Me, I just want to get a 10 and flee this school!" he complained, hands on his head.

"Calm down, Aimso," replied Kpegnan, holding back a smile. *"Look, it's simpler than you think. You just have to follow a logic."*

And with infinite patience, he explained to him, diagrams and all, how to solve systems of linear equations, how to memorize trigonometry formulas in songs, all while making sure to simplify every notion so that his friend could retain it easily.

As for Léopold, his destiny had taken a different turn. After a successful trial with a professional football club in France, he had to put his studies on the back burner to seize this opportunity. Also selected for the junior national team, he was getting ready to represent the country at the Under-20 World Cup.

For her part, Yvette, although intelligent, had trouble keeping up in physics and chemistry. She understood the theoretical concepts, but the practical exercises threw her off completely.

"Little brother, explain this story of the force of gravity to me again, because me, I just see formulas dancing in my head."

"Look, Yvette," replied Kpegnan with a benevolent smile, *"imagine you are holding a mango and you let it go. Why doesn't it go up and why does it fall? Well, it's because the earth pulls it, that is gravity!"*

She burst out laughing. *"Ahh, so if I drop my notebook and it falls, it's Newton who is right, hein. White folks are really something huh?"*

"Exactly!"

Thanks to his patience and his accessible teaching methods, Aimso and Yvette made considerable progress throughout the year. They had adopted Kpegnan as their private tutor, and he never refused to help them, even when it meant sacrificing his own revision time.

The study sessions at the boarding school were a spectacle in themselves. In the large study hall, everyone tried as best they could to concentrate, but the atmosphere was rarely studious from start to finish.

Some students, dead beat from the day, would subtly doze off on their notebooks, heads resting on crossed arms, until a supervisor came to wake them up with a wooden ruler tapping on the table.

"Hey, you over there, is this a dormitory?!"

Others, as exams approached, downed whole cups of black coffee to keep their eyes peeled, reciting their lessons in low voices like prayers.

As for Kpegnan, he was always the center of attention, surrounded by students in distress, explaining a lesson here, giving a tip there, and correcting an exercise hither and thither.

Even the supervisors had noticed. One evening, while he was in the middle of an improvised class with a small group of students, Monsieur Bouazo, the strict *maître au pair*, walked by them and stopped.

"Kpegnan, are you planning to open a school here or what?" he threw out, half-amused, half-exasperated. *"Sorry, Sir, we're just revising before hitting the hay."*

The supervisor nodded. *"Alright, carry on, but at 10 PM sharp, everyone in bed!"*

They all exchanged a conspiratorial look and went back to the grindstone.

As the baccalaureate approached at high speed, Kpegnan, always diligent, was more studious than ever, but unlike his classmates, he never practiced the "*2k pi*" method, that grueling habit of studying all night until dawn. He had exhausted every math exercise in the Vuibert collection and, having nothing left to prove to himself, he now dedicated his time to helping his classmates who were struggling to keep up. He didn't see the bac as a hurdle, but as a mere formality.

Kpegnan had tried, as best he could, to get Aimso interested in studies, pushing him to do his exercises before going out. Thanks to this imposed discipline, Aimso had managed to scrape a passing grade in the second term.

Over the moon, he showered Kpegnan with gifts, grateful to the one who had believed in him when he felt incapable himself.

"The secret to success is consistency, not burnout,"

Kpegnan liked to repeat.

And in a few weeks, he would prove to the whole world that his destiny was written in golden letters.

But one day, as he was returning from the refectory, a sad event turned his daily life upside down. He received a telegram from the village. The message was short and brutal: *"Grandfather deceased.*"

Kpegnan stopped dead in his tracks. The paper trembled between his fingers. Even if he had expected it, he refused to accept the obvious. A veil of sadness darkened his look. *"He's the one who should have been here to see my success."*

Thanks to the unwavering support of his friends Léopold and Aimso, he found the strength to weather the storm. But one thing was certain: he was going to pass his baccalaureate, come hell or high water, in honor of his grandfather.

The school year was marked by a few teachers' strikes, unhappy with their living conditions. However, despite these disruptions, classes resumed and everything followed its course.

Meanwhile, in Tenably, another milestone event was brewing, but Kpegnan was still in the dark.

In the small village, under a starry sky, Djekobou, her heart heavy and her body exhausted, was on the verge of giving birth to her first child. She was surrounded by the village midwives, her mother by her side, holding her hand firmly.

Since morning, she had felt violent cramps, but now, the pain was becoming unbearable. She was lying on a mat, legs spread, short of breath. The contractions were getting closer, the suffering reaching its peak.

"Aaaah! Mama! It's pushing inside me!" Djekobou screamed, clinging desperately to anything within reach.

"Breathe, my daughter, courage!" repeated Makoura, her voice trembling with emotion.

Djekobou howled in pain, her voice shattering the silence of the night. Between screams, she let out inaudible words, sometimes even profanities, so unbearable was the suffering.

But Kouity, the experienced village midwife, remained as cool as a cucumber. She had seen it all before. *"Go on, push! Push even harder!"* she encouraged in a firm voice. *"I can see the baby's head, just one last effort and it will be over!"*

Djekobou gathered her last ounce of strength. With a final scream, she felt a weight escape her. A new cry, fragile but powerful. A baby had just seen the light of day.

"It's a boy!" announced old Mawa with a beaming smile.

Kouity delicately took the newborn, gave him a few little taps, then cleaned his still-bloody face. Then, she stuffed a substance into his nostrils to clear them. The women present let their joy explode, singing praises and prayers to wish the newborn a long life.

In the household, it was an explosion of joy. Djekobou's mother began to sing and dance: *« Po ya ti blê ô pô hê gbô, po ya ti blé ô pohê gbô... »*

The women accompanied her in chorus, clapping their hands, stomping the ground with their feet, transforming this birth into a true celebration.

When Djekobou finally took her son in her arms, she felt an indescribable happiness. She kissed him endlessly, examining his fragile little face, trying to guess who he resembled. Although it was still too early to discern his features, one thing didn't lie: his ears tick out, exactly like Kpegnan's.

Djekobou, in tears, caressed her son's cheek with infinite tenderness. *"He is so beautiful..."* she whispered, exhausted but fulfilled. *"We go call am Potey,"* she declared proudly. Then, in a whisper, she sighed: *"Imagine say, I near-abort this small angel..."*

Only she knew, and only Kpegnan knew. No one else was in the loop about the true identity of the child's father.

Amani, for his part, was bursting with pride. A son! A boy! He felt fulfilled, strong, fully accomplished. To celebrate this happy event, he showered Djekobou with gifts and went so far as to suggest she come and move in with him.

When, one weekend, his wife decided to pay him a visit, Amani preferred to take the bull by the horns to avoid any confrontation. He chose to break the news to his wife himself, for fear she would hear it through the grapevine.

"Darling, I have decided that the young girl will come to live here with the child." She widened her eyes, flabbergasted, as if she had just received a violent blow. "*say what?*" Her tone oscillated between disbelief and anger.

"I am not asking for your opinion; I am informing you." An icy silence fell between them before she breathed, her voice trembling: *"I thought you loved me and you dare do this to me?"*

He shrugged, indifferent. *"So what? What does love have to do with it?*" She clenched her fists, trying to contain the storm brewing inside her. *"I cannot accept it. You must make a choice."*

Amani stared at her for a moment, his look impassive, then dropped in a cold and detached voice: *"If you force my hand to choose, you are going to lose me. Think carefully."*

Tears sprang from his wife's eyes. *"Why do you treat me this way? Is it my fault if I cannot bear children?*" She collapsed in sobs, inconsolable.

The school year was a rollercoaster of emotions. Between exhausting days of classes, revisions late into the night, sometimes unjust punishments, and small moments of solidarity, Kpegnan was forging a determination of steel.

He knew he carried his family's hope, that he had to do his uncle and grandmother proud, and above all, he wanted to prove that he could succeed despite all the difficulties.

With Aimso and Yvette by his side, he was learning that school wasn't just about grades, but also about mutual aid, laughter, and unbreakable friendships. And in a few weeks, he would pass the ultimate test: the baccalaureate. But for now, he was content to live each day intensely, hoping that his efforts would eventually pay off.

The days went by with a particular intensity at the boarding school. The shadow of the final exams loomed over the high school, and every student felt the mounting pressure. The corridors had become quiet; light conversations had given way to relentless revision. Nights were short, punctuated by the scratching of pens and the murmurs of students reciting their math formulas or key historical dates.

Kpegnan, for his part, approached this period with apparent serenity. He knew he would succeed. His precocious intelligence and his ability to quickly assimilate lessons ensured him a comfortable lead. But he didn't want to just pass: he wanted to shine, to snag the best grade, and prove to everyone that he was the cream of the crop.

Every morning, he got up before the crack of dawn to revise in peace. He spent hours solving equations, working on his physics-chemistry formulas, and polishing his essays.

"Kpegnan, are you sure you're not a hidden genius?" joked Aimso, yawning after a long revision session. *"He doesn't just want to pass, he wants to crush everyone!"* added Yvette, shooting him an amused look. *"Leave me alone, I just want to make sure I leave here with honors,"* replied Kpegnan with a confident smile.

Dawn had broken over Daloda, plunging the boarding school into a gloomy atmosphere. It was the big day, the one everyone dreaded and awaited with palpable nervousness: the baccalaureate. The atmosphere was heavy; anxiety and stress were written on every face. Even the best students didn't escape the worry.

In the courtyard of the exam center, the candidates had grouped into small circles. Some feverishly re-read scribbled notes, others murmured mathematical formulas, hoping to engrave them one last time in their memory.

Kpegnan, however, remained calm. Sitting apart on a bench, eyes closed, he mentally reviewed his revisions. For him, the math exam was just a formality. His only apprehension: knowing if he would manage to keep his cool.

Aimso, on the other hand, seemed far less tranquil. *"Kpegnan, my brother, today I feel math is going to fry our brains..."* he whispered, approaching.

"You did revise though, right?" asked Kpegnan, a bit concerned. *"Yes, but not enough! But I have a last kata. Look at this..."* he said with a confident smile.

He slightly pulled back his shirt and revealed small cheat sheets, carefully folded in the lining of his sleeve.

"What is that?" Kpegnan was astonished. *"My brother, why break my head? You, you are sharp, for you it's easy. Me, I just need a helping hand."*

Kpegnan's look turned grave. *"Aimso, do you really think you can pass an exam relying only on scraps of paper?"*

"Bah, it's just for math. I can't remember the formulas, and this will be enough to save my grade," replied Aimso, shrugging his shoulders.

Kpegnan shook his head. *"No. You should have applied yourself and learned. When you cheat, you are stealing from yourself first."*

"Oh really?" replied Aimso ironically. *"Me, I just see that the teachers want answers, not moral lessons. What I want is to pass the BAC."*

"And when life comes to question you with its real questions, will you also pull a paper hidden in your sleeve?" Kpegnan threw back. Aimso, troubled, lowered his voice. *"You talk as if a little cheat could decide my conduct in the future." "Yes,"* replied Kpegnan firmly. *"Because cheating quickly becomes a habit. And habit shapes the man you will be tomorrow. Shortcuts seem easy, but every easy way out leaves a mark. As they say: 'Idleness in youth is the source of all disorders in life.'"*

Aimso remained speechless, staring at the ground. *"I understand... But I don't want to fail. And anyway, I want to become a politician. I don't think it's incompatible."*

"Count on your own strength," replied Kpegnan calmly. *"Succeeding or failing without cheating is knowing at least that you fought by yourself. And that is where true glory is born."*

A bit embarrassed, Aimso resumed: *"My brother, but it's too late. I'm not ready. If I don't cheat, it's failure guaranteed."*

"Aimso! Are you crazy? What if you get caught? You risk expulsion!" Kpegnan was indignant. *"I don't have a choice. Otherwise, it's another year to start over!"*

Kpegnan sighed and concluded in a tone tinged with disappointment: *"Know one thing, my brother: cheating can offer you ephemeral success, but it robs you of your learning. It prepares a future where you will always have to hide your weaknesses. True success is built in effort, never in fraud."*

Kpegnan hadn't managed to talk Aimso out of his plan. The bell rang, and the candidates joined their rooms in a heavy silence. Soon, the supervisors entered, distributed the exams. The atmosphere became icy and stressful for the candidates: the exam had just begun.

Everything seemed to be going normally, until the moment Aimso almost got caught. As he was trying to discreetly unfold one of his papers, the head supervisor, a man with a piercing expression, approached him. Abruptly, he stopped right behind him.

"You, over there! Don't move!" Aimso's blood ran cold. His fingers hurriedly closed over the paper, which he hid by pretending to scratch his head. *"What are you hiding?"* asked the supervisor in a harsh voice.

Silence fell in the room. All eyes converged on Aimso, whose forehead was covered in sweat. *"Sir, I... I'm hiding nothing. It's just... a sudden migraine!"* he stammered. The supervisor stared at him for a long time, then finally nodded. *"Alright. But watch yourself."*

Aimso inwardly breathed a sigh of relief. He had just escaped by the skin of his teeth.

The exams ended, giving way to the long and unbearable wait for results. The days stretched out like weeks. Kpegnan, sure of himself, spent his time playing football, while Aimso, usually mocking and talkative, became taciturn, eaten away by uncertainty.

Finally, the long-awaited day arrived. At the crack of dawn, the courtyard of the Catholic high school filled with students with beating hearts. The headmistress took the microphone and announced in a solemn voice: *"all candidates, please come forward!"*

Kpegnan stepped forward with a firm stride; Aimso seemed to recoil with every step.

They began by proclaiming the honors:

"Kpegnan Ninsemon: highest honors." "Igaro Laure: honors." "Dineamin Roger: honors At the call of his name, Kpegnan's heart leapt. He remained motionless for a moment, incredulous, before a

broad smile lit up his face: he had succeeded, and with flying colors!

But the joy was not shared. In the crowd, cries of disappointment erupted. The exam had been ruthless this year, and many saw their dreams collapse.

Suddenly, a scream split the air: *"Ahhhh! It's not possible! Yet I worked hard!"* It was Aimso. His name hadn't been cited. Hope was now reduced to the list of those eligible for the make-up exam. *"My brother, they did combine again... I'm waiting for the make up session. If even there they don't say my name, I go scatter here!"* he raged.

"Calm down, it's going to be okay," Kpegnan tried to appease him. When, finally, his name was pronounced among the candidates kept for the make-up session, Aimso just let out a brief cry: *"Yes!"*

By his side, Yvette let out a deep sigh: "*Me too... second chance.*" Kpegnan took them both by the hand: *"Don't lose heart. You still have a chance.*"

But Aimso sighed: *"My brother, me, I wanted to be done with it once and for all. Now, I have to suffer again."*

"It's not the end of the world," replied Yvette, regaining her energy. *"Kpegnan, you are a whiz. We knew you were going to shine."*

"It's thanks to you too," he replied humbly. *"Come on, focus for the make-up. And this time, no cheating, Aimso!"*

The latter raised his hands, falsely offended: *"I won't tempt the devil again, believe me!"*

From then on, Kpegnan put his success at the service of others. He spent his days helping his friends revise, proving to them that knowledge is shared, and that true success is savored in solidarity.

The nights of work resumed, even more intense. Aimso, this time, hung on with a newfound ardor. He refused to get a wink of sleep, for fear of forgetting what he had learned. *"Kpegnan, if I fail again, I'm going to cry like a baby!"* he confided the night before. *"You won't fail, trust me,"* replied Kpegnan with assurance.

The next day, Aimso and Yvette faced their final tests, determined to give it their best shot. Then came the day of truth. When the list was read, Aimso jumped up hearing his name: *"I passed!!!"* he screamed, his voice covering the entire courtyard.

He turned to Yvette, who had also just been admitted. She screamed with joy and jumped into Kpegnan's arms: *"We did it! We did it! Thank you, my son Kpegnan, you are an angel!"*

Kpegnan replied with a wide and luminous smile. That day, he understood that his success was worth nothing without that of others. *"I told you so! Now, no one can stop you!"*

Aimso fell to his knees, raising his hands to the sky. *"Lord, thank you! Never again will I see a bac subject in my life!"* Yvette, eyes shining, breathed a sigh of relief. *"We suffered, but it was worth it."*

Kpegnan looked at them with pride. His school year was ending on a perfect note: not only had he excelled, but he had also helped his friends succeed. That day, they left the boarding school as true heroes, their diploma in pocket, hearts swollen with hope and excitement, ready to face the challenges of the adult world.

Before leaving for good, Kpegnan wanted to leave a trace of his passage. In the gloom of the dormitory, he lit a candle, then, with the melting wax, he carved his name on the ceiling. A final symbolic gesture, like a simple promise: never forget these years marked by friendship, trials, and dreams finally accomplished.

The sun was beginning to set over Daloda, casting a golden light on the upscale neighborhood where Kamone's villa was located. That evening, the excitement was at its peak. To celebrate the success of Kpegnan, Aimso, Yvette, and their classmates, Kamone had organized a big party in her sumptuous house.

From the entrance, the atmosphere was electric. A gentle breeze made the white curtains of the terrace dance while bursts of laughter and music resonated throughout the courtyard. The villa, a beautiful residence with white walls and large glass windows, offered an ideal setting for the celebration. The garden was lit by multicolored lanterns, and at the back, a large table garnished with succulent dishes was already attracting the foodies.

Guests arrived one after another, dressed to the nines. The girls wore carefully tied loincloths or elegant dresses, while the boys had put on their well-ironed shirts and impeccable trousers.

Kamone, always smiling and elegant in a fitted wax dress, welcomed every guest warmly. *"Welcome to my home! Tonight is your night. Have fun, eat, dance, this is your moment!"*

Kpegnan, a bit intimidated by so much attention, couldn't help but smile. He glanced at Aimso, who was already working the room, probably looking for who to dance with first. Yvette, for her part, shone in a beautiful red dress, fully savoring the moment after so much stress.

On the large table covered in loincloths with striking patterns, set up under a tarp supported by reed wood poles, a true feast awaited the guests: *baked chicken,* golden brown, accompanied by a spicy sauce. Crispy fried fish, Kpegnan's favorite specialty. Steaming *attiéké*, served with slices of onion and fresh chili. *Foutou* accompanied by *palm seed sauce*, which scented the entire garden. Sweet fritters and ice-cold *bissap* juice, perfect for sweetening palates.

But the party wouldn't have been complete without a wide choice of drinks carefully selected by Kamone. The young graduates and guests could quench their thirst with: Perrier, a sparkling water prized by the most refined. Tonic, for those who liked a bitter touch. Fanta, the favorite sugary drink of the youth. Ginger juice, homemade, with just the right amount of kick and freshness.

But for the older guests and Kamone's teacher friends, the table was also garnished with well-aged whiskey, served in small elegant glasses.

Among them, one man particularly attracted attention: Mister Zébédé, Yvette's companion. Regional bank agency manager, Mister Zébédé was the embodiment of elegance and refinement. Always dressed with care, that evening he sported a perfectly tailored beige suit, a glittering gold watch on his left wrist, an elephant hair bracelet on his right wrist, and a subtle touch of *Brut 33*, the perfume whose woody and virile scent floated around him.

A glass of whiskey in hand, he was chatting in a low voice with Kamone's teacher friends, his poised tone and measured gestures reinforcing the aura of mystery and power he naturally exuded. It was whispered that he was married, but that his wife resided in the capital. So he didn't hesitate to spend time in Daloda alongside Yvette, whom he cherished particularly.

"Honey, you look resplendent tonight," he murmured to her, offering her a glass. Yvette, radiant, simply smiled, aware of the curious looks around them. When the music rose in intensity, the atmosphere became electric, and bodies began to sway to the rhythm of the catchy melodies.

In a corner of the terrace, the Disc Jockey, set up behind a table covered in vinyls, handled his turntable and belt-drive deck with confidence, spinning large 33 rpm records under the crackling needle. With a precise hand, he queued up the hits of the moment: Sam Mangwana, Franco, Seigneur Rochereau, James Brown, Ernesto Djédjé, Prince Nico Mbarga, and many others, whose voices resonated through the powerful speakers set up in the four corners of the garden.

The familiar crackle of the vinyls added a nostalgic and authentic touch to this night of celebration, where every note made the hot air of Daloda vibrate.

Aimso, true to form, was the first to jump up. "Tonight, nobody sits! We're celebrating our bac the right way!" he exclaimed, grabbing Kpegnan by the arm.

In no time flat, the dance floor caught fire. The girls executed rhythmic steps with grace, while the boys tried as best they could to follow the tempo.

But it was Aimso who stole the show. An accomplished dancer and born showman, he strung together perfectly mastered moves with ease, captivating everyone's attention. He knew how to impress the ladies, alternating between elegant steps and exaggerated hip swaying, triggering both admiration and bursts of laughter. His energy was contagious, and soon, everyone was swept away by the fever of the rhythm.

For his part, Kpegnan, usually reserved, let himself get sucked into the atmosphere. But as is paradoxically the case for good, studious students, dancing was not his strong suit. His disorganized steps and shaky movements claimed more victims than admirers. Every time he attempted a move, he stepped on his unfortunate partners' toes.

When the disc jockey played Marvin Gaye's "Sexual Healing," Yvette left Kpegnan no escape. She grabbed his hand firmly and declared: *"You, today, you are dancing with me! Hold me tight, but above all, spare my feet!"*

Kpegnan, trapped, attempted a few hesitant steps, narrowly missing crushing Yvette's foot, who reacted immediately*: "Easy! You don't dance this fast!"*

Amidst the laughter and cheers of the guests, he tried his best to follow the rhythm, his look betraying extreme concentration. On the sidelines, Zébédé, comfortably settled with his glass of whiskey, watched the scene with a small smile on his lips.

After several hours of laughter and dancing, Kamone took the floor. *"Tonight, we are celebrating our graduates, in particular Kpegnan, Aimso, and Yvette. You have worked hard, you have persevered despite the difficulties, and today, you are the pride of your families and your school."*

A thunder of applause rang out. Then, she turned to Kpegnan. *"My little one, your mother would have been so proud of you. You have shown that hard work and discipline always pay off. May this success be only the beginning of a great destiny."*

Kamone's words touched Kpegnan deeply, and he felt his eyes well up. *"Thank you, Tantie... and thank you all. This success is also thanks to Aimso and Yvette, my boarding school brother and sister. I promise you we will go even further together!"*

The guests exploded in cheers.

While the party was in full swing, Kamone had a memorable surprise in store, perfectly suited to Kpegnan's tastes: a group of young *Aloukou* singers, that rhythmic musical genre he appreciated so much.

Suddenly, the percussion resonated, and the group made its entrance to the cheers of the guests. Dressed in bright loincloths, they belted out catchy songs, accompanied by rhythmic dances that immediately captivated the assembly. The *tam-tams* vibrated, voices rose, and in an instant, the courtyard transformed into a true live spectacle.

The graduates, seated in the center, were honored with improvised lyrics paying tribute to them, celebrating their perseverance and success. Kpegnan, carried away by emotion, discreetly tapped his foot to the beat, savoring every note of this music that reminded him of the evenings of his childhood in the village.

Then, to top it all off, three masked dancers entered the scene, executing a spectacular choreography symbolizing strength and grace.

The atmosphere was electric. Guests stood up one by one, letting themselves be carried away by the cadence, while the songs and *tam-tams* rang out in the night of Daloda.

The party continued until the wee hours of the morning, offering Kpegnan and his friends an indelible memory, rooted in the rhythms and culture that had cradled their youth.

That night, they were no longer stressed final-year students, but young adults ready to conquer their future.

The party at Kamone's was an unforgettable moment, an evening where laughter, music, and emotions had intertwined. But in the wake of the festivities, a new reality set in: the future started now.

The bac results had made a big splash throughout the country. Among the best graduates in the land of lagoons, Kpegnan figured at the top of the national ranking. His name had been plastered in the newspapers, and very quickly, news broke: he had obtained a scholarship of excellence to pursue his studies in France!

Kamone, proud of him, helped him prepare his documents, while Yvette and Aimso listened with admiration. But he wasn't the only one with big plans.

A few days later, while they were chatting in a *maquis* at Zébédé's invitation, Aimso dropped a bombshell. *"My brother, I have something to tell you."*

"What is it?" replied Kpegnan.

"My father made me a promise: if I get my bac, he sends me to study in Canada!"

Kpegnan's eyes went wide. *"Hein?! Aimso, is that serious?"*

"Very serious! Did you think I was joking? That's why I suffered so much with that math! But thanks to you, I succeeded. In a few months, I'll be in North America, me too!"

They burst out laughing, then Yvette added: *"And what about me? While you go across the water, me I am going to stay here. It is time for me to look to build a family now."*

The two boys turned toward her. *"For me, that is enough like that, long studies. I am going to enter the CAFOP to become a primary school teacher."*

The Center for Educational Training and Development, CAFOP was the school that trained the country's future teachers. Yvette wanted to pass on her knowledge to future generations, and her success in the bac finally opened this door for her.

"You too, you are already a true intellectual!"

joked Aimso.

They burst out laughing, but deep down, they felt a pang in their hearts. After so many years spent together, their paths were about to separate.

"So it's decided," said Kpegnan, looking at them. "For me, it's France, Aimso Canada, and Yvette becomes a teacher here."

"Exactly," confirmed Yvette with a nostalgic smile.

They held hands, sealing an indestructible

friendship despite the distance that would now separate them. *"No matter where we are, we'll see each other again one day, that's a promise,"* added Kpegnan.

"Yes, and that day, we'll party even bigger than at Kamone's!" concluded Aimso, laughing.

Life had just offered them the first pages of a brilliant future, and each was ready to write their own destiny.

After the euphoria of the party and the announcements of their future departures, Kpegnan knew it was time to return to the village. Before flying off to France in a few months, he had to spend time with his folks, to reconnect with the roots that had forged the man he had become.

Kamone, as benevolent as ever, insisted on driving him back. *"I want to make sure you arrive safely and especially that your grandmother sees for herself how much her grandson has become a man."*

So, they hit the road to the village in her Citroën. The journey was peaceful, but charged with emotion. Sitting in the front, Kpegnan watched the landscapes roll by, his heart heavy and his mind elsewhere.

Kamone, sensing his unusual silence, glanced at him. *"You're thinking too much, Kpegnan. What's eating you?"*

He took a deep breath before answering. *"Tantie, I am happy, but at the same time... I'm scared. France is far away. Boarding school was already a big change, but now, I'm leaving for another continent."*

Kamone smiled, placing a reassuring hand on his neck. *"It's normal to have cold feet, my little one. But look at how far you've come. You passed your bac with flying colors, you worked hard, and this scholarship, you didn't*

steal it. Believe me, you'll land on your feet over there too. You are a fighter."

Kpegnan cracked a smile. *"I hope that from where he is, Grandfather will be proud of me."*

They continued their journey, leaving Daloda, the memories of boarding school and parties behind them, to find the rocky lands of Kpegnan's native village.

The moment the Citroën entered the village, a wave of emotion seized Kpegnan. Children ran behind the car shouting his name; other villagers raised their hands in greeting.

His uncle Téhé and his grandmother Nanhan were already waiting for him in front of the family courtyard. The colossus Téhé had eyes shining with emotion. As soon as Kpegnan got out of the car, he walked slowly toward him and grabbed him by the shoulders.

"My son, you have returned." Without a word, Kpegnan threw himself into his arms. *"Uncle, I succeeded,"* he whispered, a lump in his throat.

Téhé, usually a man of few words when it came to affection, placed a hand on his head to bless him. *"I knew it. You are a true son of this earth. And now, you are going to represent our family over there, among the Whites. You must show that we are men of value."*

Nanhan, for her part, discreetly wiped away a tear before exclaiming: *"But before all that, come eat, my son! I prepared your favorite dish."*

The whole village was buzzing. News traveled fast: *"Baha's son passed his bac with honors and is going to France!"*

After the family discussions and parental blessings, he had to cross paths with Djekobou and Potey, their son.

Evening was falling when Kpegnan arrived at Djekobou's place. His heart was beating faster than he would have liked. When she opened the door, a brutal emotion overwhelmed him. She hadn't changed much, except for the depth and maturity in her eyes. In her arms, a fragile little being slept peacefully.

Kpegnan squatted slowly and contemplated the infant. His blood. His son. Only he and Djekobou knew the truth, and at that instant, he understood the magnitude of this secret they would carry forever.

"He looks like you," he whispered, his throat tight. Djekobou lowered her head. *"It is rather you he looks like. Look at his ears."*

Then she added with a sad smile floating on her lips: *"He will grow up here without you. I only hope you will never forget us."*

A silence settled in. Kpegnan wanted to speak, to promise that he would return, that he would never forget them. But could he swear such a thing when an ocean was about to separate them?

He reached out a finger toward the baby's small hand. The child instinctively grabbed it. Kpegnan felt his heart clench. He was leaving, but he was leaving a part of himself behind.

In the days that followed, Kpegnan rediscovered the carefree nature of his childhood. He walked the familiar paths of his village, the ones his feet knew by heart, ran to the river where he fished and bathed. He listened to the tales of the elders, lulled by their voices charged with wisdom and memories. With the village youth, he shared bursts of laughter and participated in inter-village football tournaments.

But this time, Nanhan was keeping a close watch. Worried, she had forbidden him to play football, dreading that a malicious injury the work of sorcerers, she said, would come to jeopardize everything. Kpegnan obeyed reluctantly, but he compensated by passionately recounting his boarding school memories and his dreams for the future.

Above all, he intended to make the most of every moment with his uncle and grandmother, to fully savor their presence. He knew that his departure for France would mark a new chapter in his life, far from his kin and this land that had seen him grow.

One evening, as they were sitting under the great tree, Téhé turned a grave look toward him and said: *"Mark my words, my son. No matter where you go, always remember where you come from. The tree that forgets its roots cannot grow."*

Kpegnan nodded, engraving these words in his heart.

The holidays had a bittersweet taste this year.

Kpegnan knew it: this stay in Tenably would be his last for a long time. In a few weeks, he would leave Africa to fly to France, where prestigious studies awaited him.

In the morning, Nanhan prepared his favorite dish. She didn't speak much, but every gesture betrayed her sorrow. Téhé, true to himself, simply gave him a friendly pat before whispering: *"Be strong, my son. The road is long, but it will take you far."*

His friends accompanied him to the bus. Bayala tried to mask his emotion with awkward jokes, but Kouia had a dark look. *"You will come back, hein?"* he finally asked. *"Of course,"* replied Kpegnan, without truly believing it.

Djekobou was there too, standing a bit back, holding Potey in her arms. She didn't cry. She was content to stare at him with an intensity that spoke louder than words.

The bus engine roared. Kpegnan climbed aboard, cast a final glance at these faces he loved so much, and then the vehicle lurched forward.

As Tenably faded into the horizon, a tear rolled down his cheek. He was leaving for a promising future, but a part of him would always remain anchored here, in this village where it all began.

And where someone, somewhere, would bear his name without ever knowing why.

Part 3

With a mix of feverish excitement and bittersweet melancholy, Kpegnan got ready to leave his native land. This day, so long-awaited, dreamt of and dreaded all at once, had finally arrived. On the plane, Kpegnan had managed to snag a window seat. As the aircraft barreled down the runway for takeoff, his heart pounded out of his chest, every beat resounding like a final farewell to his homeland.

The plane taxied slowly at first, then picked up speed abruptly. A gut- wrenching anxiety took hold of him. His fingers dug into the armrest, and when the machine finally left the ground, he squeezed his eyes shut and said a silent prayer. As if his body were rejecting this brutal uprooting, his stomach tied itself in knots, and a strange sensation washed over him.

Through the porthole, he watched the houses, streets, and fields shrink into tiny, blurry specks beneath the vastness of the sky. He felt as though he were leaving a piece of himself back there, on that soil he wouldn’t see again for a long time.

Around him, the other passengers seemed perfectly at ease. Some were already glued to their screens, others chatted with soft laughter. *How can they be so calm?* Kpegnan wondered, while he couldn't even relax a muscle, let alone soothe the fear gnawing at his mind.

Out of the blue, an unusual sensation invaded his ears. First a slight pressure, then a dull hum that intensified rapidly. For a first-time flyer like him, everything felt dialed up to eleven, bordering on alarming. The roar of the jet engines echoed in his head like a deafening drum. Instinctively, he brought a hand to his ear and tapped lightly, hoping to shake off the discomfort.

Through the small, open shutter, he discovered a mesmerizing spectacle: clouds stretching as far as the eye could see, a dazzling white under the sun. But the beauty of the landscape couldn't wipe away his discomfort. With every shift in altitude, the pressure mounted.

A little later, as he tried to get his bearings in this new universe, a flight attendant with a picture-perfect smile came down the aisle, followed by a steward pushing a cart loaded with meal trays. When his turn came, Kpegnan looked down at the tray handed to him: a piece of chicken drowning in a thick sauce, a cold roll, a portion of cheese, and a yogurt. He stared at the spread, but his stomach, still in knots from anxiety, wanted nothing to do with it.

He brought the cheese to his nose. A sharp, aggressive smell wafted off it. He put it back immediately. He looked at the whole thing without a shred of appetite. It all seemed bizarre, foreign, tasteless. Even the water served in the little plastic cup seemed bland to him. In any case, he wasn't hungry. Before boarding, he had feasted on a hearty plate of *attiéké* with fish. So, he settled for just eating the yogurt.

For the rest of the time, he remained lost in thought, staring into the void. His mind was still clinging to images of his village, the sound of his grandmother's voice, the smell of the steaming agouti she used to prepare for him with so much love.

In his head, he also couldn't stop imagining Paris: the grand avenues, the lights, the buildings he had only ever seen in movies and stories.

Just as he was trying to distract himself by leafing through *Fraternité-Dimanche*, the newspaper he'd bought at the airport, a sudden jolt shook the aircraft. His blood ran cold. He dropped the paper and held on for dear life to the seat in front of him.

The plane shook and pitched, like a canoe tossed about on a raging river. Kpegnan felt a cold sweat trickle down his spine. Every bump amplified his panic. He closed his eyes, praying under his breath: *"Lord, I don't want to die in the sky... not like this."*

A female passenger next to him gave him a compassionate look. *"It's normal, young man, it's just a bit of turbulence,"* she said with a reassuring smile.

But to him, there was nothing normal about hanging by a thread in the void, thousands of meters above the ground. Every vibration, every sudden movement was a threat.

The flight seemed to drag on forever. He checked the screen in front of him over and over, counting down the remaining kilometers to Paris, hoping to see this nightmare come to an end.

Then, after what felt like an eternity, the lights of Paris finally appeared through the window, sparkling like an ocean of fireflies in the dead of night.

Suddenly, a voice rang out: *"Ladies and Gentlemen, this is your captain speaking. We thank you for choosing Air Afrique for this journey. We are now beginning our descent towards Paris. Landing is expected in a few minutes. We ask that you return to your seats, fasten your seatbelts, and return your tray tables to the upright position. The temperature on the ground is currently 20 degrees, the weather is cloudy. On behalf of the entire crew, we wish you a pleasant stay and hope to have the pleasure of welcoming you aboard our Air Afrique flights again. Thank you for your trust."*

When the wheels finally touched the tarmac, he felt his body go limp with a long sigh of relief. He had made it.

As passengers stood up to grab their luggage, Kpegnan sat there for a moment, his backpack hugged tight against his chest, his regard lost through the small glass window. France was there, right in front of him.

Stepping out of the aircraft, he felt the first blast of cold air whip across his face. The air was different, drier, crisper than back home. On the jet bridge leading to the terminal, he walked slowly, as if wanting to savor every second.

He immediately felt lost in this sea of people where everyone walked at breakneck speed, dragging noisy suitcases behind them. Announcements rang out over the loudspeakers in rapid-fire French. He went with the flow of passengers to passport control.

Standing before the border police officer, he felt his heart hammering in his chest. The man in uniform scrutinized his passport, looked at him for a moment, then stamped the page without a word. *"Welcome to France,"* he dropped in a neutral tone.

Kpegnan finally let out a breath. He had arrived. He set foot on French soil with only one certainty: his life would never be the same again.

Kpegnan collected his suitcases, slung his small bag over his shoulder, and followed the stream of passengers into the vast Charles-de-Gaulle airport. The world surrounding him looked like something straight out of a movie. The futuristic architecture of the airport, with its immense corridors and glowing signs, was a radical departure from his native land.

He stopped for a moment, fascinated by the hustle and bustle around him. He watched men in well-tailored suits walking with a brisk pace, briefcases in hand, while women in elegant dresses and perfectly coiffed hair exchanged words in sophisticated French. A little further away, a group of young people in bell-bottom trousers and shirts with multicolored patterns laughed while swapping audio cassettes. In a corner, a group of white people, short in stature and with slanted eyes, were conversing in a bizarre language. Everything was new, loud, and a bit overwhelming for Kpegnan.

The smell was different, too. A mix of tobacco, strong perfume, and gasoline hung in the air. Kpegnan soon found himself next to a man taking a long drag on a Gitane, the blue smoke drifting lazily into the hall.

He now had to find a way to get to Paris. He spotted a line of passengers buying tickets at a counter, where an agent in a dark blue uniform, cap tilted slightly to the side, was handing out tickets with a nonchalant air.

Ticket in hand, he followed the crowd toward the train that would take him to the capital. He descended into the underground station, where the smell of metal and coal mingled with dust and dried urine. The lighting was dim, and graffiti covered the concrete walls. A white bum, sitting in a corner, held out his hand to passersby, mumbling a few incomprehensible words. Kpegnan looked away, ill at ease. *"A white man begging?"* he wondered, taken aback.

When the old, creaking train arrived at the station, he got on and sat on a faded red velvet bench. The cabin was filled with travelers buried in their *France-Soir* newspapers or reading the latest news in *L'Aurore.* A few young people were whispering about a certain Claude François, while others discussed the power of Valéry Giscard d'Estaing.

The train lurched forward and, through the window, Kpegnan watched the first gray buildings of the Parisian suburbs roll by. He felt a shiver run down his spine, not from the cold, but from excitement. Paris was there, so close. A city he had heard so much about, a city of promises and mysteries.

Soon, he would see with his own eyes those grand illuminated avenues, those crowded cafés where people sipped black coffee while discussing politics, those immense booksellers set up along the Seine, and perhaps even the Eiffel Tower.

But for now, he was content to observe, to soak it all in. He was no longer just an African student landing in an unknown country. He was an explorer, ready to discover a new world.

Upon his arrival, Kpegnan had spent the night in a modest youth hostel located in the heart of the 14th arrondissement. Early in the morning, just before heading to the train station, he lingered for a moment at his bedroom window. From up there, he scrutinized the busy street, fascinated by the ballet of passersby.

What struck him most was the uniformity of the faces. All the passersby were white. No trace of a familiar face, of a brother from back home, of a reflection of himself in this cosmopolitan city. A question flashed through his mind, sudden and nagging: *But where do the Blacks live in Paris?*

The October cold, sharp and biting, caught him off guard. He, accustomed to the gentleness of a milder climate, shivered under his jacket. Yet, to his great surprise, elderly people, looking sprightly, were jogging in tracksuits, and some even went so far as to wear shorts.

At the train station, Kpegnan had gone down to the basement, his arms burdened with two heavy suitcases. In front of him lay an escalator. A marvel of modern technology, he thought confidently.

Without hesitation, he placed his first suitcase on the step and prepared to set down the second. But, instead of going up, the first suitcase came right back at him. "*But... what kind of witchcraft is this?*" he muttered, surprised.

He grabbed the suitcase, took a deep breath, and tried again. Same result. He put the suitcase down, and it came back down. He put it back, and it returned. A real tug-of-war. Sweat beaded on his forehead, but he refused to give in.

The travelers around him had started to slow down, surprised and captivated by this impromptu show. Some exchanged amused glances, others smiled discreetly behind their newspapers. Kpegnan, however, was too absorbed in his battle with the diabolical machine to notice the spectacle he was providing. He persisted, wiped his brow, puffed loudly, and redoubled his efforts.

"Merde! What kind of story is this? It's not possible! They should have at least provided stairs!" he grumbled, placing both suitcases down at the same time this time, determined to triumph over the stubborn staircase.

Fatal error. Instead of going up, they tumbled toward him at full speed, forcing him to scramble backward to avoid having them smash into his feet. He nearly tipped over and fell on his neck, and his cry of surprise in his mother tongue, *"Siè djô"*, triggered general hilarity.

His combat with the infernal staircase had lasted for long minutes, under the laughing gazes of the passersby. Some didn't even bother hiding their laughter anymore.

It was at that moment that a young man, who was coming down that very staircase, stopped in front of him and, with a sympathetic smile, said to him: *"Sir, it would be easier on the other side."*

Kpegnan blinked, bewildered. He finally looked up and spotted, just a few meters away, a second escalator. That one, sure enough, was going up.

He stood rooted to the spot for a moment, realizing the absurdity of the scene he had just caused. Then, without a word, he headed, his dignity in tatters, toward the correct staircase, this time without the slightest difficulty. Behind him, laughter still rang out.

Once on the platform, Kpegnan tried to forget his humiliation.

On this October morning, the Gare du Nord in Paris was buzzing with the coming and going of travelers bundled up in their coats. The air was crisp, heavy with the smell of coffee and pastries wafting from the kiosks. Kpegnan, a bit lost in this crowd, clutched his train ticket in his hand. The illuminated board indicated his imminent departure for Clermont-Ferrand.

When he boarded the Intercités train, he looked for his seat near the window. The carriage was simple, with worn fabric seats and luggage racks that were already quite full. After a final whistle, the train moved off slowly, then gathered speed as it left the Parisian greyness behind.

Through the window, the landscape changed rapidly. The gray buildings of the Parisian suburbs gave way to golden fields, then to forests where the trees displayed their autumn colors. The red of the maples, the orange of the beeches, and the brilliant yellow of the poplars formed a living painting. From time to time, the train passed through small villages with stone houses, church steeples pointing toward a sky heavy with clouds.

The journey lasted about three and a half hours. At each stop, passengers got on and off, bringing a draft of cold air with them every time the doors opened. Inside the carriage, the atmosphere was calm. Some read newspapers and magazines, others dozed off, rocked by the motion of the train.

The further the train advanced toward the south, the more rolling the landscape became. The plateaus of Auvergne began to take shape, with their gently rounded reliefs. At times, Kpegnan caught glimpses of cows grazing in lush green meadows, isolated farms bordered by hedges.

Approaching Clermont-Ferrand, the imposing silhouette of the Auvergne volcanoes appeared on the horizon. The Puy de Dôme, majestic, stood tall under a pearl-gray sky. A fine mist covered certain hills, giving the landscape a mysterious air.

Finally, the train slowed down and entered, with a dull rumble, the heart of the Clermont-Ferrand station. Kpegnan gathered his things, still stiff from the journey, and stepped down onto the platform. A cool wind whipped his face, laden with that mixed smell of hot coffee and cold tobacco floating in the air. Around him, passengers dispersed quickly toward the exit.

Suitcases in hand, still marked with airport tags, he approached the forecourt, looking out for a taxi. That was when he spotted a young girl with large glasses, busy but calm. He approached, hesitating, to ask for directions. She looked at him for a moment, her eye sliding toward the luggage tags, then, with a frank smile, she understood.

"You just arrived? Are you a student?" "Yes," replied Kpegnan. *"Come on, come with me, I'll take you to the university residence."*

Kpegnan hesitated for a split second but ended up accepting. He climbed into the small car without ceremony. Inside, another young girl welcomed him with a broad smile, as if they already knew each other. "I'm Jeanine. And you?" *"And I'm Lachaise." "My name is Kpegnan, and you can call me by my first name."*

Thanks to the two young girls, the first hours of his arrival went off without a hitch, and very sweetly.

When the little gray Beetle pulled up in front of the Dolet university residence, Kpegnan cast a circular glance around, still dizzy from the trip. At his side, the young woman from the station got out first. She took a deep breath of the damp Clermont-Ferrand air. *"Well, here it is!"* she announced, smiling.

Numbed by the unexpected October cold, Kpegnan shivered. Without a coat, he instinctively tightened his collar and stepped cautiously out of the vehicle, pulling his suitcases with him. He glanced at the austere building with its dull yellow walls. Lachaise, noticing his discomfort, took a denim jacket and a scarf out of her trunk and handed them to him.

In front of the entrance, a group of students was smoking and laughing, their animated voices contrasting with the silence weighing on him. *"You'll see, it's no palace, but you get used to it easily!"* added Lachaise.

Together they walked through the glass doors to find themselves in a cramped hall, where the smell of old paper and central heating hung in the air.

At the residence reception, the other girl, Jeanine, was already handling the formalities. She spoke fast, winking at the concierge, a middle-aged woman with a tight bun sitting behind a counter cluttered with files. Kpegnan stood back, polite, attentive, a little disoriented.

The lady barely looked up before asking in a neutral tone: *"Name?" "Kpegnan, Ninsemou,"* he replied, trying to hide his stress.

The receptionist leafed through a dusty register, drew a line with a pen, then handed over a key attached to a metal tag that was too heavy to be practical. *"Room 308, third floor. The elevator is in the hallway over there, but it's often out of order."*

Lachaise, clearly used to this kind of brisk welcome, grabbed one of his suitcases and signaled for him to follow.

Kpegnan hesitated when he saw the elevator. He had never seen one before. The cabin took a long time to open, and Lachaise finally suggested taking the stairs. *"Come on, chin up! Three floors is nothing,"* she joked.

But halfway up the stairs, Kpegnan began to feel the fatigue. His suitcases seemed to double in weight with every step, and he was panting while Lachaise climbed with disconcerting ease. *"You don't have lead books in there, do you?"* she said with a laugh.

Finally, they reached the third floor. The corridor, dimly lit by a yellowish light, stretched out before them. The numbered doors were marked with traces of tape and discreet graffiti. A background noise combining muffled music and bursts of laughter escaped from some of the rooms. Tired from the long journey and still a bit disoriented, Kpegnan paced the corridors of the Dolet residence, looking for his room number. He dragged his khaki canvas suitcase, his eyes sweeping over the austere walls of the building.

When he finally found room 308, Kpegnan put the key in the lock and pushed the door open. The interior was spartan: two small single beds with rough sheets, a worn wooden desk, a metal wardrobe that creaked slightly when he opened it, and a window overlooking a courtyard where a few students were smoking down below despite the cold.

He put down his suitcases and sat on the bed, which let out a sinister creak. Lachaise, leaning against the doorframe, observed the room with an amused smile. *"Welcome to your new home."* Kpegnan took a deep breath. He was here, in his room, ready to start a new life.

When he left his room to walk the young lady back, a warm voice rang out behind him in the hallway: *"Hey, you! You new here?"*

Kpegnan turned around. A tall, slender young man, dressed in a red sweater and baggy trousers, was approaching with a friendly smile. *"Yes, I just arrived,"* he replied in a weary voice. The other nodded enthusiastically and offered his hand. *"Welcome to Dolet, my brother! I'm Diop, from Senegal. And you?"*

Kpegnan shook his hand, but instead of answering directly, he declared calmly: *"Kpegnan, from Africa."* Diop raised an eyebrow, amused. *"Yes, that much I can see, but where exactly?" "I am African, that's all. The little patch of earth where I was born is called Tenably."*

Diop smiled warmly and gently tapped Kpegnan's elbow with immediate camaraderie. *"Ah, you, you're a true Pan-Africanist! You refuse to play the border game, huh?" "Borders are just lines drawn by others. Me, I am from this land called Africa, not from one of those little pieces of land they left us called countries."*

Diop observed him for a moment, impressed by this answer. *"I like that, my brother. Here, you'll see, there are many of us who think like you. At Dolet, we are Africans first and foremost, not just Senegalese, Ivorians, or Malians. You'll feel at home in no time."*

Before Kpegnan could reply, another voice interrupted them. *"Salam! I'm Karim, from Algeria."* A young man with a smiling face, dressed in a light djellaba, had approached and was extending a friendly hand to Kpegnan, who shook it warmly. *"Pleasure to meet you, Karim." "You just arrived?"* asked Karim. *"Yes, and I think I've never had such a rough time in my life as I did with those stairs and this cold,"* replied Kpegnan, laughing. *"Welcome, then! Come have some tea with us later, we'll explain how things work around here,"* proposed Karim.

Kpegnan nodded, grateful for the warm welcome. Behind him, Lachaise, the young girl who had been playing the Good Samaritan since his arrival, smiled as she watched the scene unfold.

"Well, I see you are in good hands. I'll let you get settled. See you tomorrow for the grocery run!"

"Thank you, Lachaise. Without you, I think I'd still be stuck staring at a broken elevator," he said with a weary smile.

She gave him a wave and vanished down the corridor.

Once settled in his cramped but functional double room, Kpegnan stretched out for a long moment, finally savoring a moment of respite. However, the solitude didn't last long.

A knock on the door, then Diop's voice: *"Kpegnan!*

Come on, we're in the common room!"

Curious, he joined them and discovered a modest room where several students were gathered around a small table cluttered with bowls of steaming tea, bread, and a plate of tinned sardines.

"Sit down, give the tea a try, it's the best cure for the cold!" a Malian student shouted with a laugh. Kpegnan sat down and accepted the hot glass Karim handed him. The tea was strong and sugary, with a slight bitterness, a comforting drink after such a grueling day.

The discussions were in full swing. Some debated African politics, exchanging views on current events and independence struggles, still fresh in some countries, and coups d'état. Others joked about the food at the university cafeteria, a daily grievance.

"Here, my brother, if you plan on eating well, you need to make friends who know how to cook!" joked Konneh, a Guinean who claimed to be a top chef when it came to peanut sauce rice.

"Otherwise, the resto U will make you lose your lunch in two weeks with their ratatouille and their cheese!" Karim added with a laugh.

Despite his fatigue, Kpegnan felt immediately at ease. He already understood what this place was: it wasn't just a residence; it was a little slice of Africa in the heart of Clermont-Ferrand.

That night, as soon as he returned to his room, he lay down on his bed with a sigh of relief. Despite the harshness of the journey, despite the biting cold and the endless stairs, he already felt a little bit at home.

The next day, Lachaise, the student who had taken him under her wing, took him to handle his first administrative errands at the prefecture and the university, then to the store to get a coat, a scarf, and shoes suited for the cold. Over the following days, she accompanied him to show him around the city a bit.

Kpegnan never admitted it, but looking back on his duel with the escalator, he told himself that he hadn't just looked ridiculous that day, he'd also had a stroke of luck!

When he arrived in France, Kpegnan was loaded with prejudices. He had been heavily influenced by Monsieur Zokou, his history and geography teacher, and by the numerous anti-colonialist authors whose writings he read with passion. His favorite artist? Bob Marley. He loved his songs, even if he didn't always understand the lyrics. What he knew was that Bob Marley hated *"Babylon,"* and that was enough for him.

But quickly, as time went by, he ran up against a totally different world. He had become suspicious, thin- skinned, and defensive. He interpreted every remark as an attack. He no longer had that natural ease that made him a leader. From now on, he withdrew into his shell, becoming taciturn and distant. French humor left him perplexed. *"Why do they laugh at such absurd things?"*

He often found his classmates' jokes out of place, sometimes even offensive. One day, Leboeuf, a student known for his mocking humor, made a snide remark upon seeing Kpegnan wearing a pair of Ferradini shoes without socks in the dead of winter. *"Not exactly the best call for winter, eh?"* Kpegnan ignored him, hoping Leboeuf would leave him alone. But the other guy insisted: *"I've got extra socks if you want some."*

Kpegnan felt anger rising within him. Rather than blowing up, he left the room without a word, swallowing his pride.

But that wasn't the only thing that disturbed him. He hated the French habit of doing *la bise*, pecking on the cheek, at every opportunity to say hello. To him, a kiss should remain intimate. He preferred a handshake. But in France, they made him understand that shaking a woman's hand was impolite. It was another facet of the culture shock he had to face.

Little by little, Kpegnan had broken his solitude by befriending the French student with the strong-willed personality: Mademoiselle Lachaise, whom he had met right upon his arrival.

She had a unique style, always decked out in big round glasses and chain-smoking Gauloises all day long. She was brilliant in math and physics, but deeply despised the engineering cycle she was enrolled in.

"What I want is to be a nurse," she would say, taking a drag of smoke. *"To work in Africa, in the forgotten countryside. That would be much more useful than all this."*

Kpegnan looked at her with a mixture of surprise and skepticism. Africa? Her? *"And your parents, what do they think about that?"* he asked.

She shrugged, stubbing out her cigarette in the ashtray. *"They couldn't care less. Or they pretend. To them, it's a passing fancy. But me, I hate their world. Their castle, their comfort. I prefer my little studio, my shabby walls. It's my paradise, the place where I feel free."*

Kpegnan scrutinized her with a curiosity tinged with perplexity. This young girl, so direct, so loose with her words, intrigued him deeply.

"And your boyfriend, does he live in your little paradise too? By the way, what are you waiting for to introduce me to him?" he threw out, a smirk on his face.

Straight to the point, Lachaise locked her eyes with his. *"I don't have a boyfriend. And I don't want one."* She paused, then added with a mischievous wink: *"I have a girlfriend instead. Jeanine... you know her well."*

Kpegnan froze, his eyebrows furrowing. *"Wait, you mean that... you are actually a couple?"* Surprised by his astonishment, Lachaise replied calmly: *"Yes. So what? Does that trouble you that much?"*

Kpegnan stammered, searching for words: *"I didn't expect it, that's all. Back home, this kind of relationship... it doesn't exist."*

Lachaise sketched an ironic smile. *"But of course it exists. You simply prefer to turn a blind eye. Do you really believe there are no homosexuals in Africa?"*

Kpegnan sighed, his voice heavy with conviction. *"Maybe, but it's an aberration. Man is made for woman. Nature established this balance. How can one love someone of the same sex? It defies logic."*

Lachaise shrugged, her tone firm. *"Love has nothing to do with norms imposed by society. We don't choose who makes our heart beat. That is a truth that no law, no custom, can erase."*

Kpegnan, getting carried away, exclaimed: *"It's against nature!"*

A frank burst of laughter escaped Lachaise's lips, tinged with defiance. *"Ah, the 'against nature' argument... Tell me, wearing glasses, using a telephone, or traveling by plane, is that natural?"*

"That's not comparable," Kpegnan retorted with annoyance. *"The union between a man and a woman is what guarantees life. Two people of the same sex cannot give birth to a child. It is the very foundation of humanity."*

Lachaise took a puff of smoke and replied in a steady voice: *"So, according to your reasoning, a sterile woman or a couple who chooses not to have children would also be an aberration? Since they don't participate in reproduction either."*

Kpegnan shook his head, agitated, unable to find an immediate comeback. *"No, but... There are roles to respect,"* Kpegnan insisted. *"Man and woman complete each other. A couple is a man and a woman. That is what is normal."*

Lachaise stared at him for a moment, then rested her elbow on the table, challenging him with her eyes. *"Normal according to whom? Your culture? Your religion? Because I grew up in a country where everyone is free to love who they want. You find it 'abnormal' because you were raised that way. But if you were born here, maybe you would see things differently."*

Kpegnan crossed his arms, his look hard. *"No. There are things that are universal. Homosexuality is a perversion."*

Lachaise lost her smile. *"A perversion? You think love between two consenting adults is a perversion? But polygamy, which you defend so much, that's not a perversion, perhaps?"*

Kpegnan tensed up. A heavy silence settled in, like an invisible wall between them. Two worlds were clashing in this tiny space: one rooted in millennia-old traditions, the other driven by the idea of individual freedom.

Lachaise continued, more incisive: *"And besides, explain this to me: if homosexuality is an 'aberration,' why has it existed forever, in all societies, in all eras? Why have kings, poets, warriors, artists, men and women of all civilizations loved people of their own sex? Were they all 'perverted'?"*

Kpegnan clenched his fists. *"It's not the same. Those are isolated cases, deviations... The norm is a man and a woman."*

Lachaise gave a bitter smile. *"The norm... but the norm changes, Kpegnan. In the past, the 'norm' was slavery. It was also that a woman had no rights, not even the right to learn to read. If we had blindly followed the norm, do you think the world would have evolved?"*

She leaned slightly toward him, eyes shining: *"The reproduction argument is the same. Not everyone is meant to have children. A couple can exist without procreating, because a couple isn't just a baby factory. Love is also an alliance, a complicity, a way to build a life together."*

Kpegnan looked away for a moment, troubled despite himself. *"You don't understand. Where we come from, it's inconceivable. It's shameful."*

Lachaise's tone grew harder. *"No, what is shameful is condemning people simply because they love differently. What is shameful is imposing silence on those who don't fit into your boxes. You say you love freedom, but your freedom stops where your intolerance begins."*

A heavy silence settled. In this silence, Kpegnan felt a dull anger rising in him, but also, deep down, a doubt. A slight unease he dared not name.

Lachaise, for her part, simply lit another cigarette, an enigmatic smile on her lips. *"One day, you'll understand,"* she murmured, blowing smoke toward the ceiling.

Kpegnan, his voice steadier, somewhat weary, tried to regain his footing: *"I would like you to understand as well that polygamy is not a fantasy. It is a millennia-old tradition, rooted, accepted. Among us, it structures society. Here, in the West, people cry scandal, but how many live in hypocrisy, juggling mistresses while swearing fidelity? At least with us, things are clear."*

Lachaise snickered. *"Oh really? A man can have several women, and that, that is legitimate. But two men or two women who love each other, that becomes an abomination? Nice logic, truly."*

Kpegnan clenched his jaw, eyes dark. *"You cannot understand. Our realities are not yours."*

Lachaise held his gaze, her tone dry: *"I understand one thing, Kpegnan. Love has no borders. No color, no gender, no culture. You want to build walls. I want to break them."*

She crushed her cigarette, stood up, and grabbed her pack of Gauloises. Her voice snapped like a slap in the face: *"You want to believe that love between two men or two women is an abomination? You are free to do so. But in that case, don't ever talk to me about freedom again."*

Kpegnan, sketching an ironic smile, shot back: *"It's undoubtedly because you've never had a taste of a man capable of making you discover other sensations that you speak and think this way. But anyway... that's your choice. I respect it, even if I have my reservations. After all... who am I to judge?"*

Lachaise left without answering, slamming the door, leaving him alone, prey to his contradictions.

Kpegnan remained seated for a long time, staring into space. He had grown up with unshakable certainties about what was *"good"* or "bad." But in France, he was discovering a world that was cracking the foundation of his convictions. Lachaise hadn't overturned his beliefs. Not yet. But she had planted a seed. A seed of doubt.

A part of him felt that he could never see the world exactly as before. Perhaps certain truths weren't as universal as he believed. Perhaps the evolution of a society wasn't measured only by its respect for traditions, but also by its capacity to accept diversity.

He sighed, stood up slowly, and opened the window. The fresh night air rushed into the room. He turned on his desk lamp and opened his notebook. Perhaps one day, he would have an answer to all these questions that, from now on, would never leave him.

Kpegnan adored the peaceful city of Clermont- Ferrand. He loved going out for a stroll when he had a bit of time. Every morning during autumn, the city woke up under a pearl-gray sky, heavy with mist. The wet cobblestones glistened under the hurried steps of schoolchildren, leather satchels flapping against their legs. In the cafés, the radio crackled in the background, playing a song by Jean-Jacques Goldman or Renaud. The smell of hot bread escaped from the bakeries, mingling with the scent of roasted chestnuts sold on street corners. Russet leaves swirled on the sidewalks, sometimes stuck to the tires of old Renault 5s.

Exiting the station or on crowded buses, Michelin employees, in gray or blue overalls, headed to the factory with steady steps, some carrying their lunch pails under their arms. Their faces were still marked by the morning cold, but already focused on the rhythm of the assembly lines and the dull thud of the presses.

At noon, shutters closed for family meals, while the city caught its breath, peaceful, slow, wrapped in the scarf of volcanic wind from the surrounding *puys*.

Kpegnan shared his room with Vial, a young man who was rather calm and discreet, but whose hygiene left a lot to be desired. Rarely did he deign to take a shower, and his single pair of leather shoes, worn by time and eaten away by humidity, gave off an unbearable odor. As soon as he took them off, a wave of stench invaded the room, seeping into the sheets and clothes.

Embarrassed, but diplomatic, Kpegnan tried to broach the subject with Vial, who settled for a smile, as if the problem didn't exist. Faced with this indifference, he took matters into his own hands: he threw the window wide open, sprayed the room with perfume, and sometimes even slid a camphor ball near the shoes, hoping to dull the smell. It was no use.

Exasperated, he ended up pestering the concierge to get a room change. After several days of waiting, his request was finally accepted. The day he moved into his new room, he breathed a deep sigh of relief. For the first time in a long while, he could breathe freely and enjoy a clean, orderly space without fearing an invasion of nauseating smells.

Lachaise, for her part, didn't hide her satisfaction at finding Kpegnan alone for study sessions. No more distractions and offensive odors. In this new privacy, the atmosphere was more conducive to work and secrets. While they buckled down to solve complex equations and decipher technical diagrams, she always found an excuse to discreetly graze Kpegnan's hand or flash him a smile.

Sometimes, she would slip him little notes scribbled on a torn piece of paper. Amused and astonished, Kpegnan discovered them with both curiosity and pleasure, although his face remained impassive.

On one of them, she had written: *"Kpegnan, my ebony wood, every time I see you, my heart falters. You have an indescribable effect on me, a sensation I cannot explain to myself. Soften your heart a little and do not fear this love reaching out to you. I desire you ardently and I don't know what to do to make you feel the same, tell me, I would really like to know."*

Lachaise was charming, very likeable, and helpful. However, she didn't fit Kpegnan's criteria. What put him off even more was her habit of smoking. But beyond these considerations, his heart was already entirely occupied by Djekobou. That is why he remained stone-cold to Lachaise's advances. Although he couldn't deny that in many respects, he wasn't indifferent to her.

Nevertheless, Kpegnan and Lachaise remained good friends. Clermont, a bubbling university town, quickly became their playground. From crowded lecture halls to well-equipped laboratories, everything was in place to offer top-quality training. But beyond the classes, this year was also one of discoveries, new experiences, and bonds forged in spontaneity.

They had befriended other students from all walks of life. Student parties, passionate debates on the future of engineering, and impromptu hikes in the Chaîne des Puys gave rhythm to their daily lives. Life was in full swing, balancing learning and levity.

One November evening, the air was crisp and damp, the paved streets of Clermont echoing under the hurried steps of night owls, bundled up or in costume, caught up in the Halloween fever. That night, Lachaise had dragged Kpegnan into this strange carnival, a celebration he knew nothing about. During the day, she had dragged him into a thrift shop, rummaged through the racks, and, without letting him get a word in edgewise, had shoved a costume into his arms.

"You'll wear this tonight. Trust me, you'll turn heads," she had thrown out with that rebellious smile he was beginning to know so well.

"For what occasion, please?" he asked, incredulous. *"You'll see tonight. We have to be ready. It's going to be a night to remember."*

During the party, Lachaise was unrecognizable. Disguised as a nightmarish nurse, she sported an apron that had once been white but was now stained with fake blood splatters, and she proudly brandished a gigantic syringe filled with a reddish liquid. With her gleaming eyes and strange smile, she looked every bit the horror movie heroine.

At her side, Kpegnan stood in stark contrast. He wore a bomber jacket that was a size too big, a leather cap, and dark sunglasses in the middle of the night. With his lost-in-the-woods look and cautious gait, he looked more like a disillusioned pilot exhausted from a long flight than a monster emerging from the night. No matter; after all, this celebration was foreign to him.

"You know, I was completely in the dark about what Halloween was until you told me about it," he admitted, adjusting his cap. *"If I knew, I would have come with a Leopard-Men costume,"* he added with a chuckle.

Lachaise smiled. *"Standard. It's not really a tradition here either. It's mostly just an excuse to dress up and act crazy!"*

They ventured into the dark alleyways, crossing paths with groups of children trying their luck at house doors. The atmosphere was joyful; Lachaise pretended to frighten passersby with her menacing syringe, triggering fits of laughter with every jump scare.

But rounding a corner, Kpegnan stopped suddenly, as if struck by a memory. He rubbed his chin, pensive. *"Hey, now that I think about it, I have heard of Halloween before, but not like this."*

Lachaise raised an eyebrow. *"What do you mean?"* Kpegnan sketched a bland smile. *"Once, a few weeks ago, a homeless man asked me for money. I refused. So he said: 'It is not Halloween yet, take off your mask, sir.'"*

Lachaise raised her eyebrows, taken aback. *"Did you understand what he meant?"* Kpegnan shrugged. *"Not right off the bat. I thought he was just crazy, but actually, he was calling me a..."*

He stopped, finally realizing the weight of the insult. Lachaise felt her blood boil instantly. *"You piece of... what an asshole!"* She put away her syringe and clenched her fists.

Her indignation kicked up a notch. She stopped and stared at Kpegnan. *"And you? You didn't say anything?" "What's the point? I didn't understand what he was implying,"* he replied calmly.

But Lachaise wouldn't cool down. Her eyes flared up, and without even realizing it, she launched into a fiery tirade against ignorance and racist stupidity. She spoke loudly, gesticulating, drawing the looks of curious passersby. *"Do you realize? This guy thought he could humiliate you just because your skin is black! And you, you don't even react! Damn it, Kpegnan, it's unfair."*

He observed her, surprised by her outburst. He wasn't used to someone coming to his defense with such fervor. Usually, he was the defender. *"Does it hurt you that much?" "Yes, because it revolts me. You are my friend, and you don't deserve that."*

Kpegnan sketched a smile. *"Thank you, Lachaise, but you know, racists don't get to me. They are just weak minds."*

Then he continued, in a calm and lucid tone: *"Physiologically, we are all cut from the same cloth: a heart that beats, blood flowing in veins, the same DNA, emotions that drive us, the same amount of gray matter. The only thing that distinguishes us externally is skin color. Admittedly, on a civilizational level, certain peoples have dominated in certain eras, but to believe that one race is superior to another is an absurdity. The real difference between human beings isn't skin color, the shape of the nose, or the eyes, but intelligence and dignity."*

Lachaise remained quiet for a moment. Little by little, the tension bunching her shoulders eased. Kpegnan's words had touched her. When she turned to him, it was with a new kind of admiration. *"You speak like an old sage,"* she said, trying to smile. *"A philosopher in a pilot's cap."*

Kpegnan, amused, replied: *"It must be the effect of the costume."*

They started walking again, slower this time. Around them, the city continued to live. Children's laughter burst out from a nearby alley. *"You know,"* Kpegnan resumed after a moment, *"it's not the first time this has happened to me. This kind of remark, or look, or that heavy silence, especially when we are together. I feel them. I understand them, even if no one says anything."*

He paused, then added: *"But that's not why I came here. I came to learn, to grow, to build something. I refuse to let this kind of thing lead me astray from my goal."*

Lachaise looked at him deeply. *"You shouldn't have to deal with that,"* she said softly. *"Maybe, but the world is what it is. Me, I choose to look at it differently. To not let it dirty me from the inside."*

"I wish I were as strong as you," she whispered. Kpegnan smiled gently: *"You are stronger than you think. You get angry for others, you defend what is right, even when it doesn't concern you directly. You are brave, Lachaise, and that is rare." "Do you think that's why we get along well?" "Maybe. Or maybe because you make me laugh with your giant syringe,"* he replied, pointing to her fake-blood-stained costume.

She laughed out loud, relieved. *"Shall we head back?"* she suggested. *"Yes, but only if you promise to get rid of your giant syringe. By the way, that nurse outfit suits you well. Is it a premonition?"*

"No promises, Kpegnan, the night is still young. And thanks for the compliment."

They walked away from the square side by side, in that companionable silence shared by those who don't need words. That evening, on the surface, nothing extraordinary had happened. However, for Kpegnan, something essential had just played out. He had seen a rare sincerity in Lachaise's eyes. A loyalty that went far beyond friendship. Something deep.

Kpegnan didn't just go to class. Every day, bag slung over his shoulder and books under his arm, he faced crowded lecture halls, professors, and homework that sometimes seemed never-ending. On weekends, without ever complaining, he proudly donned his dishwasher's apron in a small neighborhood restaurant, tucked away in an alley. There, in the stifling heat of the kitchen, amidst the steam of washing up and the incessant clatter of plates, he washed mountains of dirty cutlery, listening with half an ear to the bursts of laughter and conversations of customers behind the swinging doors.

Yet, he could have settled for his scholarship or chosen more comfort. Lachaise, a girl from a wealthy family, often offered her help, but out of pride, or perhaps to preserve that independence he wore like armor, Kpegnan refused. *"I came here to fight, not to hold out my hand,"* he would repeat with a stubborn smile. He wanted to succeed on his own, without moral debt, without feeling like a charity case.

Every franc earned by the sweat of his brow was carefully put aside. Not to give in to certain whims or to treat himself to fleeting comfort, but for his family back in the village. Faithful to this duty, he often went to the post office, filled out forms diligently, and sent money orders to Djekobou and his uncle Téhé. In this way, he carried with him that quiet pride of immigrants who never forget where they come from, nor the loved faces left behind. With every transfer, he felt a little more worthy of those who had placed so much hope in him.

One winter Sunday morning, Kpegnan decided to go to a Catholic parish. When he crossed the threshold of the large church for the first time, he expected to find the noisy and vibrant fervor of African services, the mesmerizing songs, hands raised to the sky, faces bathed in tears and hope. But the immense nave echoed with an icy silence. A few old people, scattered on massive benches, mechanically chanted the lyrics of a hymn. Their weak voices were lost in the echo of the vaults.

Kpegnan felt a wave of unease. This house of God seemed orphaned of joy. Where were the young people, the families, the children dancing, drumming, singing until ecstasy? Here, the empty benches seemed to weigh heavier than stone.

So, his mind wandered: *Why, in Africa, do the churches never empty? Why this burning fervor, these whole nights spent in prayer and song, this visceral need to hope beyond daily misery? Was it poverty that pushed his people to take refuge in the divine? Or did the African soul, more sensitive to invisible mysteries, refuse to get used to the silence of the world?*

A doubt crossed his mind: *What if, in the West, faith had slowly died out because men believed they already had everything? Whereas in Africa, people still prayed because everything was lacking?*

He pulled his coat tight, shivering as much from the cold as from this revelation. For the first time, he felt like a foreigner not only because of his language or skin color, but because of his way of believing. Returning from the service, he went to Lachaise's place.

Lachaise, lying on the bed, an amused smile: *"Why the long face? You just came from church, didn't you?" "I am somewhat disappointed by what I saw there. It contrasts with what I was used to seeing back home." "You still hope to find here what you left in Africa?"*

Kpegnan, sitting on the edge of the bed, pensive: *"It's not just Africa, it's God. Back home, when we pray, we feel a presence. The songs, the cries, the tears. It's as if the sky opens up. Here, I feel like God has gone on vacation."*

Lachaise, sitting up, ironic: *"Or maybe He never existed, as many people here think. Have you ever asked yourself that? That it might just be an invention to keep people quiet?"*

Kpegnan, raising his eyebrows, a bit offended: *"How can you say that? You think that way too? When I see miracles, healings, and people transformed. You think that's just hot air?"*

Lachaise, shrugging her shoulders: *"Me, I'm more spiritual than religious, that's all. When I observe the universe, I believe in the existence of a creator. But as one of my philosophy teachers in high school used to say, while it's undeniable that God created man, one must recognize that he got rid of him ages ago. Man is now an orphan, because God is dead."*

Kpegnan, stunned: *"Really? Is that what you think too?"*

Lachaise added: *"Here, people live without God and they get by just fine. No need to wait for paradise to be happy. Even in Africa, I think you have your own beliefs, if I'm not mistaken?"*

Kpegnan, calmly but firmly: *"Yes, but when we invoke the spirits of the ancestors, we entrust the final word to God. For me, faith is a force that is bigger than I am, that keeps me standing even here, far from everything. Without God, I would be nothing."*

Lachaise, observing him for a long time, softening her voice: *"Maybe, but I choose to believe in man, not in an invisible being. I believe more in freedom."*

Kpegnan, smiling sadly: *"And what if, deep down, freedom and faith weren't incompatible? If true freedom was precisely knowing that you aren't alone in this world?"*

A silence hung heavy. She looked away, troubled.

He lowered his eyes.

Over the months, the university year took on the appearance of a true rite of passage. Everyone left a part of themselves behind, certainties, illusions. Then came the first midterm exams, falling like a guillotine on the euphoria of the early days. Some stumbled under the pressure, others hit their stride. Kpegnan, brilliant and methodical, quickly distinguished himself by his rigor and consistency. Lachaise, more instinctive, compensated with a surprising adaptability and contagious energy. Together, they formed a formidable duo, supporting each other in difficult moments and constantly challenging each other to push their limits.

When the end of the year came, they crossed the finish line with flying colors, admitted to the next level. The time had finally come to savor a well-deserved vacation.

Summer was settling little by little in Auvergne, and the small student city of Clermont-Ferrand was gradually emptying of its inhabitants. Lachaise suggested Kpegnan stay in France to spend the holidays with her, all expenses paid. Despite his pressing desire to return home, he didn't hesitate long before accepting this tempting offer from Lachaise.

To his great dismay, Lachaise chose the Provence- Alpes-Côte d'Azur region as their destination. *"We'll start the holidays with Avignon first,"* she announced enthusiastically. *"Why not Paris? I would love so much to visit that mythical city,"* exclaimed Kpegnan. *"France isn't just Paris, you know that well, my friend. I don't understand this fascination so many people have, especially Africans, for that city." "I'd just like to pose next to the Eiffel Tower and send the photo to my parents." "Come on, don't give me that look, for goodness' sake! I propose something else, I am sure you will love it. Since you keep talking to me about your famous history professor, I am certain this getaway will please you." "Okay, as you wish."*

The next day, the day of departure, when Lachaise came to pick Kpegnan up, he noticed she had swapped her usual jeans for a very short and daring skirt. They hopped aboard her Volkswagen Beetle and set off on the road to Provence.

The journey was a revelation for Kpegnan. Through the window, he discovered a splendid France. Vast plains stretched as far as the eye could see, crossed by an impeccable highway. Peaceful cows grazed at the foot of green mountains, indifferent to the noise of cars and trucks speeding by. The fields were perfectly aligned, the crops tended in a mathematical order.

"That is what a developed country looks like... Here, nothing is left to chance. When will our countries reach this level?" he mused with a mix of admiration and vague sadness.

After a few hours of driving, Lachaise suggested a stop to relax and drink a coffee at a carefully maintained rest area. Usually, she took the opportunity to smoke, but this time, she settled for a nice little hot coffee. She had stopped smoking cigarettes to please Kpegnan.

The latter, attentive to the slightest detail, scrutinized his surroundings. Every element stood in stark contrast to what he was used to. Yet, out of pride, he kept his thoughts to himself, refraining from making a single comment to Lachaise. This trip only strengthened his determination to succeed in his studies and, one day, contribute to the development of his country.

Upon their arrival in Avignon, Kpegnan discovered a charming little city where ancient architecture rubbed shoulders with a lively crowd taking over the streets with effervescence.

"Why are there so many people in such a small town?" he asked, curious. *"These people come from all over for the Festival of Arts and Performance that starts tomorrow. My parents have a pied-à-terre here. That's where we'll be staying before exploring other places,"* explained Lachaise.

The next day, she showed him the treasures of Avignon: the majestic Palace of the Popes, the Rocher des Doms offering a breathtaking view, the famous Pont d'Avignon, and many other historical gems.

Fascinated, Kpegnan contemplated these monuments steeped in history, though he couldn't help but compare them to those in his own country, often left to rot.

In the evening, they attended a play as part of the festival. From the very first scenes, the audience was won over. Laughter erupted, spectators applauded to bring the house down, and Lachaise followed every line with passionate attention. But Kpegnan remained stone-faced. He struggled to follow the plot, feeling alien to the surrounding excitement.

He discreetly swept his eyes across the room and noted, with a touch of bitterness, that he was the only black man in the audience. A feeling of isolation took hold of him, accentuated by his inability to grasp the nuances of the show.

At the end of the performance, the room was still buzzing with laughter and cheerful commentary. Lachaise turned to him with a radiant smile. *"So, what did you think?"* she asked.

Kpegnan hesitated for a second before answering, sensing that he was at a turning point of his journey.

After Avignon, they hit the road toward Vaison-la- Romaine, passing by the majestic Pont du Gard. There, facing this immense

Roman aqueduct, Kpegnan stopped, eyes wide, unable to hide his admiration.

"It's incredible. How could those ancient builders show such ingenuity?" he asked, flabbergasted. *"The Romans were brilliant engineers, geniuses ahead of their time,"* replied Lachaise. *"Yet, there were also great scholars and mathematicians in Africa... But us, aside from the pyramids of Egypt, where are our works of ingenuity? We have no comparable works back home."*

A heavy silence settled in. Then, Kpegnan continued, his voice full of bitterness: *"We are only scratching the surface of our potential. We settle for the minimum. African ingenuity is still in an embryonic state. We don't ask ourselves enough questions. Look, for example, for centuries our ancestors believed the ocean marked the end of the world. They didn't even try to see beyond it."*

Lachaise, ill at ease, sensing the tension in his voice, tried to nuance his words. *"There are great works in Africa, I am certain of it..."*

Kpegnan sketched a bitter smile. "*A few vestiges, yes. But most modern infrastructure is nothing but colonial relics, poorly maintained and falling into ruin. Bridges collapsing, roads that are impassable... nothing that bears witness to our own genius."*

"I understand your bitterness, Kpegnan, but look around you. Things are evolving. You mustn't lose hope. Education and knowledge can change everything. You'll see, Africa will progress."

Kpegnan shook his head. *"We snatched our independence in pain, yet we are still lagging behind. Why so much waste despite our riches? Unlike René Dumont who said that 'Black Africa is off to a bad start,' I think it never really took off."*

Lachaise took his hand, seeking to soothe him. *"My father always told me that the intelligence of Africans is undeniable, but that their attachment to traditions and emotions sometimes holds them back. In my opinion, colonialism left deep scars and largely contributed to this state of affairs."*

Kpegnan stared at her for a moment before letting out a short, bitter laugh. *"Your father isn't totally wrong... but that is only part of the story. Traditions are not intrinsically a brake on development. It is their rigidity and their inability to adapt to modern challenges that can create blockages. As for colonization, my professor Zokou often said: 'One can doubt the purity of intentions. For it was nothing other than exploitation under the guise of civilization.' But today, lamenting serves no purpose. We must move forward, step by step, with a long-term vision."*

His gaze drifted over the millennia-old aqueduct. He took a deep breath and said: And in his bubbling mind, a single idea resonated:

"I do not despair of my continent, this Africa of intrepid warriors, of great healers and fetish priests with mystical powers. This Africa whose legends my uncle and grandparents told me, where one never really dies... One simply traverses time, becoming the wind that blows, the forest that whispers, the bird that sings. This Africa of solidarity, where equity is privileged over the frantic race toward individualism."

Lachaise nodded gently, touched by his vision.

"That is a very beautiful way of seeing things."

Kpegnan resumed, with a glimmer of determination in his eyes: *"The colonizers pillaged our riches. We must conquer what they have that is most precious: knowledge. We must invade their research centers, their universities, learn, master, then build and grow. Admittedly, we are moving forward slowly, at a snail's pace, but I am convinced that one day, yes one day, perhaps in several centuries, we will catch up."*

Lachaise squeezed his hand a little tighter and whispered: *"I am sure you are right. I am certain that you will play a role, however small, in this transformation."*

Kpegnan nodded slowly. There was no simple answer. But in the wind blowing over the stones of the Pont du Gard, he felt the stirrings of a new line of thought, a realization. And sometimes, that is all it takes to start moving forward.

After their stay in Avignon, Vaison-la-Romaine was their last stop in Provence-Alpes-Côte d'Azur. Nestled between verdant hills, rolling vineyards, and lush forests, the town exuded a timeless charm.

Lachaise knew how much Kpegnan loved nature. She was intent on showing him this magical place, a blend of Antiquity, the Middle Ages, and modernity. And she was not disappointed. Upon their arrival, Kpegnan was captivated by the landscapes. The olive groves stretched as far as the eye could see, forming a brilliant green carpet under the summer sun. He marveled at every detail, soaking his spirit in this peaceful and harmonious beauty.

But beyond the discoveries, this trip marked much more than a simple tourist exploration. These vacations were the cement of a budding love. The friendship between Kpegnan and Lachaise had morphed into a serious, more intimate relationship. They fell irrevocably in love. Between them, everything became obvious. One could no longer do without the other. It was no longer a simple student complicity.

Returning from this unforgettable trip, Kpegnan made a major decision. He left the university residence, and Lachaise gave up her small studio. Together, they settled into a two-room apartment in the heart of the city. Their student complicity had gently slid toward a deeper intimacy, a committed relationship, made of shared laughter, gazes that no longer hid anything, and whispered promises.

Part 4

In the village, time trickled away.

Kpegnan's absence had left a gaping void in Ténably. It had already been a year since the young prodigy had left for France, carried away on the wings of a scholarship that was the pride of the village. But behind the songs of glory and the prayers of encouragement, daily life had resumed its course, with its joys, its sorrows, and its struggles.

The child, the fruit of his love with Djekobou, was growing like a weed. His first steps made the women erupt in laughter and applause. His resemblance to Kpegnan left little room for doubt: the same broad forehead, the same sharp looks, the same sticking-out ears. Djekobou clung to these features as living proof of the faithfulness of her heart.

As for Nanhan, Kpegnan's grandmother, she lived her days in a sorrowful listlessness. Seated in front of her hut, her wrinkled eyes would lose themselves in the dusty road, hoping at every moment to see the slender silhouette of her grandson emerge. His absence weighed heavily on her. In the evening, she murmured prayers to the ancestors, asking them to watch over him over there, so far from his native soil. But deep down, she dreaded that he might be swallowed up by that strange world and that he would little by little forget his roots.

Amani, who sincerely believed himself to be the little boy's father, stepped up his visits and promises, and Djekobou played her role impeccably. She received him, smiled, sometimes refused certain gestures she deemed dangerous, but accepted the money, converting the humiliation into tangible resources for the baby.

Meanwhile, Amani's ex-wife, a woman whose departure had caused quite a stir in the village, was rebuilding her life far from prying eyes and gossip. Less than a year after the separation, word got out that, far from the village, she had given birth to twins, fruits of an affair that had nothing to do with Amani. The rumor ran wild and spread like wildfire. For some, it was proof that the sterility was perhaps not on the woman's side; for others, it was a shame that fell upon Amani like an ironic twist of fate.

Amani, despite all his gifts and his guilt, was therefore not the father. The man who was paying believed he was repairing a wrong which, in secret, could not be pinned on him, and Djekobou's manipulation, which was intended to be a lifesaver, took on a cruel dimension from then on. Djekobou wondered:

If the truth were to come out, who would be broken? Amani, humiliated and morally ruined? Or herself, dishonored?

Djekobou reproached herself for nothing. Her conscience was clear. For her, this was Amani's sentence for having violated her.

One day, an old schoolteacher, a former colleague, passed in front of Amani, a broad smile plastered on his lips.

"Hey, Amani, did you hear the news?" "What news?" he replied, annoyed at not having been taken into confidence. "Your ex-wife! She gave birth, over there, in the city. Not one, but two! Twins, a boy and a girl. Hale and hearty!"

The old man departed, leaving Amani rooted to the spot. His heart pounded in his temples; his breathing became heavy. He felt a cold chill invade him.

Twins? His mind first refused the evidence. Then a deadly sentence, which he thought buried, resurfaced the one his wife spoke the evening she left the house, tears in her eyes:

"The problem, Amani, is not me."

Back then, he had brushed her words aside with a wave of his hand, convinced the fault lay with her. Today, the truth imposed itself with the brutality of a slap in the face. It wasn't her. It was him.

A bitter taste filled his mouth. He went inside hurriedly, slammed the door, and collapsed onto the bed. His eyes latched onto a small child's shirt, bought long ago for Djekobou. His stomach tied itself in knots.

In his mind, two visions blurred together: the bursts of laughter of the twins he would never have, children of another man; and Djekobou, whom he had believed to be carrying his legacy.

Then a terrible doubt seized him: *what if this child was not his? What if she was playing him, just as life had once played with his pride?*

He sat up abruptly, knocking over the chair. In his eyes, rage mingled with despair. For the first time, Amani understood that he was not merely a victim of chance: he was a captive of a truth that no wealth, no authority could abolish.

Sometime later, Amani was posted far away, to a school in the North. But before his departure, he had insisted, demanded even, to take the child with him. *"It's my son!"* he clamored with the pride of a man seeking to salvage his honor. Djekobou had listened to him, then, with a firm look and her arms tightened around her little one, she had cut him off:

"This child is not yours. He is Kpegnan's. I can no longer live in this lie. Go where you want, but he stays here, with me."

That day, Amani felt annihilated, his pride trampled a second time. He left the village without another word, dragging behind him the burden of his humiliation.

In this atmosphere of nostalgia, Djekobou was the object of much desire, but she did not yield.

She had taken a vow of chastity, like a promise to Kpegnan. Her love, she dedicated entirely to him and to the child they had conceived. She resisted temptations, rumors, and advances. Even in moments of loneliness when the absence became heavy, she stood her ground, head held high, persuaded that Kpegnan's return would finally give meaning to all these sacrifices.

Youl Bloffeur, the singer of the Aloukou band, was the boldest. He, who had always desired Djekobou, had sniffed out an opportunity. A smooth talker with a charming smile, he multiplied the occasions to cross paths with Djekobou. He often offered doughnuts to little Potey. When he saw her at the stream, he complimented her on her walk. During the evening gatherings, he cast lingering glances at her and slipped a few improvised verses dedicated to her into his songs to trouble her heart.

Thus life flowed in Ténably: between Potey's innocent laughter, Nanhan's discreet tears, Amani's grudges, and Youl Bloffeur's seductive songs. Everyone, in one way or another, lived in the aura of Kpegnan, whose absence was more present than many a presence.

One moonlit evening, after an Aloukou rehearsal where his husky voice had electrified the village square, Youl Bloffeur approached Djekobou at the stream. She was filling her bucket, focused, avoiding his eyes.

"Still clinging to your ghost from France?" he threw out with a smirk.

Djekobou raised her head, annoyed.

"Carry yourself from my front, Youl Bloffeur. Go find toothpick make you brush that your mouth wey dey smell tobacco and Banji there."

A burst of laughter rose among the young women drawing water nearby. Youl Bloffeur, stung to the quick, puffed out his chest.

"Is it me you are insulting? You think you're clever because you're keeping a promise to a man who left you behind, illiterate that you are! You're dreaming, Djekobou. Kpegnan, over there, he's discovering real life. You think he'll wait for you? You are naive."

She replied immediately, her eyes flashing:

"Han han, na that one self. I go wait am pian."

Youl Bloffeur clicked his tongue, vexed, but he did not back down. He stepped closer, his eyes shining with a strange glint.

"Listen well. You think you can resist me? Me, Youl Bloffeur, I have powers of which you ignore the strength. No woman, I say, no woman has ever resisted my charm when I have decided. You will see, you too, you will fall."

Djekobou looked him up and down, her full bucket in her hands.

"Just try small, you go see."

Then, with a brusque gesture, she hoisted her bucket. Youl Bloffeur remained planted there, humiliated by this resistance he had not foreseen. But deep down, he had not said his last word.

One moonless night, Djekobou was returning from her sick aunt's hut in a settlement near Ténably. The bush rustled with unsettling sounds. Suddenly, Youl Bloffeur surged onto the path, dressed in a black loincloth, cowrie shells suspended around his neck. His eyes shone with a disturbing light.

"You can no longer avoid me, Djekobou," he whispered in a grave voice. "I have done the ritual, I have invoked the spirits. You will be mine tonight."

He raised a small calabash filled with a reddish liquid that he sprinkled in front of her, murmuring incantations. Djekobou felt an icy shiver traverse her body. Her legs seemed to want to give way; she seemed drawn toward him by an invisible force.

Then, in a desperate burst, she screamed*: "You don fall down in Jesus name! Jesus Christ, save me oh!*

At that instant, a violent gust of wind rushed between the trees. Youl Bloffeur's calabash tipped over, shattering on the ground. His cowrie shells snapped, scattered in the dust. He staggered, his eyes losing their shine. He muttered a curse and fled into the night, his voice broken by rage and shame.

The next day, Djekobou, still trembling, confided in the pastor of the village church. She thought she would find spiritual support in him, a compassionate ear. But as she spoke, she felt his regard sliding, insistent, over her features, over her curves.

"My daughter," he said with a smile that was anything but pastoral, all the while caressing her hands, *"The Lord has blessed you with rare beauty. If you came to my house more often, I could pray specially for you, at length."*

She backed away, her heart sinking, a bitter disgust rising in her throat. Even here, she was not safe.

Alone in her hut that night, Djekobou burst into sobs. Temptation, pressure, loneliness everything seemed to gang up against her. But she remembered the vow she had made to Kpegnan, her oath of love and fidelity. She hugged her child against her and, despite her tears, repeated again and again:

"*My heart na for you, Kpegnan. Na you alone I dey for.*"

The temptation was immense and unbearable, but Djekobou resisted, holding on to her love. Every gesture, every look from Nanhan gave birth to a dull tension within her, a conflict between desire and loyalty. She felt her heart beating fit to burst, every fiber of her being pushing her to yield, and yet she held on.

Nanhan, fascinated by Djekobou's reputation for purity, broke the silence one day: *"If you manage to hold out, it is certainly thanks to the excision. You see, your father was wrong."*

These words hit Djekobou full force. In the evocation of painful memories, she perceived at once a provocation, a brutal truth, and a profound misunderstanding. Her determination wavered for an instant, then she pulled herself together, conscious that this battle against herself remained the only proof of her love and her strength.

In Clermont-Ferrand, within Kpegnan's silences, a persistent presence remained, a truth he managed neither to flee nor to face. For, thousands of kilometers away, he knew that Djekobou continued to wait for him. She still believed that his heart beat for her alone, that nothing and no one had been able to erase the tenderness that had bound them forever. This certainty she maintained in his absence weighed on him like an invisible burden. Every thought of her awakened the same haunting question: *what would he tell her when he returned to the country?*

For him, Djekobou remained the deep, immutable love. The one that had traversed years and borders. The one that withstood silences, longing, and kilometers. She was the constant presence in his mind, the discreet breath that still animated his heart despite the distance and absence.

Yet, he knew he could not keep the truth silent forever. A day would come when he would have to reveal everything to her: to write, to speak, to lay himself bare. Even if a part of him still trembled, prisoner of the illusion of a fleeting love, Kpegnan sensed that he could not escape this confession. Honesty demanded that he confront his own contradictions. Courage required that he look his love in the face, that he dare to name what he truly felt. He nourished, perhaps naively, the hope that Djekobou would understand.

However, he was overwhelmed, torn between two irreconcilable truths. How to make her understand that here, in this foreign winter, Lachaise had not been a whim, let alone a betrayal? She had been a necessity. A fragile but vital refuge against the freezing cold of exile, against the harsh loneliness of a life without bearings, far from his land and his people.

With Lachaise, he found a form of breathing room. She offered him a shelter, imperfect, certainly, but real. She bandaged his exile, plugged the breaches opened by absence. Yet, she replaced no one. Neither Djekobou, nor what they had shared. She was but a provisional answer to the gaping void left by his estrangement.

So, one sleepless night, while Lachaise slept peacefully in the room, Kpegnan, exhausted, his soul eaten away by guilt, finally let urgency take over. His hands trembled, his heart beat heavily, but he picked up the pen. In this silence charged with truth, he wrote to Djekobou.

My dear Djekobou, Good morning or good evening, depending on the position of the sun.

I hope with all my heart that you are well, and that our little POTEY is growing hale and hearty.

I imagine your worry... My silence has surely weighed heavy. But know this: it never meant oblivion. Since my arrival, I wanted to focus, to tame this unknown world and let myself be absorbed by my studies.

Today more than ever, I felt this compelling need to write to you. To open my heart to you.

My first winter here was an ordeal. A biting cold that seeps right into the bones. Days so short one would think we were plunged into an endless night. After classes, I took refuge in my room, where even the artificial heat of the radiator failed to warm my soul. This mechanical, oppressive heating gave me a migraine and made me miss the tepid softness of our African nights.

When summer arrived, I awaited it like a deliverance… but what a disillusionment! A blazing sun, a heavy, suffocating heat, without the slightest breeze to soothe the ardor of the days. Here, everything is extreme, everything is out of proportion. But I will end up getting used to it.

Despite everything, I have good news to announce: I am moving on to the second year, with honors. I would have liked to see you smile upon learning this, to imagine you jumping for joy while telling me, as you used to do:

"That's good, but you can do better." So I promise you, my sweet, next year, I will do even better.

My darling, your absence weighs on me. The nostalgia for home gnaws at me, a little more each day. I only have to close my eyes to see you again, to relive our memories.

Our long walks in the forest, lulled by the song of birds and the distant cry of monkeys.

Our endless conversations, under the benevolent light of the moon, at the edge of the school, alone in the immensity of the night.

Our stifled laughter, when we hid, during the Booms, behind the straw fence to watch the older ones dance and kiss in secret, our joy during the soccer tournaments between villages.

And that old woman, do you remember her? The one who chased us away as soon as she saw us too close to each other behind her hut, shouting that we were *"too young for those things"?* Her name escapes me, but I am certain that you, you remember…

And that stormy night. Do you recall? We were curled up against each other, trembling, convinced that our final hour had come.

That night, we made a promise. To never separate.

Today, the ocean divides us, the kilometers pull us apart, but my heart, it remains anchored to yours, like the roots of the same tree.

My darling, I miss your laugh. Your jokes too. I can't wait to read your words.

Here, everything is fine, despite my initial apprehensions. Apart from the climate, I have nothing to complain about.

There are people from the four corners of the world here. People are respectful, polite, although everyone stays with their community. The West Indians together, the North Africans together, the Black Africans together. The Whites, they are more open, but also more wary. Here, it takes time to be accepted.

I have a female friend here, her name is Lachaise. She is white, very kind, and she takes good care of me. Do not worry: she is only a comrade, nothing very serious, but one never knows, for I will not lie to you, she pleases me well. However, I resist, but, if I waver... If I succumb to temptation, it would only be with the body, never with my heart. Never could she replace you in my heart. I think of you every day. And I will always keep my promise.

My love, since we were friends, I already loved you. But it was a sweet, carefree love, woven of complicity and innocence. With time, it transformed into something much deeper, more burning.

Perhaps you do not know it yet… But you are the queen of my heart. I do not imagine a single second of life without you. You are in me, encrusted in my soul, and only God could tear you away.

Your love consumes me, a sweet sickness of which I do not want to be cured.

Do you continue to go regularly to church, as you promised? Do you respect your vow of chastity?

In any case, I trust you, for I know you are serious and faithful. I am certain that boys run after you, but never will you yield. Always be wise and save yourself, for I still care for you. Remain pious, for only God is in control.

On my side, I go to church less and less. At every mass, I see only old people certainly in search of a place in paradise. The young have deserted the places of worship, I don't know for what reason. Here, faith seems to be dying out. Back home, it is still alive, vibrant, rooted in every drumbeat and every prayer murmured by the light of a candle or a hurricane lamp.

How are my friends Kouia and Bayala? And our dear Kémessié, still just as hilarious? Tell her that her jokes and her famous *"dumb"* questions miss me terribly. I have a keen desire to see you all again.

Do not forget to pass on my greetings to the grandparents, to my darling uncle Téhé.

From now on, I promise you, I will write to you more often. In the meantime, I am sending you these few photos to help you wait.

A thousand kisses, a thousand hugs. Kiss everyone for me.

I embrace you very tightly. Your better half.

Kpegnan sealed the envelope, then held it between his hands for a moment. A wave of emotion swept through him, stirring up both impatience and dread. He burned with the desire to receive an answer.

But suddenly, a thought imposed itself upon him:

how would Djekobou react?

He wanted to believe, deep down, that Djekobou would understand that sometimes, the body could betray without the heart or the soul stumbling. Yet, he knew that words, however sincere, would have little purchase.

No matter the strength of the justifications or the weight of the arguments, he had broken an oath. And it was this betrayal, naked and irrevocable, that gave birth to his fear of Djekobou's response.

More than a month after he sent it, the letter finally arrived in the village.

When Djekobou recognized the familiar handwriting on the envelope, her heart skipped a beat. A tidal wave of emotion overwhelmed her. Hands trembling, she seized the letter, pressed it against her chest, her eyes glistening with tears, before opening it with caution.

Inside, a surprise awaited her: photos of Kpegnan. The moment she spotted them, her heart raced. He was there, right in front of her, smiling, well-dressed, looking fit as a fiddle.

Without waiting, she sprang up and ran to her in-laws'.

"He has written! He has written!" she cried out,

breathless, brandishing the photos.

When they saw Kpegnan's face, a ripple of relief ran through the gathering. The elders exchanged looks, the children leaned in for a better view, and the neighbors, drawn by the commotion, came to share this moment of joy.

"He is well! Look how healthy he looks!" murmured Kpegnan's grandmother, caressing the photo with her fingertips.

Faces lit up with sincere smiles. He was far away, but he hadn't forgotten his own.

That day, under the palaver tree, Kpegnan's letter was read aloud, every word resonating like a balm on the hearts that had waited for him so long.

I no even sabi where I go start. The day I see your letter eh, my heart do gbou gbou! I happy so tay I squeeze am on my chest before I open am. Night time, I sleep with am on top my mat sef.

But you too, my darling... try write small-simple na! That your big-big French, me I no dey catch all. I even call school master make he explain me. But wetin I understand be say: you dey fine, and na that one I want.

I been fear for you because of that their cold for there. Dem say the cold for that side, e dey beat person well-well! But I happy for you oh.

But I say eh! Which kind cloth be that? The one you wear inside the small photo there, e no fine koraa! You come look somehow. With that your big jacket and that your ugly cotton cap, you look like old village man. Dem force you wear that one? E no fit you one bit.

Your small Potey dey fine oh. E don dey sharp now. E like paper too much, e go turn like you sef! E sabi count small-small and e don start sing already: "Frère Jacqueu, frèreJacqueu..."

E wan go school, but e still small. Every morning, when e see other children dey go, e go cry sotay you go think say e eye wan commot.

Nanhan dey fine, but she vex. She talk say since you commot here, you no dey send letter again. She say make you dey send letter with photo everyday. She old oh, you no sabi tomorrow. Even Uncle Téhé sef dey vex, e say you don forget am.

My darling, take care for that side oh. You say Lachaise do what? Which kind name be that again? White people too dey strange, vrai-vrai. I no even understand her palaver well. You say she do what? Even if she be stool, armchair or whatever, she for leave people dem their husband quiet. Darling, na you alone I dey count on.

I know you boys, that your matter, you no dey hold body, but do am softly. If you leave me, I don finish. The way I dey keep myself because of you, and people dey laugh me say I be foolish... Don't leave me for White woman oh! Dem say White people get plan, but me I know say you no go do that thing!

I dey wait your comeback, but I tire eh! I no even get eye for another boy. But people dey disturb me here too much. Dem say I dey waste good nyash like this for nothing.

Kémessié talk say she no fit stay one week without doing it. You know say that girl craze small oh!

One Dioula man sef dey there, money full him body. E get Peugeot wey e cover with tarpaulin. E dey beg make I be him third wife. Say if I gree, e go fix my mama house, then carry me go capital with Potey. You think say I even watch am? The way I sack am eh, e shame catch am.

Kémessié, you say she be your good friend there, she dey talk say I be stupid. She say make I leave you, go marry the man because of the money. She says if I no want, she go go take the man herself. I tell her make she take am cadeau. She says she go braiquer him by herself. That girl no get brake.

Since you commot, many things happen for here. Too much sef. Plenty men don die. Dem say na "witchcraft credit" wey dey worry the village. Everybody dey fear now.

You remember that small Senoufo boy, the one wey get plenty pimples for skin and people dey call am *"Vié Galeux"?* Snake bite am, e die. Bloké too, your small good friend wey get clubfoot for left leg, him too don die.

And then Moussa the driver, serious accident catch am. Him two legs don break, him motor spoil finish.

But good news dey too oh. Kémessié don born again, girl pikin. The pikin fine! She come like white baby sef.

She say her daughter go marry our Potey later. Me, I just laugh am!

Darling, we play ball for sub-prefecture. E hot no be small, but we still win cup! See Bettega, that small Maraka boy na him score two goals. We happy sotay! But that fake referee, the way he cheat for them, he no fair eh! E refuse the goals. Kouia and Bayala wan beat am serious. Dem push am down. Even me, when e fall, I knack am one big côcôta for head.

Our players wan scatter field, but Uncle Téhé say make we leave matter. Night come, we do penalties- penalties. And since God no dey sleep, dem miss three, we no miss one. Instead make dem shame go house, dem dey shout say we do (juju).

Darling, dem transfer Amani go North. With that him big head, he say he wan carry Potey go with am! I tell am sey the pikin no be him own! I vex sotay I swear. He say na lie. E just dey shout dey call me "Toutou brodel." Me too I no miss am, deh!

Now we get new director one Voltaic man, Mister Zoungrana. Him thin-small, but him good man, and him get Renault 4. Na him dey drop me and Kémessié go junction every morning. You know Kémessié oh… she don take the mister already!

Kehi, that good-for-nothing wey fail Brevet three times e don enter police! Dem say him uncle *"make corridor"* for am. And Fla Gnron, that light-skin girl wey dey follow you up and down she don get husband oh! Dahomean man. Me I fit breathe now! The way she dey worry me eh, I been wan gbasse her self.

People contribute money to fix village school. Me, I take one thousand franc from my small klaklo money give. Dem mix pôtô pôtô with cement only. No painting sef.

One day, one big-belly man come village. He say he wan be deputy. He say if we vote for am, he go put tar for road, put light, put pump, no more going stream. Me I know sey na lie, but people dey follow am hot-hot. He dash village chief one moto.

Darling, everybody dey wait make you send something. Timothée want Magres shoe and fine jersey. Me, I want good Paris perfume, nail polish, and cloth for pikin. Old Bonfils her granddaughter dey come December you must buy suitcase. Nanhan, your grandma, want your heavy English bedsheets for this hot weather here, hmm. Uncle Téhé want good gun to chase agouti wey dey chop all him rice. Kémessié want make you find White man give her but not old White man oh! She want fine White man with blue eye, hair-full head, like that singer she paste for her room.

My love, I stop here today. But a beg, no laugh me. You know, say me I no talk big English. Next time I go beg one master make e write for me.

Send me plenty photo. I dey wait for you. No, leave me. Goodbye, my heart.

Your Djekobou.

Djekobou applied lipstick and pressed her lips to the bottom of the letter before slipping it into the envelope. Her heart was beating hard.

Upon receiving the letter, Kpegnan expected anger and reproaches, but Djekobou, true to herself, always funny, trivialized his relationship with Lachaise.

It had been nearly two years since Kpegnan had been in France. Two long years of waiting, of sporadic letters, of promises.

But today, he was coming back.

That afternoon, a bush taxi a veritable heap of scrap metal, ground to a halt in front of the village entrance. The door slammed, and a slender young man, his complexion bronzed by the sun, dressed in bell-bottom trousers and a white shirt plastered to his body, stepped out of the vehicle with a suitcase in hand.

Kpegnan was there.

The villagers, taken by surprise, suspended their activities for a moment. A murmur ran through the assembly.

"It's him! It's Kpegnan! He has returned!"

But he, without wasting a second, walked with a firm step toward the family hut.

In front of the house, his grandmother, Nanhan, was pounding rice in a deep mortar, helped by two of Téhé's wives. The old lady, stooped with age, raised and lowered her pestle with measured slowness.

When she spotted her grandson, her breath caught in her throat. The pestle slipped from her hands and fell into the dust.

"Come and see, my White man has arrived! Look how clean he is!" she cried out, her voice trembling with emotion.

The women came running, bursts of laughter and exclamations erupting from all sides.

"Come suckle, my son!" Nanhan called out, opening her arms to him.

Kpegnan burst out laughing and held her tight against him for a long time, breathing in the familiar scent of shea butter ingrained in her skin.

Then he pulled back slightly and looked her over, a glimmer of worry in his eyes.

"Nanhan... you have lost a lot of weight! Are they not feeding you well or what?" he asked, his look stern.

Nanhan shrugged, a toothless smile on her lips.

"Is it you who was feeding me before?" she retorted, laughing.

Around them, laughter rang out. But in Kpegnan's heart, a certainty took root: time had passed.

Meanwhile, at the stream, Djekobou was still drawing water. She was still unaware of her beloved's return.

When a woman from the village shouted the news to her, she dropped her calabash into the water. Without thinking, she hiked up her *pagne* and started to run.

Hardly had she arrived in front of the family house than she saw him.

Kpegnan. Her heart leaped in her chest.

It was really him, even more handsome than she had imagined.

Without hesitating, he jumped at her neck and hugged her against him with a fervor that made her whole soul shiver.

"Here, give me a kiss, my darling," he said in a teasing voice, a mischievous smile on his lips.

Djekobou smiled and pushed him away gently.

"This kissing business, leave it there eh! When I bite you, you will see!"

Kpegnan laughed heartily.

"You, you will never change!"

She stared at him, marveled.

"You dey smell fine oh! And you dey shine like that! I jihi Paris people! You must do something, you go carry me go there too."

He gently caressed her cheek, fixing her with his eyes.

"I wanted to see you so much. You have gained weight, eh! What are you eating? And our little Potey?"

Djekobou smiled tenderly. *"E dey farm with him grandma, dem dey come just now."*

Days passed, but time flew too fast. Already, his departure was approaching. But this time, Kpegnan did not want to leave just like that. Before returning to France, he had made a decision: he was going to marry Djekobou.

One night, under the pale light of the moon, he went to her house, accompanied by his little uncle Sea. It was time to make their love official.

To honor Djekobou's family, Kpegnan came with arms full of gifts: two sets of *pagne* wrappers for his mother-in-law, and a transistor radio for her uncle, the one who had married her mother after the death of her biological father.

Perplexed, Djekobou's stepfather asked him: *"To what do I owe this honor, my son?"*

Kpegnan, with a respectful look, replied: *"It is a courtesy visit. Since my return, I have not yet come to see you. It was time to remedy that."*

"Welcome home, my son. Is everything going well in the Whites' country?" "Yes, everything is fine over there. And here, how are things?"

The old man sighed. *"Nothing too serious, but the harvest was not good this year. The birds devastated all my rice."*

Kpegnan nodded, pensive. *"A pity... But it is only a difficult season; we must redouble our vigilance next time."*

The next day, in accordance with custom, the ritual abduction of Djekobou was organized with the complicity of both families. At nightfall, young men from Kpegnan's village, sent by his family, went discreetly to the young girl's parents' house. Stifled laughter, hurried footsteps, and conspiratorial whispers: everything was bathed in a subtle harmony between laughter and reverence.

Djekobou feigned light resistance, as tradition demanded. Her friends laughed out loud while encouraging her, while the boys carried her away almost by force. Her protests, more theatrical than sincere, hinted at the impatience and pride pulsing in her heart.

Taken to Kpegnan's family home, she was installed in a reserved hut, placed under the vigilant guard of the future husband's aunts and cousins.

Two days later, according to the ritual, Djekobou's brothers launched a fake search expedition. Armed with sticks and loud words, they scoured the village, knocking on huts, questioning passersby, until they reached the house of Kpegnan's parents, where the young girl was *"held captive."*

They were welcomed by Téhé, Kpegnan's uncle, seated on a bamboo bench, wrapped in a large, heavy boubou. With Olympian calm, he greeted them in a falsely naive tone: *"My young brothers, to what do I owe the honor of this visit?"*

The eldest of Djekobou's brothers replied in a firm and theatrical voice: *"We know that your son has abducted our sister. We demand her immediate return."*

Téhé crossed his arms, unperturbed, and replied after a measured silence: *"Your sister? She is not here. Continue your search."*

The brothers exchanged a knowing look before insisting: "Do not take us for naive people! She is here. We will not leave without her. Let us search the hut."

"I tell you she is not there. Have you visited all the huts in the village?" replied Téhé, inflexible.

"She is definitely here, and you can keep her if you wish. But there is a price to pay."

A murmur ran through the audience. The elders, seated in a circle, nodded gravely: tradition was following its course.

Still master of himself, Téhé bowed: *"Wait while I check."* He took a peek, then returned: *"Indeed, she is there. What is this price, then?"*

The eldest brother announced: *"A bull, five new pagnes, one hundred thousand francs, and a kola nut. Everything must be paid immediately, otherwise we leave with her."*

A long discussion then opened up. The elders took turns speaking, seeking to lighten or increase the burden. Laughter, protests, and exclamations punctuated the negotiation. Finally, after much palaver, Kpegnan's family accepted the conditions.

In a solemn gesture, the bull was led into the courtyard, the pagnes unfolded before the assembly, and the money deposited in a calabash as a sign of respect. Djekobou's brothers bowed: custom had been honored.

The union of Kpegnan and Djekobou was now sealed: the marriage could be celebrated in the dignity and jubilation of the people of Ténably.

The long-awaited day arrived. The two families gathered in a festive atmosphere, marked by joy and respect for customs. Under the appatam, carefully decorated, the ceremony took a solemn and symbolic turn.

Two young girls, chosen for their striking resemblance to Djekobou, were draped in a cloth covering their bodies and faces. A silence, heavy with suspense, fell upon the assembly, disturbed only by the muffled beating of drums. Kpegnan was then invited to step forward, blindfolded according to tradition. His challenge: to recognize his beloved solely by touch.

The rule was clear: if he made a mistake, he would have to pay a fine, proof that he did not know the one he was about to marry well enough.

But Kpegnan, sure of himself, barely brushed the arms of the two young girls. Then, he shook his head. *"None of them is Djekobou,"* he declared with assurance.

At that instant, an explosion of joyful cries rose from the assembly. Women struck up traditional songs, while the real Djekobou came out of a hut, radiant, veiled in grace and modesty. She was handed over to Kpegnan, under the sustained applause of the village. The union was celebrated in love and trust.

Another rite followed: a chicken was sacrificed as custom dictates and reserved for the bride's family. The eldest stood up and shouted: *"This chicken here, is what chicken?"* Another answered, smiling. *"It is the in-laws' chicken."* Then, following the ritual, he asked: *"Where is the bone of the chicken?"* He was handed the bone as a symbol of alliance between the two families.

Finally, Kpegnan took out an aluminum ring, handed it to Djekobou's father, and declared: *"Let this be the symbol of my commitment."*

But before Djekobou and Kpegnan could retire, a capricious aunt interrupted the ceremony. She demanded, in an imperious tone, that she be brought the molars of a virgin lioness and a four-legged hen. Faced with the impossibility of satisfying this far-fetched request, Kpegnan's parents first begged her, then handed her a one- thousand-franc note and a brand-new pagne. Thus, Djekobou officially became his wife.

And that day, under the cheers, the dances, and the songs of the village, their story entered forever into legend.

A few days later, Kpegnan took the plane back to France, his heart full of promises and hope. He left behind his village, his family, Djekobou, and his little Potey.

Years passed. Five years of effort, of invisible sacrifices, and of tenacious resilience. Upon his arrival in France, Kpegnan discovered a world different from the one he had left behind. Far from the warmth of the village, he faced the harshness of winter, loneliness, and the twists and turns of a society where he constantly had to prove his worth.

Despite the obstacles, he cleared the stages one by one with brilliance. His seriousness impressed the professors; his determination commanded the admiration of his classmates. Where others buckled under pressure, he held firm, carried by an inner strength stronger than exile, more tenacious even than doubt.

Through sheer hard work, he obtained his engineering degree with honors, even finishing as valedictorian of his class. A pride for his school, and a shining symbol for all those who still doubted the power of dreams coming from elsewhere.

Hardly was his diploma in hand when major French companies jostled for position: reputable engineering firms, ambitious multinationals, all wanted to secure the talents of this young man with an exemplary record. He was handed a radiant future on a silver platter. But in his heart, a question remained suspended: did this success far from his people really have the same taste as the one he had imagined as a child, in his native village?

France did not need one more engineer, he told himself. His duty called him home. He knew that it was in Africa that he would be most useful.

Meanwhile, Lachaise, his long-time friend, who had become much more than that, carried within her an even deeper transformation. She who, formerly, believed only in love between women, had surprised herself by desiring a future with a man. And that man was Kpegnan.

She dreamed of leaving with him for Africa, of starting everything anew beside him. But Kpegnan hesitated. This return to the country was not a simple trip. He had to find his bearings first, prepare the ground… and above all, confront a burning truth he had never dared to tell her.

A few days before his departure, he took his courage in both hands and announced his decision to Lachaise.

"Darling, for this trip, I prefer to go alone. You can join me later."

A heavy silence fell between them. Lachaise looked at him, trying to read beyond his words. *"Why could we not travel together?"* she asked, surprised.

Kpegnan looked away. *"It has been a long time since I left the country. I don't want to just land with you like that. I have to go... prepare the ground."*

"Don't worry, darling, I will know how to adapt. It doesn't bother me at all. As soon as we arrive, we could stay at the hotel while we quickly find a roof."

Kpegnan shook his head. *"That is not the problem." "Then, what is it?"* she insisted.

The atmosphere, initially light, became heavy in the space of a few seconds. Kpegnan inhaled deeply, searching in vain for the right words, but knowing that no phrasing would make the truth more acceptable.

"Actually... that is to say that... I have another wife... and a child."

A glacial silence fell upon the room. Lachaise, rooted to the spot, her eyes riveted on him, seemed not to understand what she had just heard. *"Excuse me?!"* Her tone was dry, cutting.

"I had promised her legal marriage after our traditional union... and I don't want to hurt her. The ideal for me would be to have you both, but I must speak to her about it first."

Lachaise felt a shiver run down her spine. *"What are you talking about right now?!"* she whispered, her voice broken by disbelief. *"You are married? Since when?!"*

Kpegnan let out a long sigh, overwhelmed. *"I care for her, and I care for you too."*

A new silence, but this time, charged with tension, ready to explode like a contained storm. Lachaise stared at him intensely, trying to understand how a man she thought was different could, deep down, be exactly like the others.

She ran a trembling hand through her hair, trying to order the chaos in her mind.

"Wait, wait... You could have told me this well before starting a relationship with me! I warned you, Kpegnan! I didn't want complicated stories!"

Kpegnan shrugged, attempting to keep his calm. *"I know, but I would like to be a polygamist. I have always dreamed of it. Back home, it is tolerated."*

Lachaise burst into bitter laughter, a sharp, hysterical laugh. *"Polygamist?!"* she repeated, incredulous. *"And you seriously think that I am going to be the second wife of a man?!"*

Kpegnan held her look, impassive. *"It is our culture, I have always told you, Lachaise. My wife Djekobou knows that a man can have several spouses. So the problem is not on our side, it is situated at your level."*

Lachaise clenched her fists and straightened up, eyes blazing with anger. *"You want to know what I think of your culture, Kpegnan?"* she spat, taking a step toward him, her voice loaded with contempt. *"I find it selfish. Unjust. And hypocritical. You men, you want everything! A woman must accept, shut up, and be happy with half a love!"*

Kpegnan remained marble-still, but deep inside, Lachaise's anger and sadness hit him full force. She crossed her arms, her eyes shining with profound disappointment, and murmured in a broken voice, to herself: *"Is it really possible to love two women at the same time?"*

Kpegnan approached her, held out his hand in a gesture of appeasement. "I don't know how you define love. B*ut yes, it is possible to love several women at the same time. I care for you sincerely. I don't want to rush anything.*

Take the time you need. Just remember that I will always love you."

But Lachaise violently withdrew her hand, as if his touch burned her. *"There is nothing to think about, Kpegnan. You have already made your choice. And I, I have just made mine."*

She approached one last time, plunged her wounded eyes into his, and murmured in a broken voice: *"Go tell the mother of your son that you have a new wife."*

Then, without another word, she turned around and walked away, head held high, without ever looking back.

"Yes, I told her. And she is delighted at the idea of having you as a co-wife," said Kpegnan, watching Lachaise disappear.

A heavy sadness invaded his chest. It wasn't simply a woman he had just lost. It was Lachaise. And deep down, he knew that no other would ever be like her.

The day of his departure, sitting in the plane taking him back to his native land, Kpegnan dreamed of Djekobou. He imagined her waiting for him, her smile dazzling, arms wide open in the market square. With a light heart, he closed his eyes, lulled by the steady vibrations of the aircraft. He had warned no one, dreaming of dazzling her with his surprise arrival.

But soon, his sleep slid into the strange. In his dream, the plane landed not on a runway, but in the middle of a vast, cracked, deserted plain. The village had vanished. In its place, bare earth, scorched by a lifeless sun.

Kpegnan stepped down, alone. The ground beneath his feet cracked as he advanced. In the distance, he spotted Djekobou, a frail silhouette swept by the wind, but when he ran toward her, she split in two: on one side, an African woman in a traditional wrapper with familiar features; on the other, a silhouette dressed in European style, cold, inaccessible.

He reached out his hand, but both figures recoiled, slowly fading into a whirlwind of dust. Around him, two worlds clashed without ever meeting. Kpegnan screamed, but no sound crossed his lips. He fell to his knees, the earth beneath him fissuring, sucking him into a bottomless void.

He woke up with a start, panting, eyes wide. Through the porthole, the night stretched out its cloak of stars. For a long moment, he remained motionless, his heart heavy with a bitter premonition: coming back was never simple. Perhaps nothing would ever be quite as it was before.

When the plane finally touched the soil of his country, Kpegnan felt his heart tighten in a strange way. The dream had not left his mind; it hovered around him like a light mist, invisible to others, but heavy on him.

As he moved through the airport, the familiar noises, the bursts of voices, the spicy scents, the humid heat should have filled him with joy. However, a small voice murmured deep within him: *what if everything had changed?*

With every step toward the exit, his former impatience gave way to strong apprehension. His smile tried to be light, but deep down, he feared what he was about to discover: *Would Djekobou still be the same? Had he himself remained the one she had loved? Or was he now just a stranger, bringing back with him a trace of a past that existed only in his memories?*

Upon his arrival in the village, Ténably stretched out before him, immutable. The huts of beaten earth, the few new buildings of brick and cement, the great tree under which the elders gathered, the market rustling with life. Everything seemed at once familiar and strangely distant.

The inhabitants had gathered, as if his arrival had been sensed. Heart beating, Kpegnan stepped out of the vehicle.

Then, a cry split the air, sharp, bursting with life:

"Kpegnan!"

A silhouette cut through the crowd, running. Kémessié, all smiles, surged forth like a tornado, arms wide open and eyes sparkling.

"Tchiee, you have gained weight, hein! What is this? The Whites fed you until?" she threw out, laughing loudly.

Kpegnan burst out laughing in turn, embracing her with a tenderness mixed with relief. This human contact, this sincere warmth, brought him back to reality. Perhaps he had exaggerated his fears.

But immediately, his regard sought her, frantic, almost worried. And he saw her. Djekobou. She stood back, her face illuminated by a soft, slightly shy smile. His heart skipped a beat. She was even more beautiful than in his memories, more real than in his dreams.

Beside her, a small boy, Potey, clung to her hand, eyes wide with curiosity. At that instant, the whole world faded away. He saw only her. Without thinking, he rushed toward her.

He lifted her lightly in his arms, closed his eyes, inhaled her perfume, and placed a long, tender kiss on her forehead. *"You are here, you are really here,"* he murmured, his voice trembling with emotion.

Djekobou laughed softly, caressing his cheek with tenderness. *"Where did you want me to be?"* she replied, eyes half-closed.

At that moment, Potey, hitherto well-behaved and calm, raised his little arms toward him. *"Papa!"* he shouted with all his heart. Kpegnan's heart exploded with love. He lifted him high in the air, eyes misty with tears. *"My son, my son!"* He snuggled him against him with a strength mixed with joy and disbelief.

In the midst of this jubilation, a strange sensation hit him, dull, familiar: a void. His instinct sought someone else. Where was she? Where was Nanhan, the one whose laughter should have torn the air, and whose arms should have embraced him like before, caressing his cheeks with her pale hands and rough palm.

Kpegnan's face froze. *"And Nanhan? Where is my grandmother?"* he asked, his voice lower.

Around him, the joy turned to awkwardness. eyes lowered. Smiles vanished. Only embarrassed murmurs answered him. It was Kouia, his childhood friend, who first dared to break the silence. He approached, looking grave, his voice tight. *"Kpegnan, you must be strong. Nanhan left five months ago."*

A blow from a sledgehammer. The ground seemed to give way beneath his feet. An immense void opened up inside him. *"Five months?!"* he stammered, throat knotted. *"And no one told me anything? Why?"*

Kouia lowered his eyes. *"We didn't want to disturb you. You were right at the end of your studies. She herself always said she wanted to let you go to the end without sorrow."*

The words resonated, empty, absurd, like slaps. Kpegnan felt a cold rage rise within him. They had stolen his mourning. They had robbed him of his last farewell. He closed his eyes, unable to hold back his tears. He held Potey against him with a feverish strength, seeking in the warmth of his child a refuge against the immense pain rising within him. He was home. Yes, he was home. But he understood, at that precise moment, that never again would anything be as before.

That evening, still stunned by the shock, Kpegnan pushed open the door of the church from which the faithful were emerging after a prayer session. He wasn't sure what he was looking for: answers, a little respite, or just a place to deposit his anger and his sorrow. The pastor, a man with tired features but a gentle look, approached him.

"My son, I know how heavy your pain is to bear. Your tears are true, your anger is legitimate. Even Jesus wept before the tomb of his friend Lazarus. Do not fear to cry out your grief: God is not irritated by your questions. He receives them... and He answers them, not with speeches, but with His presence."

"No! You know nothing at all!" Kpegnan cried out, his voice trembling with rage. "Presence? What presence? Me, I see only the void! What else are you going to tell me? That it is God's will? That death is part of life? But I will never see Nanhan again! And you would want me to thank God for having snatched her from me? Is that it? Easy to say, when it is not your family disappearing before your eyes!"

"Death is never easy, Kpegnan. But there comes a moment when we must learn to accept it."

"Accept what exactly?! That God snatches everything from me? My parents, my grandparents... And I am supposed to continue believing in Him? What is the use if He lets those we love leave without letting us say goodbye?"

"God takes nothing from us, my son. He accompanies us through the pain. And that pain there, it is the very proof of your love for her. Do not let it destroy you and make you lose faith. Make it a strength. Ensure that her love continues to live in you." Then he added: "God was there, Kpegnan. In every memory you have of her, in every lesson she taught you. Death does not truly separate us from those we love. It pushes us to keep them alive differently."

Kpegnan looked away, eyes drowning in tears he stubbornly tried to hold back. No words came. Anger still rumbled within him, but another presence was settling in, dull and heavy: an immense, dizzying void. A void he would have to, sooner or later, tame.

The pastor did not move. He remained there, calm, anchored in an imperturbable serenity. *"Come, get on your knees, so that together we may praise the Lord our God,"* he said softly.

Kpegnan hesitated. His heart still struggled between revolt and surrender. Then, slowly, despite himself, he yielded. He knelt beside Pastor Mahan.

Then Mahan took his hands in his, bowed before him, and, in this inhabited silence, raised a prayer.

"Almighty Lord, Creator of heaven and earth, You, the great Comforter, here is Your child Kpegnan, heart heavy and broken by the loss of his grandmother, she who carried him in her love and who now rests with You. You, the Eternal who makes young shoots sprout so that the forest never dies out, You see his tears, You know his sorrow. Give him the deep peace that only Your Spirit can offer. Remind him, Lord, that his grandmother has crossed the threshold of life to enter Your eternal rest, far from all suffering, and that her love remains alive by his side. May Nanhan's words, blessings, and gestures be like seeds in him, which will continue to bear fruit. May he walk with this strength and know that he is never alone, for Your Spirit accompanies him. Sustain him in this ordeal, surround him with Your presence like a fatherly embrace. Strengthen his faith, raise up his soul, and transform his pain into hope. In the name of Jesus Christ. Amen."

In Clermont-Ferrand, every evening, in the solitude of her room, Kpegnan's face returned. A few months already. Since that suspended moment at Roissy with his dreams, his singing accent, his promises half-serious, half- worried: *"You will come, one day."*

She had believed it. Then she had doubted. Then she stayed. But the seeds planted that day had grown in silence, nourished by memories. She then decided to write to him.

My dearest Kpegnan,

It is with a heart in tatters that I write to you today. My hand is trembling and my throat tightens under the weight of what I have to tell you. If only you were here, just here, for even a moment, so that I could dive one last time into your eyes before breaking this silence that has been devouring me since your departure.

You left, and since then, I am no longer the same. Kpegnan, I cannot forget you. You must know it, once and for all: I love you. With a boundless love, too big for me, too vast for this imperfect existence that promised us nothing. This love is all I have left. It is my strength and my weakness, my refuge and my torment.

Here, in Clermont-Ferrand, life goes on, as if nothing happened. The streets are the same, the faces too. But for me, each day is heavier than the last. I believed that time would soothe the pain of separation. I was wrong. It grows, it settles in, it gnaws at me.

And you, my love, how are you over there? Sometimes, I wish the world would stop. That we could freeze time, go back, find what we have lost. But life waits for no one, and it moves forward, without giving us a choice.

These words burn me, Kpegnan, for they say everything I dare not confront. Inside me, it is chaos: the shame of not having known how to stop your departure, the doubt of not knowing what you still feel, the fear of having lost you forever. And in the middle of all that, a stubborn hope that refuses to die.

Every night, in the glacial cold of Auvergne, I close my eyes and I imagine you near me. But even in my dreams, you move away. Your voice fades, your image dissolves. I call out, I reach out my hand, but you no longer answer.

Perhaps this is it, the true end of a love: this long and icy silence that settles in before even the word *"goodbye"* is spoken.

This was not the future I had imagined for us. I hoped, without saying it too much, that you would change your mind, that polygamy would remain a distant idea. I still believed in it. Perhaps a little too naively. It is true that I did not want to share you, and I did not want to lose you either. But sometimes, one must choose.

Kpegnan, will you come back? Or have you already turned the page?

I have a glimmer left, not a burning fire, but a soft light that still allows me to speak to you, to look for you in memories. I would like, just once, to meet your regard, to understand if the love of Avignon still lives in you, or if it has dissipated in time.

I weep for you softly, without anger. If you can, come back. If you want to, come back. But if everything is finished for you… then, goodbye to us both.

Lachaise

Kpegnan remained motionless for a long time. Every word weighed heavy. He read it a second time, more slowly, unable to detach his mind from this voice he thought he heard between the lines, this voice he knew so well. He felt his throat tighten, and a heavy ball form in his chest.

He hadn't foreseen this. Not this lucidity. Not this pain so well expressed. She spoke of courage, of memories, of that night in Avignon, and suddenly, it was he who was troubled.

He sat down. Silence invaded him. A part of him wanted to flee this truth, the other wanted to reach out across time, paper, and return to where everything was still beautiful. Lachaise was not shouting. She was not begging. She loved him, still. And that shattered him. He remained like that, for a long time, his eyes lost in the void. Then, slowly, he picked up his pen.

My dear Lachaise,

Since that day our eyes crossed at the train station in Clermont-Ferrand, nothing has ever been the same for me. I remember it as if it were yesterday. There was that something in your way of walking, in the softness of your voice, in the discreet light of your smile. That day, everything tipped over. My heart, my life, my certainties.

I had come to France to study, to build a future. But I did not yet know that I would meet the one who was going to turn my world upside down.

I fell in love with you with time, Lachaise. A deep, powerful, limpid love. A love that has only grown, despite the challenges, despite the silence, despite the distance.

You have been much more than a companion: you have been my refuge, my awakening, my light. By your side, I felt at ease, safe. You opened my mind, offered a tenderness I had never known. You loved me unconditionally, supported me tirelessly, and protected me even from myself.

Certainly, I am with another, but there is not a day when I do not think of you. Not a night when your memory does not slip into my dreams. I imagine you, alone, in that harsh Auvergne winter, and my heart tightens. How do you manage to endure those cold nights, without my arms to embrace you, without my voice to soothe you? Me, I spend mine hoping for a change of mind on your part, asking myself if one day, we will be able to find each other again without losing ourselves.

I will never forget you, Lachaise. You are part of me. You are inscribed in my memory, in my skin, in every beat of my heart.

Yes, I know. I know that I hurt you. That my departure left you in uncertainty and pain. I had to make a difficult choice, to return here to the native land, where my roots call me, where responsibilities await me. But I never erased you from my life. Never.

You must know one thing, with honesty: I still care for you. But there is a truth I cannot ignore. In my culture, in my current life, polygamy is not taboo. It is not a betrayal of love, but another way of living it, with respect and clarity. If your heart finds the strength to accept this reality, then I see no obstacle to us being together again. I am ready for anything to rekindle the flame of our love. You will remain forever a true love. See you very soon, if destiny allows us.

For months, Lachaise had remained in silence. Kpegnan said he still cared for her, however he had not renounced being a polygamist. A heavy silence, which had nothing peaceful about it. She wandered between a thousand thoughts, unable to find clarity. Kpegnan's letter, his chosen words, his grave but tender tone, had stirred something deep within her. But instead of bringing an immediate answer, it had opened a breach: that of hesitation.

She felt divided, torn between two contrary impulses. On one side, a visceral attraction to him, this inexplicable bond that resisted time and distance. On the other, fear: fear of losing herself, fear of reliving the wounds of the past, fear that her love would not be sufficient to bridge the differences, the absences, the life choices.

Every morning, she woke up with the sensation of a weight on her chest. She reread Kpegnan's letter again and again, hoping to find an answer she couldn't formulate. She oscillated between bursts of desire to go for it, to drop everything for him, and moments of withdrawal, where doubt took the upper hand. Was she ready to follow him in his choices, to accept his contradictions, to love him despite everything?

She avoided gazes, deep conversations. The world around her seemed blurry. The nights were the hardest. She thought back to their shared moments, to his promises, to his look. But something still prevented her from writing.

It was in this inner tumult, this quiet storm, that after long months of reflection, Lachaise finally made her decision. She could no longer stay there, waiting for her fears to dissipate. She knew they would never leave. She had to move forward despite her fears. *Come what may*, she told herself.

So, she picked up a pen. And the moment the ink touched the paper, her heart lightened a little.

Hi Kpegnan my ebony wood,

The silence has been long, I know. Too long certainly. But I want you to know that I am fine, despite everything. But, there is one thing your absence has taught me, a naked, tenacious truth: I need you. Desperately.

Deep down, something tells me to believe that you sincerely care for me. As for me, I have lived enough to know that dreams do not always turn into gold, that desires, as strong as they may be, are not always enough to bring into existence what we hope for.

I searched for my place for a long time. I searched for it in books, thinking a beautiful sentence would be enough to give me roots. I searched for it in cities, believing that by walking fast enough, I would end up escaping myself. I searched for it in grand speeches about freedom, exclusive love, perfect equality. Brilliant words that rang hollow when I thought of you.

And then there was you. You, with your laughter that makes the air tremble, your silences that weigh heavier than my certainties, and your way of loving without measure.

At first, I resisted. I screamed that I would never be the one who accepts half a man. That love, true love, is lived by two or is not lived at all. I wanted to fit you into my world, tidy, well-drawn, with its rules and its codes. But the more I pushed you away, the more that world became a desert.

So, I understood. It is not my world I miss when you are not there. It is you. You who give meaning to gray days. You who make the dust dance under the sun. You, with your sweet madness, your docile tenderness, and even your contradictions that shake me up.

So, yes Kpegnan, I accept. I accept your world, with its contours that I don't always understand. I accept to share, to doubt, to grumble too, because I prefer a thousand times to live in your world, with you, than to live in mine, without you.

I am coming, Kpegnan. With my suitcases full of ideas too big, of tangled dreams, and of fears too. But above all with this love for you, stubborn, faithful.

If loving is learning a new language, then I am ready to stutter until my words sing to your rhythm.

Yours. Unconditionally. And without return.

When Kpegnan read Lachaise's letter, his breath suspended. He reread certain passages several times. "I prefer a thousand times to live in your world, with you, than to live in mine, without you." These words pierced him through and through. He felt at once honored and suffocated by so much love despite the shock of separation. Finally, he told himself, she had understood. A feeling of pride and joy invaded him. And he resolved to answer her.

Hello my darling,

I am deeply moved to reconnect with you. Your silence weighed on me. Not like an ordinary absence, but like a void charged with everything that was left unsaid. Since my last letter, I hesitated for a long time to pick up the pen again. I preferred to leave you this space so you could think freely, far from me. Today, it is with a light heart and a soul in jubilation that I address these words to you.

You say you are coming with suitcases full of ideas, dreams, and fear. Me, I await you empty-handed, but with a heart wide open. Your letter passed through me like a season: sweet, burning, unpredictable. It awakened in me everything I had repressed, everything I no longer dared to hope for.

I always thought there was only a thin line between love and hate, and I believed you had already crossed it. And here you are talking about us finding each other again. I want you to know how filled with joy my heart is at the idea of seeing you again. I long to hold you against me once more. You are, still and always, in your rightful place: at the bottom of my heart.

You speak of your well-drawn world. Me, I live in a world where lines tremble, where certainties crumble, but where love never hides. A world I long thought incompatible with yours. Today, here you are, ready to tread upon it without understanding all its codes, but with enough courage to lay your heart down there.

You say that you accept. But it is I who am overwhelmed. For your *"yes"* is not a surrender, it is an act of bravery. You could have left, slammed the door, and taken your light with you. You choose to stay. To love me in my complexity, despite it.

I have always loved you, Lachaise. But today, I admire you.

I know it will not be simple. That there will be days of shadow, tense silences, questions without answers. But I promise you one thing: you will never be a half. You will never play a secondary role. In my way of loving, there is no division, only expansion. My love is not a cake one shares; it is a flame one multiplies.

You say you are ready to stutter until you make the words dance. Me, I am ready to teach you the music of my world, to listen to you invent yours, and to create with you a new language, built on "us." Come back, Lachaise. Or rather, come. As you said.

I await you. Whole. Moved. And ready. Finally.

A few months later, Lachaise took the firm decision to join Kpegnan, without soliciting anyone's opinion.

The days preceding Lachaise's departure had slipped by in a fog. Every morning, she woke up with that strange sensation of being suspended between two worlds: one she knew by heart, the other she was only imagining.

For her, everything was fading into a goodbye. Her apartment, that messy refuge where books, forgotten cups of coffee, and old socks piled up, had taken on the airs of a mausoleum.

Cardboard boxes had invaded the living room. Lachaise folded, sorted, threw away, sometimes without really looking at what she held in her hands. Every object seemed charged with a memory, every drawer an emotional ambush.

Kneeling before an old metal box, she carefully arranged photos, several of which were with Kpegnan. Some were crumpled, others still bore words scribbled in haste on the back, vestiges of happy moments. She slipped them one by one into a rigid envelope, like one gently closes a chapter, or perhaps, on the contrary, like one prepares to reopen one.

Jeanine, her forever friend, helped her without saying much. She contented herself with folding clothes, taping boxes, just being there. From time to time, she threw out a small sentence to lighten the atmosphere, but even her humor seemed to float in a room that was too empty.

After a while, she sat on a box, rested her eyes on her, and asked softly: *"You're really going to do it, huh? This trip to Africa. You've thought it through?"*

Lachaise paused in her motion. She remained motionless for a moment, then raised her head, eyes shining with both fear and determination. *"Yes. I am going to find him."*

Jeanine raised her eyebrows, dubious. *"You're sure Kpegnan is waiting for you?"*

Lachaise nodded timidly. *"Yes. He told me. We've been writing regularly for a while, but... that's no longer enough. I can't take it anymore; I miss him so much."*

Jeanine stared at her for a moment, then smiled gently, a smile where tenderness mingled with worry. *"Go then, but don't forget: love, even when reaching toward the other, always begins with a walk toward oneself."*

Silence took its place again, but this time, it vibrated with hope.

Lachaise had seen her friends again, without great ceremony. A coffee, a meal, a few charged silences.

The eve of her departure, in the middle of spring, she walked for a long time in the quiet streets of Clermont, covered in a coat that was too thin, her heart too full. She stopped in front of the bookstore where she liked to loiter for hours, in front of the tobacco shop at the corner of Rue de Rabanesse, looked one last time at the Puy-de-Dôme, and stopped one final time at her parents' home.

The day of departure, Lachaise stood facing the large bay window of Roissy Charles de Gaulle airport. Behind her, Paris stretched out, majestic, noisy, reassuring in its immobility.

She sank slowly into her seat, fingers clenched on the armrest, heart beating to the rhythm of a thousand conflicting emotions. She was leaving. Over there. Toward that end of the world where everything seemed to her at once raw, untamed, and strangely bewitching.

She was turning her back on Paris, on its streets charged with history, on its cobblestones heavy with memories. On the boulevards bursting with light, on the train stations trembling with hurried lives. She was also moving away from her native Auvergne: from the blue mountains waking at dawn, from the tranquil cows in the pastures, from the biting cold and the unique taste of the Saint-Nectaire cheese she cherished so much.

For what? For whom? For Kpegnan. For a life still blurry, suspended between hope and doubt. A life dreamed of as much as dreaded.

The plane tore itself from the ground in a dull roar, ripping through the sky. And with it, Lachaise's stomach knotted, her past moved away. Had she made the right choice?

In a few hours, she would set foot on foreign soil. A land where the rules are not those of her books, where love has other contours, other flavors. A land that was perhaps waiting for her or that would reject her.

But it was too late to back down. Lachaise was flying toward the unknown, heart beating for a man and for a dream she hadn't finished inventing.

Africa.

A continent she had known only through Kpegnan's stories, pages of books, or the cold, distant images of a black-and-white television. She had imagined the landscapes, the scents, the heat that sticks to the skin, but would reality align with her dreams? She glanced out the porthole. The sky was immense, endless. Just like the unknown awaiting her. When the plane began its descent, a golden light set the horizon ablaze. The African sun. Brutal. Splendid.

As soon as her feet touched the tarmac, a moist heat welcomed her, suffocating. The air, dense and humid, saturated her lungs with unprecedented smells: kerosene mixed with the hot dust of the earth. She inhaled deeply. She scrutinized the sky, which had nothing of the pale blue she knew in Europe. Here, it blazed, raw, dazzling, insolent in its intensity.

Inside the hall, Lachaise was struck by this singular contrast: a discrete modernity but impregnated with Africa. Light walls, varnished counters, illuminated signs, and everywhere, the emerald green and white uniforms of Air Afrique, worn by the hostesses with elegance. The air conditioning diffused a semblance of coolness, but at moments, heavy whiffs of perfume, tobacco, sweat, and kerosene crossed the air, reminding one of the harshness outside. The loudspeakers crackled, in a nasal French, solemn announcements: *"Air Afrique, the flight from Paris has arrived."*

Upon her exit, the tumult assaulted her. In front of the esplanade, a horde of Peugeot 404s and 504s aligned along the roadway honked in an impatient concert.

Porters in dark-colored shirts hailed travelers. Whole families waiting for their loved ones were massed under the sun. They waved their arms, shouted names, and threw themselves toward their own in a burst of joy.

All around her, life buzzed. Men shouted, gesticulated, almost grabbed each other, while taxis called out to each other with blasts of the horn. Everything vibrated, everything rustled, everything overflowed.

Lachaise, in the middle of this tumult, felt tiny. Foreign. Swallowed up. Nothing like Europe, where every gesture seemed regulated, where every minute was framed. Here, chaos seemed an art: it had its own laws, its own savage beauty. A wave of panic rose to her throat. *What if she couldn't make it? What if Kpegnan was wrong about her?* Her eyes desperately sought a landmark, a sign, in this unknown ocean.

Suddenly, a voice pierced the din. *"Lachaise?"*

She turned around. And when she spotted Kpegnan, her heart relaxed, her face lit up. A smile. A breath of relief. The first step had just been crossed.

Kpegnan took her hand and murmured: *"I admit, I missed you terribly."*

She replied in a breath: *"Me too... Without my stubbornness, I know that what we had would have lasted. Under the effect of anger, one says words that go beyond thought... But I realize today that I was stupid. I should never have turned my back on you nor let you leave like that."*

Then he leaned in, placed a tender kiss on her lips, and added: *"All is well that ends well. We can pick up where we left off. I knew it wasn't a goodbye. You are welcome."*

The journey, from now on, would know no return.

The time had come to adapt, together.

A few days later, it was the big departure for the village. Kpegnan insisted that Lachaise discover with her own eyes the land that had seen him grow up. He wanted her to soak up the African culture first, to feel the rhythm, the heat, the roots.

Aboard a Peugeot 404, they crisscrossed the red roads through the bush. The landscape scrolled by, vibrant, unknown. Every turn moved her a little further from her world and brought her closer to a new home.

When the car stopped at the village of Tenably, a joyous crowd awaited them. Elderly women threw handfuls of white flour as a sign of welcome and blessing. Others unrolled *pagnes* on the ground to honor her. A little intimidated, Lachaise let herself be carried by this fervor and, with the help of Djekobou who whispered softly in her ear: *"Don't worry, here is your home."*

Lachaise's first days in the village were a total immersion into a new world. Woken at the first light of day, right at the piercing crow of the rooster, she observed with curiosity the life waking up around her. The women, already in motion, relit wood fires, while shirtless children ran barefoot between the huts.

As the days went by, guided by Djekobou and the village women, she lent herself to the game of learning. The pestle in her hands, she advanced timidly toward the large mortar.

The cassava *foutou*, a firm and elastic mass, resisted under the clumsy blows she attempted to deal it. Every stroke of the pestle reminded her how much this gesture, yet so fluid for the others, required force and coordination. Around her, laughter burst forth while she struggled to keep the rhythm. Lachaise laughed too despite the fatigue, conscious that behind every burst of laughter vibrated an invitation to persevere.

"Softly, Lachaise, otherwise you will mash someone's fingers here oh!" Kemessié joked.

Then came the turn to cook the *Kpélé*, that sticky and fragrant sauce, whose stringy texture and intense smell baffled her at first before seducing her senses. Little by little, she adapted, learning to handle the wooden ladle and to dose the spices under the approving eyes of the other women.

Kpegnan observed her from afar with a discreet smile at the corner of his lips. When Lachaise had a sudden fever, Kpegnan could have cut her stay short, brought her quickly back to the city, but she contented herself with Nivaquine and she quickly recovered her health. Kpegnan wanted her to take the necessary time for her adaptation. To feel, understand, touch the very essence of his world.

To his great surprise, Lachaise lent herself to it with unexpected enthusiasm. She laughed with the young girls, admired the dexterity of the elders, tasted every dish with sincere curiosity. Even the free and bold presence of sheep and goats strolling without constraint like full members of the community, sometimes inviting themselves right into the kitchens, did not bother her. On the contrary, she seemed fascinated by this harmony between humans and animals, this almost instinctive cohabitation.

Lachaise savored every instant of this simple and authentic life. One of her favorite moments was the open- air shower, in an enclosure of woven branches and old rusty sheets, open to the sky. Under the pale light of the moon, she poured hot water on her skin using a cup, savoring every drop, every breath of wind. The steam rising gently from the bucket mingled with the nocturnal noises: the cry of owls, distant barking, the murmurs of the bush. This natural concert did not frighten her; on the contrary, it filled her with profound quietude. What Lachaise dreaded above all was having to relieve herself behind a pile of rubbish, under the hungry gaze of pigs, then using a maize stalk to wipe herself.

In this simplicity, she found an unsuspected peace. Everything was elementary, truly primitive, but incredibly soothing. She felt a little accepted by this universe. Returning to her hut, draped in a *pagne*, she smiled.

During her stay in the village, Lachaise had not limited herself to learning local traditions. Very quickly, she had felt the need to go beyond smiles and daily gestures to open deeper, more urgent discussions. Among the subjects that upset her: female genital mutilation and early marriages.

She could not look away nor keep silent. Every time she crossed a little girl in the village, carefree and lively, she thought of those, too numerous, whose innocence was broken in the name of a centuries-old tradition. She thought of the atrocious pain inflicted without anesthesia, the infections, the traumas that marked bodies and minds for life. She also thought of all those women deprived of the right to dispose of their own bodies, in the name of honor or purity. So she spoke.

In the circles of women, in improvised kitchens, she explained, with simple but hard-hitting words, that this practice was not a rite of passage but violence. That it had nothing to do with faith, nor love, still less with dignity. She shared testimonies, numbers, stories of women who had dared to say no, of countries that had banned this practice, of communities that had found other ways to honor their daughters.

At first, the looks were suspicious, sometimes closed. But Lachaise did not waver. She knew that silence kills more surely than blades. Little by little, some women dared to speak. Mothers confided their doubts, others told of their wounds long buried. The taboo was cracking. An awareness was being born.

Lachaise did not want to impose her vision. For her, defending these bodies, these stolen childhoods, was a duty, a necessity. But she knew the fight would be long.

Over the days, she discovered with curiosity and sometimes stupor the social structure of the village. Polygamy, which she would have perceived elsewhere as an exception, imposed itself here as a deeply rooted norm. The majority of men had several wives. But what troubled her even more was the age of certain young girls, married when barely out of childhood. Gazes still childlike, frail bodies, naive smiles already bore the label of *"woman"* and the weight of a marriage often imposed.

One evening, under the great silk-cotton tree (*fromager*), the elders had gathered as was their habit.

The fire crackled in the center of the circle. Women were roasting plantains just nearby. Lachaise, invited by Djekobou, sat there with humility, but her heart beating. She knew she was about to cross a line.

A heavy silence settled in, until the eldest finally took the floor: *"My daughter, they say you talk a lot with the women. That you ask questions about our customs."*

Lachaise sucked in a breath of air. She looked each one in the eye, with respect but without deviation: *"Yes, father. I listen. And I speak. Because I believe that certain traditions do more harm than they uplift."*

A murmur ran through the circle. The eldest frowned slightly. *"What do you mean?" "I am speaking of excision and early marriages."*

A man, seated to her left, had a nervous twitch. A woman, in the back, lowered her eyes. *"These are customs, my daughter. They have existed since our ancestors. Who are you to judge them?"*

"I am no one to judge," replied Lachaise calmly. *"But I am a woman. And I know other women, here or elsewhere, who have suffered all their lives because of these practices. Who have lost their health, their joy, sometimes even their life."*

"You do not understand our world. Here, an uncircumcised girl is not a woman. And among us, a girl married early is one less burden for the family. It is also a way to preserve her honor before it is compromised. For a young girl free for too long is a risk. A scandal can soil the entire lineage. Early marriage is security."

Lachaise sat up straighter, firmer: *"Is that really what it is to be a woman? To suffer in silence? To lose one's childhood? Why not let the girls choose? Study? Decide their life as the boys do?"*

A heavy silence fell again. Then an old woman spoke softly: *"When I was your age, I did not have the choice. I was married at twelve. I was cut too. I obeyed. I bled. And I buried two daughters dead from the same rite. Perhaps it is time to listen to this young woman."*

Téhé, hitherto mute, spoke softly and in a calm tone: *"My daughter-in-law, to be a woman is not only to choose. It is to carry. To carry the home, the continuity, the earth itself. What you call suffering, we call sacrifice. And sacrifice is part of our honor. We do not refuse girls the right to dream. But, here, one learns early that life is not made only of individual choices. It is made of duties toward the family, toward the clan, toward those who came before us. If every girl decided alone, like the boys, who would keep the memory? Who would transmit our values? The modern world wants equality, but forgets that certain things stand upright because the women, precisely, accepted to hold firm."*

Lachaise replied politely: *"I understand, father. I understand what the word 'sacrifice' represents here. And I do not reject the idea of carrying, of transmitting, of honoring what our mothers carried before us. But I ask a simple question: must sacrifice be synonymous with imposed suffering? Can we speak of honor when what is transmitted is pain, fear, silence? Girls too can keep the memory, but with books in their hands. They can transmit values, but without having to bury their childhood. It is not betraying tradition to make it evolve. It is saving it from oblivion, from rejection, from the pain it sometimes inflicts without meaning to. What I want is not to break what we are. It is to open a door. So that those who want to study, dream, choose, can do so without denying their traditions."*

The elders looked at each other. Some nodded, others looked away. Lachaise's words had just broken something. A wall. A taboo.

The eldest remained mute, his look, initially hard, had veiled over. Then he spoke in a weary voice: *"You speak with the verve of a generation that has known neither war, nor famines, nor exiles. We built walls to survive. Rules, to hold together. Sometimes at the price of pain, yes. But how to know where protection ends and where oppression begins?"*

He sighed then added: *"A door, you say. And what if in opening it, it was the whole house that collapsed? If you want to open a door, then show us that there is still a solid house behind it. Not a ruin, not an oblivion. Something that resembles us... that elevates us. Talking costs nothing. Listening neither. What you say, my daughter, we must reflect upon it. But know that changing a world demands more than words. It demands time. And courage."*

Lachaise lowered her head, touched. She had heard the fear in the eldest's words, but also a breach. She spoke with softness, but a new determination in her voice:

"I do not come to destroy the house. I come so that it may have windows. So that one breathes a little more in there, so that one sees a little further. I propose a new rite, father. A passage toward adulthood that does not wound, that does not take, but that reveals. A ceremony where girls affirm what they are, what they want to become. Where they learn for a year, with the women of the village, what it means to be responsible, free, and dignified. At the end, they choose their path: marriage, studies, a trade, or all three. And it is their choice that is honored. It is not less sacred. It is just more just."

She paused, then looked in turn at the elders, the women, the young girls in the back. *"Tradition is not a pen. It is a fire. If we stifle it, it dies. If we feed it with wisdom, it lights the way for a long time."*

"So let us speak, father. Again and again. Until silence no longer kills."

The face of the eldest lingered on Lachaise, then on the faces around the circle. He saw the fear in some eyes, the hope in others. Then he straightened his back, curved by the weight of years, and spoke with wisdom:

"You come to shake things up, yes, but you do not come to uproot. That is why I listen to you. Your word is not unanimous. Not yet. But it has sown a seed. And in this earth, even ancient, seeds know how to pierce the crust of time. Go. And build without destroying."

Part 5

After three months of immersion, Lachaise had grown fond of this simple, warm way of life. She now knew every face, every alleyway, and every sound of the village. Leaving this universe so soon left a strange taste in her mouth, a bittersweet mix of nostalgia and excitement.

Alongside Djekobou, she took her seat in the car Kpegnan had chartered specifically for them. The engine purred softly, carrying away memories that were too vivid to fade.

Upon their arrival in the city, the contrast was stark. The uproar of honking horns, the feverish hustle and bustle of the markets, modern buildings rubbing shoulders with old neighborhoods, everything seemed to be moving at breakneck speed, dizzying and relentless.

Kpegnan's official villa, elegant and spacious, was waiting for them. The moment they crossed the threshold, they discovered a refined interior, carefully arranged for their comfort. Every detail seemed well thought out. Yet, amidst this hushed harmony, Lachaise felt her heart still beating for the village, raw, vibrant, imperfect, but terribly alive.

And so, their new life began. Months went by.

Djekobou had considerably improved her command of French thanks to intensive literacy classes. As the wife of a high-ranking executive, she was fully aware of the stakes and had thrown herself into learning with determination, showing true grit. Djekobou, always energetic and full of life, wasn't one to settle for being just a housewife.

"Me, sit around doing nothing? Impossible!"

She opened a large African restaurant named *"Le Coin,"* where she served traditional dishes from the village, drawing in customers from all over the city. Her restaurant quickly became the talk of the town; even politicians and celebrities became regulars.

Lachaise, for her part, poured her energy into social projects to help underprivileged girls pursue their studies. She launched a scholarship program and set up a training center for young women wishing to learn a trade.

Little Potey was growing up straddling two worlds. He was enrolled in an international school, where Lachaise regularly stepped in as a substitute teacher.

Every evening, over a hearty meal, they laughed and shared stories of their day. Kpegnan, through his attitude, had fostered a spirit of coexistence built on mutual respect, transparent communication, and a fair division of roles.

Then one morning... news dropped out of the blue.

Lachaise was pregnant. It was a huge surprise, the emotion indescribable. Kpegnan was over the moon. Djekobou, laughing heartily, placed her hand tenderly on her co-wife's belly.

"So, Madame Paris, are you ready for the baby crying at 3 a.m.?" she joked.

Lachaise laughed too, her eyes sparkling with happiness.

"I think I am."

A few months later, in a room cradled by softness, Lachaise gave birth to a magnificent baby girl. A mixed- race child with golden skin, light curls, and big, sparkling blue eyes. When he held her in his arms for the first time, Kpegnan felt his heart bursting with love.

He held her delicately, studied her for a long time, and then murmured:

"She will be called Gnansou."

In that precise instant, he felt his heart swell with immense love. In this little being, he saw the union of two worlds, two histories. Gnansou was more than a child; she was a symbol. Living proof that borders can vanish when love is sincere.

One evening, in the garden of their home, under the infinite sky, Djekobou was helping Potey with his exercises. Just beside them, Lachaise was tenderly rocking little Gnansou, who was fast asleep against her chest. With her fingertips, she caressed her daughter's tiny hands.

The two women conversed in hushed tones.

"My sister, can you give me a hand for a second?

This arithmetic problem is a tough nut to crack for me."

Lachaise approached, glanced at the exercise, amused.

"Let me see. It's not that complicated, though. Potey should be able to solve it on his own. We need to let him try. He's getting lazier by the minute, don't you think?"

She paused, then added, more seriously:

"Comfort is a beautiful thing, but get too used to it, and it ends up numbing the soul. And Potey, he's let himself go a bit too quickly."

She sighed.

"And worse, at his age, he's already fallen in love."

Djekobou turned her head, astonished.

"In love? With who, then?"

"A young mixed-race girl in his class. Diamond. A minister's daughter," Lachaise added with a smile mixed with worry. "A sharp little thing, smart as a whip, and already sure of herself. He spends his time writing her name in his notebooks instead of doing his homework."

Djekobou started to laugh, shaking her head.

"Well then, our Potey is aiming high! But he'd better aim right in his exercises first!"

Potey, lying on the sofa, pencil in hand but looking distracted, was watching the birds on the flowers with more interest than his notebook. He had taken a shine to this sweet life, paced by heavy meals, modern toys, and tender words. He was no longer the curious and resourceful little boy from the village. A certain softness had crept in, insidious and invisible.

Kpegnan watched them from the terrace, a smile full of gratitude on his lips. His family united, vibrant. He had dreamed of such balance, and life had offered him even more. His home embodied a polygamy made successful through adaptation, love, and the refusal of cultural hierarchies.

He opened his eyes wide and whispered:

"I am fulfilled."

But the outside world called him back quickly. An important delegation from Tenably was waiting for him in the living room. He stood up reluctantly, cast one last look at the scene, and slipped away quietly.

"This garden is really peaceful, especially in the evening. You can hear the crickets singing," said Lachaise, looking at Djekobou with gratitude.

Djekobou nodded:

"Yes, here, everything breathes tranquility. It's different from the commotion of the village, but also different from what you knew in France, surely. You know, Lachaise, your husband forgot again to tell me last time that he was going on a mission, and he comes back as if nothing happened," Djekobou threw out there with an amused smile.

"Oh that, Kpegnan and his organizational skills. He warned me the night before last, but he must have assumed you already knew," replied Lachaise.

"We'll have to make him sit down one day to set up a calendar," joked Djekobou.

"Yes, but he'll always find an excuse to dodge the discussion, you know him better than I do, my dear," Lachaise retorted.

They continued to chat, drifting from light subjects to deeper discussions about their lives, their children, and their respective plans. They had found a balance, a way of coexisting that surprised and fascinated those around them. After all, it wasn't every day that two women so different united around the same man without tearing each other apart.

Then Lachaise set her glass of bissap on the table and looked at Djekobou with sincerity.

"You know, I've never thanked you," she said softly.

Djekobou raised her eyebrows, amused.

"What for?"

"For everything," Lachaise replied with a smile.

"When I arrived here, everything seemed so far from my world: the culture, the traditions... I didn't always know how to behave, but you were there. You could have seen me as a threat, a rival, but you took me in like a sister. You made things so much easier for me."

Djekobou shook her head, an affectionate smile on her lips.

"We are bound by much more than a marriage, Lachaise. Life put us on the same path, and we chose to make it a strength rather than a burden."

Lachaise took her hand, grateful.

"Thanks to you, I feel at home here."

Djekobou gently squeezed her hand in response.

"And I am happy to have a sister to share this adventure with. Love is bigger than jealousy. I knew that if I resisted, it would only hurt Kpegnan and drive us apart. So I chose to accept and to learn to love you too."

"You are an exceptional woman, Djekobou. I think without you, I never would have found my place here."

The two women laughed, aware that they formed a united family and that beyond cultural borders, their love for Kpegnan and their children had bound them in a way few people could understand.

Years passed. Kpegnan's seriousness, his intelligence, and his charisma impressed the country's high authorities.

One day, Kpegnan's phone rang.

"Monsieur Kpegnan, we are calling you from the Presidency of the Republic. An official summons has been sent to you."

His heart raced.

The next morning, dressed in an impeccably tailored suit, he went to the Presidency.

In the President's sumptuous office, he was handed an official document, sealed and solemn. He opened it on the spot.

"Congratulations, Monsieur Kpegnan. As of today, you are officially the Minister of Public Works and Urban Planning."

Silence settled in. The words resonated within him with an unreal echo.

"Me... Minister?!" he stammered, his voice barely audible. He didn't want to explode with joy just yet.

The old President smiled, looking upon him kindly.

"Who else? Your track record is exemplary. We have faith in you. The country needs people like you."

"The official announcement will be made tomorrow. Congratulations, Mister Minister."

When he went home that evening, he found Djekobou and Lachaise on the terrace, busy chatting as always. They were laughing. Potey and Gnansou were running in the garden. He observed them for a moment, his heart swelling with pride and love.

Djekobou fixed her eyes on him. "*What's going on? You look weird...*" Kpegnan took a deep breath.

"I've just been named Minister."

A moment of silence.

Then a cry of joy burst forth, pure and loud. Djekobou rushed into his arms.

"I always told you, you were born to accomplish great things! With you, the sky is the limit."

Lachaise, more discreet, smiled tenderly.

"You fully deserve it, honey."

Potey came running immediately, his eyes shining.

"Papa! Does that mean you're going to have lots of money now, like Diamond's dad? I want a racing bike."

They burst out laughing. Gnansou toddled toward her father and grabbed onto his leg, all smiles.

"No, my children, it's not about that! It means you will see me rarely. But we are going to build an even more beautiful life together, I promise you."

Under the dark night sprinkled with stars, Kpegnan looked up, his heart at peace. He knew, in that precise moment, that he had fulfilled his destiny.

The days passed, paced by his new responsibilities. Every evening, despite the fatigue and the heavy decisions he had to carry, he came home to find his sleeping children, the looks and small cares of his wives, and the warmth of his home.

Destiny smiled upon him once more. A few months after his nomination, Djekobou gave birth to twins, two healthy boys whom he named Dehi and Gnahé. A nod to his roots and a wish he'd held since adolescence.

They dined together, laughed, shared anecdotes, and talked about their plans and dreams. Kpegnan, like a good husband, spent time equally with each of his wives. He included both in important decisions regarding the budget, family projects, and the rest. The two women shared the household chores and the raising of the children.

Sometimes, they organized huge parties where the whole family, friends, and relatives from the village came to celebrate their happiness.

A soft night stretched over the garden where Kpegnan sat, surrounded by Djekobou, Lachaise, Potey, Gnansou, Gnahé, and Dehi. He turned his eyes toward the sky, breathing in deeply, a feeling of peace washing over him. For the first time in a long time, he felt in perfect harmony with himself.

He thought back on everything he had been through: his departure for France, filled with hope but marked by doubts. His return to the country, tinged with uncertainties and the fear of no longer recognizing his bearings. His love for Djekobou, the unexpected surprise of his relationship with Lachaise. His meteoric rise, up to his recent nomination.

A sincere smile lit up his face. He squeezed Djekobou's hand on one side and Lachaise's on the other.

"Life is beautiful, and it's just getting started."

Lachaise placed a tender kiss on his cheek, while Djekobou laughed softly, resting her head against his shoulder. Potey, exhausted by the excitement of the day, had already fallen asleep, huddled against his father, while Gnansou, their little mixed-race daughter, fought against sleep, her thumb in her mouth.

A few weeks following his appointment as minister, Kpegnan made a pivotal decision: to return to Tenably to celebrate this honor and receive the blessings of his village.

It had all begun there, on that red earth that had watched him grow. He couldn't fully savor his success without paying homage to those who had supported him and carried him in their prayers.

Word was sent to Tenably: *"Your son Kpegnan is returning! He has made it; he has become a big man in the country!"*

At this news, the village came alive with unparalleled excitement. Preparations were in full swing. Traditional dance troupes rehearsed their choreography. The drums were tuned, ready to resonate throughout the region.

The great chief ordered a clean sweep of the village streets. *"A son of the soil is returning in triumph; everything must be spick and span!"*

Welcome arches made of palm fronds were erected, colorful banners hung high. The griots were already clearing their throats, ready to sing the praises of the prodigal son.

Finally, when the long-awaited day arrived, Kpegnan's convoy, accompanied by Djekobou, Lachaise, Potey, Gnansou, and the twins Dehi and Gnahé, left the capital at the crack of dawn, bound for Tenably. The journey was long, but his heart beat with excitement and pride.

As they neared the village, the drums became distinct. In the distance, a massive crowd waited at the entrance.

As soon as the car slowed to a crawl, cries of joy erupted: *"Kpegnan is here! Our son is back!"*

Women, decked out in their finest loincloths, spun around with grace, balancing calabashes perfectly on their heads. Men beat the drums with fervor, chanting his name with pride. Children ran around the convoy, laughing their heads off. The griots, for their part, struck up powerful songs, deep with meaning, in Kpegnan's honor. Songs so vibrant they made the very air shiver.

One of these songs, intoned by the master of the spoken word, Bah Oulahi, brought goosebumps to the skin and filled eyes with-held-back tears.

"Listen, children of Tenably, lend me your ears. The village son has conquered the world. His name travels on the wind. But his roots, they dive deep into the land of the ancestors.

He was born near the sacred river. His mother brought him into the world while the drums were already whispering his destiny. His first steps followed the invisible tracks of the forefathers. He walked through darkness, faced the spirits, and one by one, he laid them low.

Then he crossed the ocean, Carrying with him our hopes and the prayers of the elders. Over there, he conquered knowledge, And it is with hands full of gold and a mind illuminated that he has returned.

Oh you, Kpegnan! You who tamed the white bird without breaking its wings. Tell us your secrets, elegant man. You, son of charmers and enchanters, your words are honey, your laughter a gris-gris.

When you pass, even the river bows down. You won the heart of the white woman like rain conquers dust. Your name is a fire that dances from Tenably all the way to France. You who seduce hearts and minds, even the white woman with colored eyes, shining like the sun, Followed you to our lands.

Tenably laughs, the jealous grow thin. The hearts of the envious burn. He who was not born here in Tenably may weep. O Kpegnan! Tell your brothers where you drew this knowledge that even the

Whites honor. For your gold serves not your glory alone. Your gold lights up the whole clan.

Kpegnan, red panther with velvet steps, Your humility is as tall as your strength. What joy to sing the praises of such a noble being! Stand up so we may celebrate you!

Here comes the Gladignon! Make way! Let the path be purified! Look at him! What style! Look at all these women, in silence, they are biting their lips. The men, they lower their eyes.

Step aside, the big man approaches! And let our children walk in the imprint of his steps. Your name, Kpegnan, will live beyond the seasons. It shall not wither. Your wealth will never run dry.

You, descendant of Pouhi, great-grandson of Gbohou, Grandson of the wise Baha, Son of Téhé, the warrior whom no weapon could ever vanquish. Lead us to where your spirit was forged. Tenably salutes you, head held high. With Kpegnan, misfortune will no longer pass our doors. Kpéhé Tchiglô, tell me why men fear you so. Go, and return again, laden with glory for your kin."

While the griots sang his praises, Kpegnan, carried away by the euphoria, could not contain himself. He rose with grace and launched into an improvised dance. Elbows raised, arms spread like wings, he evoked an eagle ready to soar into the heavens. Then, in a fluid motion, he spun around, adopting the supple, feline gait of a panther. A thunder of applause greeted this fusion of power and elegance.

When Lachaise and Djekobou joined him on the dance floor, the moment became magical: a true collective ecstasy seized the assembly.

Shortly after, as Kpegnan was taking his seat, an unexpected apparition sent shivers through the crowd. Making a majestic entrance onto the square, Pôya Klaha appeared, the great mask of happiness, whose outings were rare and steeped in solemnity. His presence was an exceptional event, bordering on myth. Feared and revered, he embodied both the benevolence of the ancients and the mystical power of tradition.

Kpegnan felt the magnitude of his achievement. He had seen this sacred mask only once in his life. He was only ten years old then. That image, both blurry and sacred, had remained etched in his memory like a dream lost in time.

And now, years later, he stood face to face with it. A chill ran down his spine when Pôya Klaha bowed before him. Faced with a moment of such rare intensity, Kpegnan stood frozen, overwhelmed with emotion. His lips trembled, his heart pounded like a drum. Memories, voices, symbols, everything tangled together in his mind. A thin tear slid down his cheek, soon followed by another. He could neither speak nor move. Only feel, deeply, the force of the ancestral bond expressing itself before him with shattering majesty.

The great mask, with his deep voice relayed by a herald, declared: *"My son, you left in quest of knowledge, and today, you return with honor and success. Your success is that of the whole village."*

He was then handed a calabash filled with pure water and sacred herbs. The mask poured a few drops on Kpegnan's head as a sign of blessing. *"May your days be long, may your reign be prosperous, and may the light of your success illuminate future generations."*

Thunderous applause followed these solemn words.

On this sun-drenched day, surrounded by his people and his family, Kpegnan felt a profound peace. He had made it, not just in his career, but as a man, as a father. And he knew this was only the beginning of a grand adventure.

An elder approached and placed a sacred scarf upon Kpegnan's shoulders, the ultimate honor, the seal of eternal recognition.

Facing the jubilant crowd, Kpegnan raised his arms and declared in a booming voice: *"My parents, I have returned! Today, we celebrate this rise together, for it is yours too!"*

A roar of acclaim made the ground vibrate beneath his feet.

While the party was in full swing, the village women busied themselves around giant cauldrons. The famous Kplê, a royal dish, simmered slowly, releasing thick aromas into the air. Beside it, a spicy okra sauce, infused with the smokiness of agouti and red palm oil, perfumed the air. Smoked fish and braised meats were laid out on broad banana leaves.

Under the imposing shade of the great fromager tree, the elders sipped palm wine from calabashes while recounting the exploits of the ancestors.

Just as the sun began to set, a strange silence suddenly settled in. Then, piercing screams and wild roars tore through the air.

The spectators jumped to their feet, their eyes fixed on the scene about to unfold. Suddenly, the dreaded *"Blahons"*, the Panther-Men made their appearance.

These initiated warriors, clad in tunics of various colors adorned with black motifs resembling the spotted skin of a panther, their feet and ankles wrapped in wide ornaments of plant fibers dyed red or black. Their faces covered by the same fabric with black patterns, they advanced with feline majesty.

Around them, men with bodies coated in clay, wearing bright loincloths around their hips adorned with beads, pom-poms, and talismans. Some wore raffia headbands, shell bracelets, and necklaces that sang with every movement.

Their ritual dance began. Wild, hypnotic.

They jumped, bounded, and spun, imitating the agility of the beast to perfection. Their cries resonated like real roars, sparking both wonder and fear. The audience, hanging on their every move, held its breath. Every jump, every spectacular acrobatic feat seemed to defy the laws of gravity.

Seated beside the village chief, Kpegnan contemplated the scene with admiration.

"My son, today, these warriors recognize you as a worthy representative of our people."

Kpegnan closed his eyes for a moment, absorbing all the symbolism of this ceremony. His destiny had just been sealed. After the Panther-Men passed, a long procession filed past Kpegnan, offering him symbolic gifts:

Sacks of new rice and corn, plenty of poultry, baskets filled with bottles of palm oil, precious fabrics with ancestral patterns as a sign of nobility, a carved wooden statuette representing a great chief, a mark of respect and transfer of power, and a white ram, offered by the elders to ensure protection and prosperity.

Djekobou and Lachaise received numerous gifts as well.

Gnansou, observing all this with a perplexed look, tugged on her mother's hand and whispered:

"Mama... do we really have to stick it out until the end?"

Lachaise smiled, tenderly stroking her hair.

"Yes, sweetie. It's a big day for Papa... and for us too."

As the drums resonated for a final dance and the songs quieted down, Kpegnan sat on a wooden chair, slightly set back. Before him, the village glowed under the flames of torches and the soothing light of the moon. Djekobou and Lachaise were by his side, absorbed by the solemn beauty of the moment. Not far away, Potey and the other children, dead tired from this unforgettable day, were sleeping soundly in Téhé's hut, rocked by the distant echoes of the party.

The square was still alive. The songs, the dances, the laughter continued to weave through the night. The elders, standing tall, raised their calabashes to the sky in his honor, and the great flames dancing in the center of the village seemed to want to rival the stars. Kpegnan watched, speechless, his heart swelling with a mix of emotion, gratitude, and vertigo.

When the party finally ran out of steam, in a final burst of drumming, he stared at the sparkling sky. He thought of those who had come before him.

He saw his grandfather again, an upright and imposing figure, whose words came back to him like a prayer:

"A man is built with his courage and his knowledge. Never forget that you are a son of Tenably."

Then, he felt the gentle presence of his grandmother, bent over a steaming dish, murmuring as she always did:

"My son, knowledge is the only wealth a thief cannot steal. Learn, and you will shine like the sun."

He imagined them there, both of them, sitting under the great fromager tree. His grandfather, holding his carved cane, nodding slowly, proud. His grandmother, discreetly wiping away a tear of joy. They were there, invisible but present, keeping watch as in the old days.

And as the dawn began to break on the horizon, Kpegnan understood that this was not an end. It was a beginning.

He had received the legacy. Now, it was up to him to pass it on. To watch over his own. To show the way, like holding out a flame, not to burn, but to illuminate.

Kpegnan was no longer just a brilliant student or an accomplished executive. He was a leader, a father, a husband, and a son of the soil whose name would remain forever engraved in the history of Tenably.

Then, his heart at peace, his gaze turned toward the future, he finally went to sleep, ready to write the next chapter of his story.

The next day, after the homage ceremony, his uncle Téhé took him aside and urged him to accept a purification session. In the afternoon, they left for a hamlet buried in the hollow of the forest. There, between knotty roots and the songs of invisible birds, the fetishist's hut stood humble and secluded. The very air seemed to hold a secret.

There, Kpegnan met Tapé Gba, a frail old man with a trembling voice but a piercing, intimidating look. The fetishist, dressed all in white, his body coated in clay and charcoal, sat motionless, eyes closed, listening to voices no one else could hear.

"You're just in time, my son," he said finally. "Before you put yourself out in front of everyone, you must be given protection. The world you are stepping into is a swamp infested with invisible enemies; one never knows where the attacks will come from. I am going to work on you so that even bullets won't touch you."

Kpegnan remained silent and obeyed. Tapé Gba intoned ancient words, a language worn by time that only he seemed to understand. He then placed his hands on Kpegnan's forehead, listing names, calling upon spirits and ancestors. Seeming to draw a border between the world and the protection, he scattered a handful of black sand in a circle around them.

He dug up a small bottle buried in the earth. His mixture, dark and thick, very spicy, burned Kpegnan's throat when he had to swallow it. He gagged down the first cup, but eventually got used to it over time. Every dawn, for a whole week, he then washed himself with an acrid and foul-smelling potion, under the merciless look of the master who, afterward, would coat his body in a paste made of bark, blackish mud, and gorilla dung. His body squirmed every time, but his soul gradually toughened.

At the end of the ritual, Tapé Gba handed him a talisman: a piece of leather sewn with red thread, adorned with cowrie shells.

"Keep it on you always," he advised. Then the old man's voice became graver: *"But listen well, my son: if a woman touches this gris-gris, it will lose its power. Worse still, it could cost you your life. So keep your eyes peeled. This talisman is your invisible wall,"* Tapé Gba concluded. *"As long as it is on you, no evil hand will strike you. But keep it far from women. You will not fall anymore. It is done. Go."*

In his duties, Kpegnan embodied the image of an exemplary young Minister of Equipment, both close to the people and rigorous in the exercise of his functions. Far from three-piece suits and high-and-mighty airs, he preferred, when visiting construction sites, to dress like a common laborer: hard hat on his head, boots on his feet, shirt sleeves rolled up. This choice of clothing was not insignificant. It translated his deep desire to be among his people, to erase the barriers between power and the populace.

He was often seen walking on the beaten earth, observing the work with attention, asking technical questions, and above all, listening. He didn't just supervise; he shared a meal eaten right on the ground with the workers, a break under the sun, a word of encouragement. This proximity commanded respect and admiration.

But beneath this simplicity hid a formidable demand for excellence. Kpegnan was a stickler for deadlines: every day counted, every site was a promise made to the citizens. The companies knew that with him, the slightest delay had to be justified, documented, and owned up to. Transparent in the awarding of contracts, he had put in place strict procedures to guarantee fairness. Corruption had no place under his ministry. He hunted it down relentlessly, convinced that you cannot build a country on backroom deals.

Through his rigor, his uprightness, and his efficiency, Kpegnan had earned the absolute confidence of the President. The latter sang his praises constantly, citing his name as an example, lauding his commitment and his integrity. Kpegnan embodied the new generation of statesmen: honest, devoted, and resolutely action-oriented.

But it was upon returning from a stay in his native village, Tenably, that Kpegnan's destiny took an unexpected turn.

He had just inaugurated, with pride, a splendid villa that had just been completed. Majestic and dazzling, it symbolized the flawless journey of a man who, despite his meteoric rise, had never turned his back on his roots. The entire village had chanted his name, danced for him, proud to see one of their own shining at the summit.

But, in the midst of this jubilation, a discordant voice arose. One of his uncles, Séhia, a distant cousin of his mother who had remained impassive throughout the ceremony, his gaze hard, lips tight, finally called out to him in a harsh tone loaded with bitterness:

"You've moved up in the world, Kpegnan. But up there, you seem to have forgotten those who watched over you when you were just a dreamer with no name. Us, who conjured the spirits for you. You shine for others and you leave us in the dirt. Me, I didn't ask you for anything, just a moped. You didn't even deign to reply.

Watch your back, up there: snakes are prowling, and they don't always hiss before they bite."

Draped in his traditional boubou, Kpegnan kept that smirk on his face, a dry, distant smile he reserved for those whose barbs deserved neither anger nor a response. But behind this mask of serenity, he knew his uncle Séhia too well: a dark man, eaten up by jealousy and bitterness, who never rejoiced in the happiness of his own kin. His jokes were merely weapons in disguise, his words false caresses hiding claws.

Kpegnan still remembered the day when, after hosting him, he had given him fifty thousand francs. Instead of a thank you, Séhia, with a dark look and a voice loaded with bile, had spat out:

"With all the money you have, this is all you give me? You are truly wicked. Keep your money!"

These words had struck Kpegnan like an icy wind. He, who was quietly paying for the schooling of two of his uncle's children... Such cruelty, this ingratitude!

Nanhan, his grandmother, had never stopped warning him: *"Beware of your uncle. His heart is not pure. He harbors a hatred for you for no reason."* In the village, whispers circulated that he was a sorcerer, that he had caused the death of two of his own sons. One day, accused by enraged youths, Séhia had nearly perished under their blows. And who had saved him? Kpegnan, yet again, who had stepped in and calmed the mob.

Yet, despite these signs, despite the warnings, Kpegnan had never taken his venomous barbs seriously. He thought he saw in him only a frustrated old man, a prisoner of his own grudges. But behind his acidic words lay a deeper darkness, a deep-seated grudge, heavy as a threat.

And that smirk Kpegnan wore, even that day, was perhaps not the best shield against the fate that was patiently tightening its grip around him.

A few days later, in the capital, doom struck. In the middle of a council of ministers, a searing pain pierced his chest. Glued to his seat, suffocating, his face ashen, hands trembling, he was rushed to the clinic.

The doctors, baffled, found nothing. No history, no warning signs, but his condition was going downhill fast. The machines remained silent, the tests revealed nothing. Yet, Kpegnan suffered, terribly, in silence.

On the President's orders, he was evacuated via emergency transport aboard the presidential jet. In France, the greatest specialists pored over his case. They examined, tested, analyzed. Nothing. Everything seemed perfect. Except him. Day after day, he was fading away. Finally, he was brought back to the country for his convalescence. Every evening, at his residence, Pastor Gouléhi, known for his gift of healing through prayer, came to intercede. Then a great healer was called in his turn. All in vain.

Then, Djekobou, worried sick, advised him to finally give in to Séhia's demand: to gift that famous moped. Resigned, Kpegnan complied and tasked his faithful driver, Brahima, with delivering it to the village.

That same day, a torrential rain lashed down on Tenably. The sky opened up in a blinding flash, followed by a dull rumble. Lightning struck with full force the hut of Séhia, the embittered uncle who had publicly cursed him. When Brahima arrived with the motorbike, he discovered the old man lying on the ground, inert, his pupils glazed over, like a convict surprised by a sentence handed down from beyond. There were no witnesses. No sound, other than the thunder which, immediately, had fallen silent.

In the village, tongues started wagging. Some saw the hand of God, others that of the ancestors. But everyone agreed on one thing: you do not cast a curse on a blessed son without the heavens, sooner or later, answering back.

The next day, in the capital, against all odds, Kpegnan got out of bed and walked in his garden for the first time in weeks. Little by little, the pains vanished, his nights found peace again. The doctors, incredulous, spoke of a miracle. Others, more discreet, spoke of sacrifices performed on the down-low, between Tenably and the capital.

It was the beginning of a new chapter. Kpegnan's recovery was, everywhere, hailed as miraculous.

Kpegnan carried within him a jealously guarded secret. Behind the polished image of the accomplished man, the respected minister, and the attentive husband, hid a clandestine passion he was living with Inès.

She was only nineteen, but already possessed a captivating aura that exceeded her young age. A former beauty queen, she wasn't just admired for her impeccable figure; it was her magnetic charm that cast a spell. Her eyes, with a deep sparkle, recalled the shifting tint of waves at sunset, while her voice, soft and fluid, evoked the soothing roll of the tides. They nicknamed her *"Inès la Belle,"* not only for her grace but also for that natural, irresistible, and insolent beauty.

Seduced beyond all reason, Kpegnan had built a small house for her by the ocean, in a discreet coastal village a few kilometers from the capital. It was their refuge, their preserved universe. There, far from prying eyes, he found both the murmur of the open sea and the simplicity of a forbidden love. He went there often, alone, in an unmarked car, tearing himself away for a few hours from the rat race of politics, the heavy burden of responsibility, and the masks he had to wear.

Their meeting had been a stroke of luck. During an official reception evening, while Inès was working as a hostess, their eyes had locked. From this spark was born a clandestine relationship, fed on stolen dates and whispers shared away from the public eyes. They often met by the sea, in an old abandoned fisherman's shack, far from the world's view. There, Inès offered him the carefree lightness of her nineteen years, and Kpegnan, in return, opened her up to a universe of forbidden dreams, woven with passion and danger.

But this secret flame came with a price. Inès, beautiful and seductive, was also capricious, jealous, and high-maintenance. Kpegnan had to juggle his obligations as a public figure, the sincere affection of his two wives, and this consuming fire he could not extinguish.

Every time he crossed the threshold of the small thatched-roof house, he found Inès, ready to welcome him with a thousand kindnesses. She knew he often came weary, his spirit weighed down by the burden of power and intrigue. So, she recreated a shelter for him: a bed carefully made, the soft light of a hurricane lamp, the smell of grilled fish or attiéké prepared with love.

Her secrets were simple but irresistible: perfumed, dressed in a light red outfit that hinted at her slender body, she would massage his shoulders with sweet almond oil, caress the soles of his tired feet, and hand him a glass of homemade ginger juice, for which she alone held the recipe. Then, to soothe his torments, she would snuggle up to him, chatty and laughing, her fingers sliding behind his ears. She loved seeing him let go, he, the minister always stiff and calculating under the eye of the cameras, becoming simply a man again, relaxed, sometimes going so far as to fall asleep on her lap.

On moonlit nights, she would slip into her swimsuit and drag Kpegnan onto the beach. Barefoot in the wet sand, they chased each other, traced their names in the fine sand, and threw shells into the waves like children. Sometimes, she would cling to his arm, refusing to let go of his hand, and whisper in his ear: *"You are mine, baby."*

Inside the house, their complicit moments extended into innocent games: card games, riddles invented by Inès, improvised dares, hide-and-seek behind the bed. Then, Kpegnan would laugh, sincerely, finding with her a youth he thought long buried.

But behind this fragile happiness, Inès's love had the force of an obsession. She refused to be just a hidden lover. In a low voice or in passionate outbursts, she repeated endlessly:

"I want to be your wife too, Kpegnan. Not just the shadow behind the curtains."

She knew he already had two wives, that he was a prisoner of traditions and society's inquisitive regard. Yet, her heart, ardent and demanding, refused half-measures. She dreamed of being presented in the light of day, of becoming the one who would share his glory and his destiny. This dull jealousy showed in her gestures: a frown when he announced he had to return to his residence, a bout of sulking when a meeting prevented him from coming at the agreed time.

So, at each visit, Inès redoubled her tenderness, to chain him further. She told herself that every stolen moment brought her a little closer to her secret dream: becoming the legitimate wife of this man she loved with a deep, devouring love.

Kpegnan's official wives, showered with comfort and care, suspected nothing. But in the coastal village, tongues began to wag. Whispers circulated about this mysterious man, often seen alone, pacing the beach at sunset.

For Kpegnan, Inès represented much more than a mistress. She was an escape, a breath of freedom, a gasp of air in the vice grip of power. But every date carried the weight of danger: discovery, scandal, the fall.

One evening, while a storm rumbled in the distance, Kpegnan was sitting on the terrace, chatting peacefully with his two wives. Yet, his mind was already drifting toward Inès. So, feigning an urgent meeting, he slipped away and went to her place, accompanied by Brahima, his trusted man.

That night, while Brahima dozed in the vehicle, Kpegnan met Inès, true to form, waiting for him, ready and radiant. In the small isolated house by the sea, alone, the thunder rumbling, the breath of the wind, and the crashing of the waves were the only witnesses to their night of passionate embraces.

But at dawn, in the rush of departure, Kpegnan made a fatal error: he forgot his talisman. That small piece of leather sewn with red thread, adorned with cowries, which he hid carefully and which had never left his side.

After he left, troubled, Inès discovered the object. Not realizing its importance, she picked it up with curiosity, then, thinking she was doing the right thing, distractedly put it away in a drawer.

The next day, when he noticed the absence of the talisman, Kpegnan's blood ran cold. Heart pounding, he dispatched Brahima to retrieve it as fast as possible. But when Inès searched the drawer, the amulet had mysteriously vanished. She turned the house upside down, in tears, swearing her sincerity. She started searching again, panicked, and convinced she had kept it safe. Nothing.

Brahima, worried and doubtful, came back empty- handed, his face grim.

Curiously, two days later, misfortunes rained down on Kpegnan with the violence of a storm. A real cabal erupted. The newspapers seized upon his name and accused him of corruption, favoritism, and embezzlement of public funds. Compromising documents circulated under jackets and boubous, anonymous testimonies popped up as if by magic. Very quickly, public opinion caught fire. The front pages and editorials competed in ferocity:

Kpegnan: The Guilty Silence. Corruption and Embezzlement: The Dark Side of a Model Minister. Rise of a Man, Fall of a Myth. Villa in Tenably: Billions Swallowed Up in the Middle of the Forest.

In the corridors of the ministry, faces turned away as he passed. Some, cautious, feigned indifference. Others, bolder, peddled rumors with malicious pleasure, as if they had been waiting a long time for the fall of the strong man.

But behind these attacks, another explanation was circulating, more obscure. Djekobou, grave and worried, whispered to Kpegnan:

"These accusations falling out of the blue may not be the work of men. This could come from jealous people, offended relatives, or the ancestors themselves. It is sorcery."

The word, heavy and disturbing, had just been spoken: sorcery. That invisible poison, which leaves no trace in the blood, but which infects one's entire life.

Lachaise, more rational, wanted to laugh it off. Yet, even she, deep down, could not totally shake the doubt.

Kpegnan, however, knew. The disappearance of the talisman and this sudden fall were not simple coincidences. Alerted, he warned his uncle Téhé. On his order, he went back to consult the old fetishist Tapé Gba. There, to his great stupor, the talisman he thought lost reappeared mysteriously, deposited in the master's hands. No one could say how. Some saw in it the action of the ancestors, others a stern warning.

Tapé Gba then ordered sacrifices to be performed in Tenably, on the very earth where his placenta had been buried. A black ox was sacrificed in the village cemetery, at the sacred spot where the great initiates and his forefathers rested.

That night, armed with his recovered talisman, Kpegnan had to remain alone in the middle of the graves. The silence weighed with an oppressive heaviness, broken only by the distant hoot of an owl. Sitting on a mat, his heart beating out of his chest, he thought he felt the icy breath of the ancestors around him. The leaves of the trees rustled like voices whispering in his ear.

And suddenly, in this nocturnal shiver, a silhouette seemed to detach itself from the shadows. He thought he saw his grandfather, old Baha, walking toward him, holding the talisman in his knotty hands.

"You carry more than a name," said the silhouette. *"You carry a people. But remember: glory attracts knives. Your steps will go further than ours, but one day, your blood will flow in the full light of day."*

The voice faded away, leaving Kpegnan trembling, torn between terror and a strange exaltation. His entire body shivered. He wanted to speak, but no sound passed his lips.

Then, the voice resonated again, grave, solemn, irrevocable:

"No one can outrun what is prescribed. Walk with courage, for your destiny lies not in how long you last, but in the mark you leave."

At the crack of dawn, exhausted but curiously at peace, Kpegnan walked out of the cemetery, the talisman clutched tight in both hands. Tapé Gba was waiting for him. The old fetishist spat the kola nut he was chewing onto the amulet, then handed it back to him sternly:

"You must not have any sexual relations for two months. If you do not stick to this abstinence, the protection will crumble."

Upon his return to the capital, a miracle occurred. As if by magic, the accusations evaporated. The newspapers ate their words one after another, some going so far as to publish editorials of apology. His political adversaries, who had heaped slander upon him, came crawling back to ask for forgiveness. The scandal vanished into thin air, as if it had never existed. Kpegnan became the people's darling once again and the pride of the old President, who had kept his faith in him despite the storm.

But Kpegnan, marked forever by that night among the graves, was no longer the same. He had seen the masks fall, discovered the hypocrisy of those around him who now bowed their heads as he passed. His face seemed more gaunt, his look deeper and unfathomable. He spoke little, was wary of everyone, and weighed every word like a verdict. And from then on, his silence commanded more respect than the most eloquent speeches.

To the people, he was no longer just a minister or a leader: he was the man who had walked through the night with the ancestors, the one who had communed with the invisible. A guide marked by a mysterious seal.

Deep down, however, Kpegnan knew it: if the ancestors had saved him, they had also sealed his fate. One day, in the full light of day, they would come back to claim him.

Before long, given his rigorous management, his unshakeable integrity, and the unfailing loyalty the President showed him,

Kpegnan was named Minister of State, while keeping his portfolio for Public Works and Urban Planning.

He was no longer just a minister, but the second-in- command of the State. He had become a major voice in the country's great directions, a heavy hitter in the government, listened to, respected, sometimes feared. Wherever he walked now, the silences were full of reverence.

Kpegnan was a competent minister, respected by the workers, dreaded by the fraudsters, with a track record like no other:

A historic number of roads built since his appointment.

Thousands of jobs created in the construction sector, offering a stable future to many families.

A level of transparency and rigor never before seen in infrastructure projects.

If, as a minister, Kpegnan could transform a key sector of the country, imagine what he will accomplish at the head of the nation! the people told themselves.

The old President, a respected figure and father of the nation, was soon won over by this young minister of barely forty, of whom everyone spoke with admiration. His integrity, his vision, and his boldness set him apart from his peers. Seeing in him the future of the country, he made a decision that would mark history: Kpegnan would be his dauphin.

At the party congress, after unbearable suspense, his name was proposed and acclaimed unanimously.

The choice of Kpegnan as a candidate for the presidential election was much more than a simple passing of the torch. It symbolized a harmonious transition between the wisdom of the old and the energy of renewal. He embodied both continuity and change, tradition and innovation.

Recognized for his unwavering commitment to the people and his pragmatic management of national challenges, Kpegnan represented the man of the people, the one who, over the years, had built a reputation as a man of action and proximity.

By entrusting him with the future of the party and the country, the outgoing President sent a strong message:

"The time has come for new leadership, while remaining faithful to the values that have guided us this far. Kpegnan embodies this vision."

His nomination also translated the deep expectations of the voters, eager to see the emergence of a dynamic, honest leader deeply anchored in the daily realities of his people.

A few months later came the long-awaited moment of the presidential election.

From the official announcement of Kpegnan's candidacy, the race for power took a decisive turn. Thanks to the democratic opening established by the old President, for the first time, several applicants threw their hats in the ring, but many were brushed aside, their ambitions judged unrealistic or fanciful.

At the end of the process, only three candidacies were retained.

The voters, therefore, faced a crucial choice between three personalities with radically different visions:

Doukou, the old comrade-in-arms of the outgoing President, was seventy-six years old. A former schoolteacher and unionist, he saw himself as the legitimate heir but had been sidelined. A man of the past, a prisoner of outdated doctrines and disconnected from popular realities, he spent most of his time dozing off during meetings, letting his ideas fade into oblivion.

Biadon, a university professor and populist candidate, banked on emotion and demagoguery rather than solid experience. His pedantry was palpable: he showed off a scholarly vocabulary, cited abstract theories, peppered his speeches with academic references that few could grasp, and displayed a very condescending professorial tone. All this to mask the emptiness of his proposals, his vague and unrealistic promises. He was counting on this illusion of erudition to seduce a predominantly illiterate electorate, convinced by the appearance of competence more than the substance.

Kpegnan, the candidate of the people, of work, and of renewal. A man of action who had earned his stripes in the field, embodying a credible and ambitious alternative.

Among the three major candidates fighting for the supreme seat, one name resonated louder than the others: Kpegnan.

Kpegnan wanted, above all, sovereignty for his country. But not a facade of sovereignty, and even less a dogmatic withdrawal. He was a sovereignist in the truest sense of the word, not a man locked in a posture of permanent defiance, but a clear-eyed patriot, deeply attached to the real independence of his people in their economic, diplomatic, and cultural choices.

For him, sovereignty did not mean isolation, but the freedom to choose one's partners without bowing to external pressure. He dreamed of a country that was master of its resources, its public policies, and its destiny, capable of negotiating on equal footing with its interlocutors, whether they came from the East, the West, or the South. Kpegnan was neither naive nor closed off. He knew that in an interdependent world, no nation is an island. But he firmly believed that cooperation only makes sense when it is founded on mutual respect, sincerity, and transparency.

Aware that a country's development depends on knowledge and competence, he bet on quality human capital. To do this, he intended to invest massively in the training of highly qualified scientists and technicians, seasoned doctors, and ingenious and creative engineers. To achieve this, he had no complex about leaning on countries with proven leads in these fields, convinced that openness to international expertise diminishes national dignity in no way, so long as the country's interest remains the compass.

Refusing disguised guardianships and lopsided deals, he pleaded for a balanced diplomacy, free of complexes, where the interests of the nation came before partisan calculations or the logic of automatic alignment. His sovereignism was not an identity posture, but a responsible vision: that of a strong state, respected, capable of conversing with the world without renouncing its dignity or its political, economic, and cultural sovereignty.

From the first days of the campaign, all indicators put Kpegnan in the lead:

Polls showed him as the heavy favorite against his adversaries.

His message of breaking with corruption and his plan for massive industrialization seduced the youth and the workers.

His direct style, his closeness to the people, and his experience as a minister made him the man of the hour.

Wherever he went, he gathered crowds far larger than his rivals.

His economic transformation program inspired confidence and hope.

His vision of a sovereign and prosperous country mobilized all social strata.

Far from hollow speeches and empty promises, his campaign was founded on facts, on his concrete achievements, and on a clear vision of the future. The streets vibrated with cries of support:

"Kpegnan President! Kpegnan, the man on the ground!"

In every city, every village he visited, the welcome was triumphant. He didn't content himself with speaking tocitizens; he walked with them, listened to their grievances, shared their daily lives.

"This country doesn't need a desk man, it needs a builder!" he declared during his first big rally.

The crowds went wild.

Never had a presidential campaign sparked so much hope, so much enthusiasm.

Kpegnan was no longer just the man of infrastructure and a job well done. He was becoming the man of an entire people, ready to write a new chapter of their history.

Unlike his adversaries who settled for stiff, formal meetings and hollow speeches, Kpegnan was in the trenches, alongside the citizens:

He visited workers on construction sites.

He exchanged views with farmers on agricultural challenges.

He discussed opportunities and economic obstacles with entrepreneurs.

He listened to teachers and students regarding the future of the country.

"I am not a man of speeches, I am a man of action! With me, no more empty promises, make way for results!" Kpegnan said before a delirious crowd.

From cities to villages, a popular fervor seized the country.

Teachers and students saw in him the guarantor of a modern and accessible education.

Workers recognized his commitment to employment and industrialization.

Farmers believed in his promise to modernize agriculture and guarantee fair prices.

Women saw themselves in his fight for equal opportunities.

"With Kpegnan, we are the winners."

But if Kpegnan was the grand favorite, the battle was only just beginning. His adversaries, aware of his meteoric rise, tried to slow him down by any means necessary:

The attempts at manipulation were as sneaky as they were methodical. Partisans of Doukou who were in the administration were hard at work setting up a massive fraud operation. Ghost names were discreetly added to electoral lists, while hundreds of his supporters were struck from the registers under the pretext of "administrative revisions." Some polling stations known to be in his favor were suddenly moved to remote locations, making voting practically impossible for the poorest. Others still were *"accidentally"* delivered without ballot boxes or without ballots bearing his image.

But the most treacherous blows came from personal attacks. Suddenly, his origins were called into question: an insidious rumor claimed that his real father was none other than a farm laborer from a neighboring country, with whom his mother had allegedly had an affair. Then, they went after his wife Lachaise, a white woman, discreet but committed, whom they accused of being an agent on the payroll of communist powers, infiltrated to destabilize the country from the inside. They even whispered that his marriage was just a facade, an "ideological setup" dictated from abroad. Some went as far as questioning his diplomas, insinuating they had been bought overseas.

Everything was done to break the man, isolate him, and bring him down not through the debate of ideas, but through insinuation, fear, and lies.

But the people were awake, and the Kpegnan wave was already in motion!

"They can try to stop us, but nothing can stop a people in motion!" declared Kpegnan, facing a jubilant sea of humanity.

The beginning of the campaign revealed an obvious truth: Kpegnan was the people's choice, the man of change, the leader of the economic revolution.

From Moikro to Toibly, passing through Voupleu, Bobodougou, Bamakro, Découpé, Dagnoa, Frappéguhé, Porogo, Tiandougou, Kpegnan had crisscrossed every region of the country.

Everywhere, crowds had acclaimed him, brandishing his image, repeating his name like a promise of the future. His landslide victory in the election left no room for doubt. Even his adversaries had resigned themselves and stopped campaigning.

On the last day of the campaign, the heat was stifling.

In the capital, a human tide had invaded the grand stadium from the early hours of the morning. It was a celebration. Old Doukou, himself a candidate, had rallied to Kpegnan's candidacy and had come to publicly offer his support. Several speakers had taken the floor to pledge their backing to Kpegnan.

Around 4 p.m., when Kpegnan stepped onto the podium, collective hysteria took hold of the crowd. Some women, moved by emotion, could not hold back their tears. The joy in the crowd was immense.

He pressed the flesh with many and hugged everyone. A young lady handed him her baby, whom he hugged very tight.

When he took the microphone, screams burst from everywhere, the audience chanting his name.

He smiled and launched out in a clear voice: *"Do you want me to introduce myself?"*

"No, no, no!" replied the crowd with one voice, in a thunder of applause.

He sketched a small smile.

"As we say back home, it is the Maggi cube that makes noise, otherwise salt doesn't advertise itself."

Laughter erupted in the crowd, breaking the tension for a moment. Then, serious, he resumed: *"I know that some of our compatriots are skeptical. They doubt politicians. And, to tell you the truth, they aren't wrong. Because very often, politicians have a conflicting relationship with the truth."*

A murmur of approval rippled through the crowd.

"But me, I am not a politician. I am a statesman."

He paused, then asked: *"Do you know what the difference is between the two?"*

The audience remained mute, hanging on his every word.

"The politician," he said, *"thinks of the next election. The statesman, he thinks of the next generation. The politician serves himself; the statesman serves. The politician talks to please; the statesman acts to build. The politician promises change; the statesman makes it happen."*

Applause broke out, sustained, profound.

Kpegnan raised his hand, asking for silence. His voice vibrated with rare sincerity:

"My dear compatriots, I, Kpegnan serving is my motto. My virtue is honesty. You want to know my plan of action? Well, it is you."

A thunder of applause rang out, mixed with shouts of encouragement.

Then, Kpegnan continued, his voice stronger, carried by the fervor of the moment:

"People of the land of lagoons, my brothers and my sisters, I thank you for your trust, for your unwavering support that carries me today. But tomorrow, the victory will belong to you. An election is never won in advance. It is conquered by every voice, by every ballot, by every citizen who believes in the future."

He raised his arm toward the crowd.

"This country is not mine alone, it is yours as well! It belongs to every child who dreams, to every mother who hopes, to every father who fights, to every youth who refuses resignation."

Emotion was overtaking the crowd. Some wept for joy. Others waved flags.

"Tomorrow will mark the beginning of a new era, an era of justice where innocence is presumed and guilt must be proved, an era of brotherhood and prosperity! Together, we are going to build a nation where everyone finds their place, a nation strong in its unity, a nation proud of its destiny."

His voice swelled even more, echoing into the neighboring streets:

"And when dawn breaks over our homeland, when the sun of a new day comes to light our faces, our children will know that we chose the path of hope."

"For tomorrow is not just an election: tomorrow is the birth of a common future, it is the writing of a glorious page of our history."

A thunder of applause greeted his words.

Kpegnan blew a kiss to the crowd. In his eyes shone that light which only visionaries possess. The light of men who know that their fight is just, even at the cost of their lives.

The crowd was jubilant. Songs rose up; flags and flyers bearing Kpegnan's image danced in the evening breeze.

Kpegnan, stepping down from the platform, moved toward the human tide cheering him on. Women ululated with joy, young people chanted his name. He shook hands, hugged more children, smiled at everyone, without guards, without fear.

His face radiated an inner peace, that of men convinced they are fulfilling their mission.

Around him, security agents tried to contain the crowd. *"Let him through!"* one of them shouted.

But Kpegnan, with a calm gesture, signaled them to stand down. *"Let them come,"* he said simply. *"These are my brothers, my sisters, my people."*

The cameras were still rolling. The national journalist filmed every gesture, every look. They saw this man, in the middle of the crowd, free, accessible, beloved.

Then suddenly, amidst the tumult of shouts and songs, a sharp crack rang out.

A solitary detonation. The music cut out. A second shot went off. Then a third, which hit Kpegnan square in the stomach.

Kpegnan stopped dead. An unreal silence fell.

His body swayed. His hand instinctively sought to rest on his abdomen.

The crowd screamed. *"They shot him! They shot Kpegnan!"*

Security agents rushed in, forming a circle around him. But he was already on his knees, breath short, face pale. His trembling fingers were stained red.

"Don't move, Excellency, hang in there!" shouted a guard, supporting him.

But Kpegnan, in a barely audible whisper, breathed:

"Let me see... my people... one last time."

Everywhere, screams, tears, chaos.

Djekobou and Lachaise, present in the stands, rushed toward him. Potey and Gnansou, incredulous, tried to fight their way through the panicked crowd.

Djekobou, hands trembling, still bathed in her husband's blood, screamed his name in a broken voice. In denial, she desperately shook the body that was slowly sinking into inertia, believing the strength of her love could call him back from the dead.

"Kpegnan! Kpegnan! Stay with me! Kpegnan! Wake up! You don't have the right to leave. You swore to me we would grow old together. Why are you leaving me? Who are you entrusting me to now?" she cried, torn apart, her face drowned in tears.

By his side, Lachaise collapsed to her knees. Her fingers clutched the icy hand of the man she loved. Sobs strangled her voice as she repeated, in a broken prayer:

"My love, you promised to stay. You promised to live. Your mission isn't over. Don't abandon me."

Kpegnan, still alive, breath broken, groped for his wives' hands. His feverish fingers clung to them.

On the ground, his regard already marked by the veil of death, he raised his eyes one final time toward the African sky, seeking to entrust his soul to it.

His voice, fragile, like a whisper carried by the wind, escaped in a final breath:

"Tell them I loved them more than my own life... These assassins believe they have extinguished a voice, killed a hope by eliminating me, but they are wrong, for there are thousands of Kpegnans. Tell them the dream does not die with me. That it continues through you."

His lips parted again, ready to deliver a final word of love, but only silence came to seal his ultimate oath. A doctor attempted cardiac massage, in vain.

The wind gently lifted his white shirt, stained with blood.

Then, nothing.

Kpegnan, frozen in eternal silence, answered no more. And their weeping, mingled with the evening wind, seemed to be the only echo of this life brutally snatched away.

The bullets had struck, and the hope of a people had collapsed with Kpegnan's body.

A heavy silence fell over the crowd, which had, in the blink of an eye, lost its hero, its hope. No one wanted to accept the obvious, the pitiless truth.

That evening, the land of lagoons lost its dearest son.

Potey and Gnansou, paralyzed by the furious crowd, by the tears and the sirens, did not understand.

In the aftermath, in an uncontrollable surge, the crowd rushed toward the alleged shooter. The guards tried to intervene, in vain. In seconds, everything tipped into unheard-of violence. Who can hold back the fury of a people torn from their dream? Fists, stones, anger rained down. The lifeless body of the assassin was dragged along the ground, a sinister offering to collective pain.

The entire country stopped that day. The people wept for the man who had dared to dream for them.

But in hearts, a spark remained. For if Kpegnan was no more, his name, his courage, and his ideal became immortal. His spilled blood did not extinguish hope; it made it grow.

And in the years to come, whenever a better future was spoken of, the name of this young statesman, become a martyr for a people, would be evoked.

Kpegnan was only forty-one years old. An age where the vigor of youth mingles with the maturity of experience. He had become more than a statesman: he was the incarnation of a hope.

The next day, funeral drums resonated in every village. Flags were flown at half-mast. A month of national mourning was decreed.

A month later, it was the day of the funeral. The entire capital was in mourning. Never had the nation known such silence.

The markets were closed; funeral drums resonated even in the most remote villages. On the walls, portraits of Kpegnan blossomed, accompanied by a single phrase: *"The struggle continues."*

The crowd poured in by the tens of thousands. All of Tenably was present. Men, women, children, all dressed in white and wearing shirts and loincloths bearing Kpegnan's image, filled the grand stadium, the very place where, a month earlier, he had succumbed to a murderer's assassin bullets.

When the casket, draped in the national flag, appeared, carried by guards, a collective cry rose from the crowd. Weeping rose like a tide.

The old President, who until then had played his role as statesman, could not contain his tears this time. Upon discovering the remains of the one he considered his son, the one in whom he had placed his greatest hopes and who could have one day carried the nation's legacy, the Head of State broke down.

His sobs burst forth, shattering the heavy silence of the crowd. Before his people, before the whole world, he could not hold back his pain. His shoulders shaking with tremors, his clenched hands twisting, seeking to snatch Kpegnan from the claws of death that had just struck with a cold breath, without warning.

His voice, strangled by tears, rose up, full of heartbreaking distress: *"My son, why you? Why now? You were the future, you were the light, and it is you who is torn from me!"*

And in this cry, it was not only a broken father speaking, but an entire bereaved nation weeping with him. Collapsing, he swore to hunt down and punish all the authors of this plot. The cameras captured this moment. The country discovered an aging leader, vulnerable, weeping for the man in whom he saw the future.

Djekobou and Lachaise, dressed in black, stood side by side, their children standing between them. They walked behind the casket, holding each other's hand, united by an immense sadness and a common, infinite pain.

During the state funeral, Kpegnan received, posthumously, the country's highest distinction. His relatives, Yvette, Kemessié, Bayala, Kouia, his aunt Kamone, as well as his former teacher, Zokou, were invited to share a testimony, stamped with emotion and memories.

Silence fell on the crowd. They awaited the most solemn moment: the funeral oration. The honor fell to his friend, Aimso.

On the lectern, a carefully typed speech awaited him, but when he approached, Aimso seized the sheets, slowly crumpled them between his trembling fingers, then raised his eyes toward the casket.

He had chosen to speak to his friend, not with written words, but with his heart.

His voice, hesitant at first, broke almost immediately: "My... my dear Kpegnan... Get up, Kpegnan, I beg you... get up! This isn't your place, not in this cold box!"

He shook his head, incredulous, tears blurring his vision. "No... no, that's not what we said, do you hear me? That is not what we said! You dared to do this to me? Me, Aimso... your brother, your partner in crime... you left me?"

A long silence. Then, in a husky voice: *"When I told you we only live once, you laughed and looked at me with that look full of fire. And you told me: 'No, my brother Aimso, we live every day, but we only die once. So let's make the most of life.'"*

He sobbed, gently striking the casket. "So why, huh? Why did you leave? Why did you leave me, genius of Tenably? Get up, Kpegnan... get up, please! You still had so many days to live, so many dreams to fulfill, so many smiles to offer this world that loved you!"

His voice became softer, even more broken: *"Yes, Kpegnan, for them, you are the great statesman, the hope of a people... But for me, you remain my childhood friend, my brother of the heart, the genius of Tenably... Garrincha, the philosopher in love. Do you remember? When Djekobou made you cry, I made fun of you: 'Boys don't cry!' And today, it is you... it is you making me cry."*

A tremor shook his body. He tried to speak again, but his words drowned in sobs. Cries rose up: *"Water! Quick, water! Call the doctor!"*

Two young men rushed over and lifted Aimso, unconscious. His hands, clenched tight, refused to let go of the casket. His lips were still murmuring: *"Get up, Kpegnan... get up..."*

The crowd grew agitated, overwhelmed. Women covered their heads with loincloths, moaning: *"Hééé, God, not two deaths on the same day! Lord, have mercy!"*

The doctor, face grave, split the crowd and knelt near him. He checked his pulse, loosened his sweat-soaked tie. *"He is breathing,"* he said in a low voice. *"But he is in shock."*

They splashed water on his face. Slowly, Aimso opened his eyes again. *"Where... where is he?"* he stammered.

They tried to hold him back, but he struggled weakly: *"Let me... let me say one more word to him... just one last word..."*

His strength abandoned him. He fell back, exhausted, into the arms of those supporting him.

Pastor Gouléhi approached, his voice soft and grave: *"The ways of the Lord are unfathomable. Death is not an end, but a birth, a passage toward the light. May the Lord grant you the peace you did not find down here."*

The weeping redoubled, mixing prayers and sobs. Aimso, revived by pain, murmured weakly:

"Genius of Tenably... when you lost Nanhan, you spoke of God's cruelty. Me, I laughed... I said: 'No, God is good.' But you have to lose a loved one to understand. Today, I understand, Kpegnan. Yes, I understand..."

He wiped his tears with the back of his hand. *"I see our nights at boarding school again, the hurricane lamp lit in the dormitory. You, you were still reading while I slept. And you told me: 'Aimso, sleep if you want, me, I want to go far.' You were right, brother... you went far. Too far."*

His voice wavered. *"You promised me we would go to the end. Together. And you left without me..."*

He sketched a smile drowned in tears. *"I remember... your first salary as a director. You called me at midnight: 'Aimso, come quick, we're celebrating!' You had made fatty rice, too salty, almost inedible... and you laughed: 'The taste of a job well done is meant to be savored, even if it's salty!'"*

A fragile laugh cut through his tears. *"You see, even dead, you still manage to make me smile."*

Then, the voice became a mere breath: *"How do I go on without you, tell me? I know you are happy over there. Nanhan welcomed you. You loved her so much. I imagine you running toward her, shouting: 'Nanhan! I made it!'"*

He raised his hand toward the casket. *"Yes, you are at peace, my brother. But us, here, we are broken. Kpegnan, genius of Tenably, you were my pride, my strength, my brother."*

One last sob. *"Get up, Kpegnan... get up! You don't have the right to leave me like this!"*

He collapsed onto the casket, screaming in a mix of despair and love: *"You are a chief, Kpegnan! You are a chief! I do not say adieu... but au revoir."*

His voice died out. His tears were still streaming when his body slumped, exhausted. Around him, not a dry eye. And suddenly, as if to seal the mourning of the sky itself, a fine rain began to fall, soft, slow...

A rain of tears upon the living. After the state funeral, his remains were returned to his family for a burial in the pure tradition of his tribe. And, whenever the future was spoken of, a name stronger than death would rise: Kpegnan.

Thus, as was, alas, the fate of so many African heroes snatched too soon from the affection of their own, taking their unfinished dreams with them, another star was extinguished.

Back at the residence after the burial, Djekobou wandered, drained of all strength, like a wreck drifting in an ocean of sorrow. Her eyes was lost in the void, her soul in tatters. Every room reflected the image of Kpegnan back to her, his voice, his laughter, his scent. Everything reminded her of the man she had just lost and buried.

Approaching a wall, she took down a portrait of him. He wore his legendary smile in the photo. Djekobou pressed the photo against her chest, heart strangled by unbearable pain; she saw no way out, no light, no tomorrow.

So, in a final impulse perhaps of courage, perhaps of surrender she locked herself in the room they had shared. On the bedside table, a blister pack of Nivaquine shone under the pale light. Djekobou seized it, tears blurring her vision, hands trembling. She stared for a long time at the photo of Kpegnan lying there, then, in a breath, whispered:

"I promised not to live without you."

And, without hesitating further, she swallowed the contents of the pack in one go. The poison thus became her refuge. In this desperate gesture, she put an end to her suffering and rejoined the one she loved, fulfilling her promise. Out of love, Djekobou had just faded away.

Later, devastated but still standing, Lachaise found the strength to transform pain into hope, tragedy into legacy. In homage to Kpegnan and Djekobou, she founded, alongside Aimso, her late husband's faithful friend, a foundation bearing their names, dedicated to education, youth, and development.

One evening, sitting on the veranda of the family home, while the children were already asleep, Aimso and Lachaise found themselves together after a long day of work at the foundation.

"Aimso," she murmured, *"sometimes I wonder if all this isn't too heavy... if life still allows me to love."* *"Lachaise,"* he replied softly, *"life does not take away your right to love; it reminds you of it. I believe it would be right for us to give ourselves a chance. It wouldn't be a betrayal, but a continuity."*

"And the children? What will they think of us?" "They will see two souls united by the love of their father, and by the same desire to see them grow up in peace."

"I didn't think it was possible to smile like this anymore, Aimso. When I look at you, I sometimes feel like the pain fades away."

"Then let it go, Lachaise. Let me help you turn it into light."

"Yes, Aimso. Let's stay together to give meaning to all this, to rebuild together what life has broken."

Aimso gently pulled her close and declared in a grave voice: *"I promise you, Lachaise. Together, we will make this past a promise for the future."*

Thus, first united by duty and memory, Lachaise and Aimso saw a discreet tenderness born between them, nourished by shared trials and hopes. Little by little, this affection became a sincere love. Their union, celebrated in simplicity and emotion, opened a new page of their story that of a home rebuilt on kindness and newfound peace.

About the Author

Jules Sehi Nickin

Jules Sehi Nickin was born in a secluded village in western Côte d'Ivoire, in the land of the Wè people, where the forest, memory, and oral tradition still shape the rhythm of life. Raised by his grandparents, he grew up between tenderness and transmission, in a world where stories were not written in books but carried by voices, silences, and the wisdom of elders. That early immersion in roots and belonging would later become the living source of his writing.

His path then led him to the city, to the demanding corridors of secondary school and the University of Abidjan, where perseverance and intellectual rigor revealed a brilliant academic journey. Admitted through a highly competitive examination to CERDI in Clermont-Ferrand, France, he trained in Development Economics and Project Analysis, learning to read the destinies of nations with the same attention he gives to the destinies of men.

A francophone author who embraced English as a second language, Jules Sehi Nickin inhabits the space between worlds, between village and metropolis, between Africa and the West, between memory and modernity. His writing carries the echo of migrations, the weight of early choices, and the fragile beauty of loyalty, friendship, and love.

In his debut novel, *Kpegnan Crépuscule du destin (Twilight of Destiny)*, he gives voice to a generation shaped by the **1980s,** torn between tradition and departure, ambition and attachment, intimacy and history. In his second book, *Côte d'Ivoire: Multipartisme... et après?*, he steps into the arena of political thought, questioning the promises, fractures, and unfinished hopes of democracy, with the lucidity of an economist and the sensitivity of a storyteller.

Now living in the United States, he remains deeply connected to the land that shaped him. Passionate about the environment, sports, and music, he draws from them the same energy that runs through his pages, movement, breath, and rhythm.

More than an author, Jules Sehi Nickin is a bridge between times, spaces, and memories, a voice carried by exile but rooted in the red soil of his childhood.

www.ingramcontent.com/pod-product-compliance
Lightning Source LLC
LaVergne TN
LVHW010647110826
845149LV00014B/2982

* 9 7 9 8 9 9 3 5 5 1 3 6 4 *